Runner's Path

Also By Paul Breen

A Sudden Interest in Shakespeare
Another One Gone

Runner's Path

A Seamus O'Neill Mystery

Paul Breen

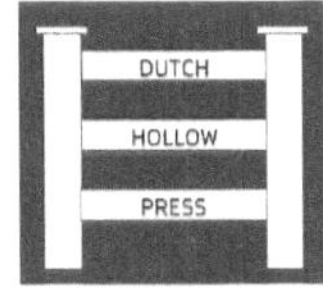

Dutch Hollow Press

ISBN 979-8-9862083-0-5 (paperback)

ISBN 979-8-9862083-1-2 (ebook)

Book Cover Design by ebooklaunch.com

For Dianna

Chapter 1
August 1998

The pounding at the door grew louder, and Seamus O'Neill's eyes creaked open. He rolled off his mattress, letting out a yawn. The only light came from the bathroom which held the apartment's lone window.

"Seamus," a woman's voice said from outside the apartment door. "It's me, Sandra."

Sandra Bartholomew was the last person O'Neill expected. He flipped on the light in his efficiency apartment. The green walls were bare except for the calendar above his mattress. O'Neill picked a guitar off the worn carpet.

"Just a second," O'Neill said. He put the guitar on its stand and stepped into his cargo shorts. He unlocked the deadbolt and opened the door.

"Are you by yourself?" Sandra asked. She sniffed and glanced at the empty beer bottles on the kitchen counter.

"Course."

Sandra stepped in and O'Neill retreated to the kitchen sink. He turned on the water and drank from the faucet.

"I have a favor to ask," Sandra said. She was dressed casually, but her makeup and hair were perfect. She looked alluring and in control, as he expected she would.

O'Neill waved her to his lone chair. He ran both hands through his straggly, black hair and returned to his mattress.

"Have you told anyone that we broke up?" Sandra asked.

O'Neill had to think. Sandra broke up with him at dinner the previous night. It wasn't a surprise, but that didn't make it easy. He spent the night at his regular bars and ended up at his apartment, drinking and playing guitar.

"I told Bip and KP," O'Neill said, scratching his forehead. "I saw them at Wando's, I think. I assume they'll tell The Johnson."

"That's it?"

"Maybe a few bartenders. One at the Red Shed for sure. That blonde kid. His name slips my mind."

Sandra let out a breath. "Don't tell anyone else."

"Why? What's up?"

"I talked to my dad, and he's still coming for dinner this evening. Afterward, he's taking me home to Chicago for the weekend. He says there is something he wants to discuss. Something life-changing. I had planned to tell him about us tonight, but I decided to hold off."

"What's this got to do with you dumping me?"

"I didn't *dump you*," Sandra said. She sat perfectly straight in the folding chair. "I simply told you what I needed you to do if you wanted to stay with me."

O'Neill wanted to respond but held off.

"Anyway, I think he's going to make a proposal to get me to leave you and move back to Chicago."

"Let me guess, you don't think he'll make this offer if he knows we've broken up?"

"Maybe not as good an offer. Dad thinks you are a bad influence. He thinks dating a musician is negatively impacting my career and my life."

"Maybe he's right," O'Neill said, reaching over and taking one of his two guitars from its stand. He sat, legs crossed on the mattress, and strummed the guitar.

"It would be different for him if you were a financially successful musician."

"Course."

"Would you go with Daddy and me tonight to dinner and pretend we're still together? He'll take me home afterward. Hopefully he has a job for me, or an allowance, or something exciting enough to get me to move back to Chicago."

"I thought you wanted to stay in Madison," O'Neill said, continuing to strum the guitar.

"I'm reevaluating everything. I'm not sure my job is leading anywhere. It's been over two years since I graduated and feel I can do more." She pulled lip balm from her purse. "It's just a favor. You would get a free meal out of it. A good meal, since we're going to the Birch Farm Café and Restaurant."

"Sure," O'Neill said, though he had no desire to eat an expensive dinner with Sandra and her father. "I'll do it for old time's sake, I guess."

"Thanks, Seamus." She rubbed her lips together and put the lip balm away. She stood and patted the top of his head. "Reservations are for six o'clock. We'll meet you there. And be on time."

The door closed after she left, but her scent remained. He played a few bars of Willie Nelson's "The Party's Over," then he put the guitar on its stand and locked the deadbolt to the apartment door. He grabbed the pen that was tied to the calendar and noted the appointment. The clock showed it was past noon. He went to the bathroom, turned off the light, and laid back down on his mattress.

It was eighty degrees and sunny on the Capitol Square. A Madison Metro Bus was idling on the street, and a pair of women in shorts passed nearby. The Wisconsin State Capitol building sat ominously across the street, towering high above the landscape. O'Neill glanced at the sun and then at the stone façade of the Birch Farm Café and Restaurant. He stuck his sunglasses into his shirt pocket and opened the door. As he stepped inside, the chaos of downtown Madison's Capitol Square was replaced by the restaurant's quiet, controlled confines. He shuffled into line behind a pair of restaurant patrons. The hostess grabbed menus and led the couple around the corner to what O'Neill assumed was the restaurant's seating area. The hostess returned shortly, eyeing O'Neill as she slid behind the podium. Mozart's "Turkish Rondo" played in the background.

"I'm here to meet a group," O'Neill said. "I expect they are already here."

"What's the name?"

"Harry and Sandra Bartholomew. I'm not sure which name they used."

Before the hostess replied, Sandra peered around the corner. She muttered a few words to the hostess and grabbed O'Neill's arm.

"You're late," Sandra said. "We have a booth."

O'Neill followed her past several tables populated by well-dressed couples. A waiter was serving one foursome, and the smell of seared meat and fish caught his attention. As they turned a corner, a tall, imposing man of about sixty greeted them.

"Dad, this is Seamus O'Neill."

"I have heard a great deal about you," Harry Bartholomew said.

"I'm sure you have," O'Neill said as he shook Harry's hand.

Harry clamped a hand onto O'Neill's shoulder, guiding him toward the booth. The lawyer was ruggedly handsome with a trusting manner that, O'Neill imagined, was a façade. "What do you want to drink, Seamus? Seamus is an Irish name, correct?"

"You know it is," Sandra said.

Harry released O'Neill as they sat on opposite sides of the table. Sandra smiled at her father as she sat next to O'Neill. She wore a black dress that matched her father's dark suit and black shoes; O'Neill wore jeans, brown loafers, and a long-sleeved shirt Sandra bought for him.

"The Irish have interesting names," Harry said. "There are a lot of Irish in Chicago, though I don't recall meeting a Seamus. Sounds more Jewish than Irish. What made your parents choose that name?"

"It's Irish for James," O'Neill said as he ran both hands through his mop of hair. "It was my father's name. Goes back, I suppose, though my mother never liked the name. She would say that James was good enough for James Joyce, but not for my father."

Harry nodded again, his thick eyebrows arching up as if catching the wind. "Interesting people, the Irish; I have been to Dublin."

Sandra's eyes widened and her cheeks flattened. "Daddy, just because Seamus has an Irish name doesn't mean he's from Ireland. He was born here in Wisconsin."

"I'm making small talk," Harry said, "trying to get acquainted with your fellow. I thought that was what you wanted. He's not what I expected. I had envisioned someone with longer hair, someone more frightening. He may be a person I can deal with."

O'Neill's gaze fell downward. He expected to endure the meal but intended to minimize interaction.

"Seamus says the parents of women he dates never like him," Sandra said.

"Perhaps it is because you're a musician," Harry said to O'Neill. "Parents fear musicians. If you have children, you will understand. What type of music do you play?"

A waiter arrived, saving O'Neill from having to answer. O'Neill glanced at the drink menu and opted for a Capital Brown Ale. Sandra ordered a martini, and Harry a vodka.

"Seamus, are you from Madison?" Harry asked.

"Madison area."

"I grew up in Chicago — Highland Park, to be more precise — and besides a few years in New York City and extended trips to Europe, I have lived in the Chicago area all my life. The city fits me like a glove, though I wish Sandra was there with me. Family is one thing I miss."

"Madison's close to Chicago, and it's a wonderful city," Sandra said. "They voted Madison the nation's best place to live a few years ago."

"That's fine if you're into whatever young, middle-class people with families are into today. Low crime, low unemployment, and strip malls, I imagine."

O'Neill wouldn't know, but he nodded. He would nod a lot during the night. He viewed it as unavoidable.

As they waited for their drinks, Harry updated his daughter on a cousin's health scare, provided details about a recent family wedding, and talked about the upcoming football season.

O'Neill hardly paid attention. He opened the menu for the Birch Farm Café and Restaurant. The menu listed various items under three separate courses, which he assumed equated to appetizers, entrees, and desserts. He studied the menu but didn't know what to order. He could pronounce bouillabaisse, but he didn't know what it was. He decided Sandra could order since she spoke restaurant French and knew what he liked.

The drinks arrived, and the beer's aroma gave O'Neill a sense of its sweetness. He took a first sip and swished the beer in his mouth before swallowing. He wanted to get through dinner without drinking much, but nerves made the task difficult.

"So, you're a musician," Harry said. "Sandra said you used to play in Chicago and Madison. It sounds like you've had an interesting musical career."

"I've been playing in bands since I was fifteen," O'Neill said.

"Would I know any of these bands?"

"I doubt it."

"Are you behind anything I hear on the radio?"

"Not unless you listen to college or community radio. I've played a lot of gigs over the years, though. I've played in a few dozen cities between Minneapolis and Indianapolis. Course, Madison is the place I've played most."

"Is Madison a town with opportunities for a musician?"

"Not if you're trying to make money. You could make more painting billboards."

"Too bad. Sandra says you're talented. She says you write and play music. What instrument do you play?"

"Bit of everything."

"A widely skilled musician and I understand you also work as a detective. You sound like a jack of all trades."

O'Neill cringed at the comment, yet Harry's smile widened.

"Being a detective must be interesting work," Harry continued.

"I'm not a detective," O'Neill said. "I just work for a detective agency."

"Oh, I didn't realize that." Harry looked toward Sandra as if expecting an explanation.

"He isn't a licensed detective, Daddy. It doesn't mean he doesn't do detective stuff."

"I write reports; get information from the internet relating to background checks; and call employers, municipalities, and banks for information and so forth. I also fix computer problems and troubleshoot. It's not that I'm a computer whiz, it's just one of my boss' shortcomings," O'Neill said.

"Sounds to me like there's some detective work there," Harry said. "Is it dangerous?"

"Not that I know of."

Harry brushed at his eyebrows and, for the first time, his smile drifted away. "You're a musician, but you're not in a band, and you do detective work, but you're not a detective. Will you get your detective license, or is this a temporary thing?"

O'Neill took a long drink of beer. He assumed Harry already knew the answer, so he thought he would get it over with. "I won't be getting a detective's license since I just do office work. Besides, I've had trouble with the cops, so I wouldn't bother applying."

"They're not strict about that kind of thing, are they?" He glanced toward Sandra and back to O'Neill. "It is probably easier than getting a fishing license."

"Wouldn't know, I don't fish."

"Neither do I."

"Why are you interested in his detective job?" Sandra asked.

"Because I want to hire him to do detective work for me."

O'Neill straightened up as a rush of confusion swished through his brain. Sweat formed on his back, and he was suddenly aware of the contour of the wooden table and its uneven varnish. He could see an imperfection in the window blinds, and he could hear ice moving inside Harry's glass. This was an opportunity, or perhaps a challenge, he had not expected. Yet he couldn't speak.

"You're serious?" Sandra said. She leaned forward and her long, black hair, which had matted against the wooden booth, broke free and flopped forward. "You want to hire Seamus?"

"Yes, I'm serious," Harry said. He laughed and his eyebrows danced about. "I am offering to hire the agency Seamus works for, but Seamus is the reason I'm proposing to hire the Ryder Detective Agency, so I want him involved. I already researched the agency, and I know that John Ryder is an ex-Madison police officer."

"Yes," O'Neill said, swallowing hard. "He worked for the City of Madison Police Department for ten years. He quit a few years ago and took over his old man's agency. His dad opened the agency before I was born. The business has a niche in the Madison market."

"You're up to something, Daddy. Why else would you suddenly want to hire the detective agency Seamus works for?"

There was a pause and Harry's folksy, caring, old chap expression reemerged, bringing along a smile. He pulled back slightly and with a blink, his gaze switched to O'Neill. When he spoke again, his voice was relaxed.

"This is a business proposition," Harry said to O'Neill. "It is a lucky stroke that a private detective from Madison comes into my daughter's life when I need a private detective in Madison. I wanted to ensure I could work with you before I made an offer."

Harry continued talking about lawyers working with private detective agencies, but O'Neill's mind was wandering.

Then O'Neill saw everything.

Harry was paying him off to get rid of him. The thought struck him with such intensity that he almost said it out loud. There was no other reason a powerful, respected lawyer like Harry Bartholomew would hire him. It was a payoff aimed at getting him out of Sandra's life, or it was a tactic to start the process. It had to be. Harry was throwing him a crumb to make the break easier.

O'Neill decided that was okay. He needed crumbs.

Chapter 2

Dinner with his ex-girlfriend and her father had played out differently than O'Neill had expected. Instead of being bored, his mind was rushing to comprehend what was happening.

"What do you think of my proposition?" Harry asked. "Will the Ryder Detective Agency take the case?"

"Taking the case will be up to Mr. Ryder," O'Neill said. "Like I said, I do office work."

"Understood," Harry said, the sincere smile remaining on his face.

"I suppose you'll want references and such."

"References are done."

Of course they are, O'Neill thought.

"I'll fax the documents to your office tomorrow morning. The contract requires your involvement. My client will pay for two weeks at your full rates. If we believe you are making progress, we will consider committing to another two weeks."

"What do you want him to do?" Sandra asked. "I mean, what is the case you're hiring Seamus to investigate?"

O'Neill and Sandra leaned closer.

"Two years ago, a woman named Andie Sheridan was murdered. She was a runner for the cross-country team at the University. In August of '96, she was running with the team." His gaze bounced between O'Neill and Sandra. "She disappeared at some point."

"I remember it," Sandra said, interrupting her father. "The University cross-country team was running through the woods in the arboretum along Monroe Street on the near west side. One woman didn't finish the run and was missing for days. Turns out she was raped and strangled. It was a big deal and creeped everyone out. Everyone expected more attacks, but there were no more."

"They never caught the killer, of course, and it's been two years," O'Neill said. "There was a lot of media coverage as I recall, and the cops presumably put a lot of resources into it. Yet it's unsolved."

"I'm not expecting you to solve an unsolvable murder," Harry said, "only to do your best. That way, my client will know I did my best. My client understands the odds are stacked against you."

O'Neill gulped his beer, deciding the drink tasted skunky, probably from dirty lines. It was odd because he usually smelled skunky beer from the start and confirmed it with the first sip. It was as if the stress of the meeting had impacted his senses.

"Who's the client?" O'Neill asked.

"His name is Adam Staley. His son was a friend of the murder victim. The son, I believe his name is Myles, doesn't like how the police handled the investigation. Hiring a private detective agency is what he asked from his parents for graduation. It is an odd request, but that's youth. His father thinks it a waste of time, but he wants to honor his son's request, so he asked me to pick a detective agency. I told him I would manage everything."

The waiter stepped in front of their table holding a notepad and a pen. Harry and Sandra picked up their menus and O'Neill whispered into Sandra's ear. After a few minutes, Harry and Sandra ordered the first course, Sandra ordering for O'Neill.

O'Neill sat dumbfounded. The next hour seemed hazy and, when the second course arrived, he guessed his meal was a fancy strip steak. It was tasty, but it was too much for him. He chewed slowly and ordered a glass of Bordeaux.

After the meal, O'Neill and the Bartholomews exited the restaurant and stepped onto Pickney Street. It was dusk in downtown Madison, but the air was still warm. The door closed and a man leaning against a light pole slipped his flat cap off his head and approached the threesome. Harry held Sandra close, barreling past and hardly allowing the man to ask for money. O'Neill nodded at the beggar but continued walking a few steps behind the Bartholomews.

When they got to Harry's Lexus in the nearest parking garage, the lawyer slapped O'Neill's shoulder, told him he enjoyed meeting him, and opened the car door. The Bartholomews planned to drive directly to Chicago. O'Neill didn't know the details but decided it didn't matter whether she was gone for two days or forever. Their relationship was over.

"Daddy is probably watching us," Sandra said after Harry got into the black Lexus. Her voice was hardly more than a whisper, but it sounded tinny in the parking garage. She put her arms over O'Neill's shoulders. "Thank you for helping me out. I appreciate it. It's great that Dad offered you work. That was a surprise."

"What's that job about?" O'Neill asked. "Is he paying me off or what?"

"Who knows?" Sandra said in his ear. "Yet it's a good thing. At least you got more than a free meal. And if he's offering you a little, who knows what he'll be offering me?"

She kissed him, and he ran his hands along her back, thinking it would be the last time he would hold her this way.

"Hopefully, we can remember the good times," she said. "And good luck getting back in with your band."

"I don't want back in," O'Neill said. She was referring to his band, Sea City Chaos. They had kicked him out ten days earlier. "Am I still keeping our breakup secret?"

"Call me tomorrow or Monday night and I'll let you know if we are officially broken up."

"None of my friends even know who your dad is. Why does it matter after tonight?"

"I want my friends to hear it from me and not from you or your friends. Just hold off until we talk again. In the meantime, you and your boss can investigate this murder. Who knows, maybe you'll figure something out."

O'Neill wanted to laugh. How would he investigate a murder? He would just give the case to Ryder and collect the twenty-five percent finder's fee Ryder promised on any job he brought in. It would be big money for him.

"Take care of yourself," O'Neill said, pulling himself away.

"You too. And stay away from Topper and his crew. They're lowlifes."

"Course," O'Neill said.

Sandra got into the Lexus. The vehicle backed out then drove past O'Neill, who stood motionless as the car's exhaust dispersed into the dreariness of the parking garage. He went to the staircase and walked down the stairs feeling empty despite the full stomach.

Chapter 3

O'Neill got to his third floor Frances Street apartment and poured a double of Grant's Scotch Whisky. He took a drink, savoring the burn as the whisky slid down his throat. After two more sips, he refilled the tumbler. He planned to wallow in self-pity, but as he stared out the window, his thoughts turned away from Sandra and toward the murder. He knew very little about their client, Myles Staley. He knew Myles had recently graduated from the University, worked in Chicago, and had a rich and controlling father. O'Neill also knew that Myles, or perhaps his father, would send a letter to the Ryder Detective Agency summarizing Myles' concerns about the case.

Ryder promised O'Neill twenty-five percent of any job he brought in. It would be good money for him, which he might use to buy a CD player that takes multiple CDs. Even if it was an unsolvable case, Ryder would love it since Harry couldn't expect results. Ryder couldn't lose and O'Neill didn't have anything left to lose.

O'Neill didn't dwell on Sandra because he thought he knew what happened with her. She was like other girls he had dated. Even though she fooled herself, she had no intention of staying with him. She initially wanted him because she thought he was artistic and sleeping with him made her feel part of it. She had seen him onstage with lights on him and people clapping. When he left the stage, people shook his hand, bought him drinks, and told him he was great. She wanted part of it.

But she snapped out of it. They always did.

O'Neill finished the tumbler as he grabbed a spiral notepad with blank pages. He summarized what he knew about the case, including the names. He put the pad in his pants pocket and, since it was sprinkling outside, put on a sweatshirt. Then he filled his flask with Scotch and stuck the container in his front pocket. He pulled it back out and took two sips as he walked to the pay phone outside the Howard Johnson's motel. He dialed John Ryder's personal number, noting the booth's faint scent of vomit. Ryder answered after only two rings.

"I got you a job with a two-week advance at full rates," O'Neill said. "I even told him you have higher rates for felony investigations, so you should create a new rate sheet. Thought I better call before you go fishing or something."

There was a pause.

"Who is this?"

"Screw you, you know who it is."

"*You* got *me* a case?" John Ryder said.

"A murder case," O'Neill said between sips of Scotch.

Ryder laughed. His laugh was a high-pitched squeal that was funny in itself. "Who the hell comes to you with a murder case? Is the case in town?"

"Yeah, the murder happened two years ago in Madison. A woman named Andie Sheridan was running with the University's cross-country team. She was raped and murdered in the arboretum."

"For Christ's sake, that murder was all over the news back in '96. The Madison Police Department kicked at it hard, but they haven't been able to solve it. Who expects me to solve that case in two weeks?"

"No one."

"You drinking, boy?"

"Course."

"Dumb question. What were you saying?"

"A friend of the murdered woman, I can't remember his name, is sure the cops bungled the investigation. The guy graduated from college and, as a graduation present, he asked his daddy to hire a private detective agency to investigate the murder. I got his name somewhere. It's Staley," he said after pulling out his notepad. "Myles Staley is the son and Adam Staley is the dad."

"How did this Staley get your name?"

"He didn't. But Daddy Staley's lawyer is Sandra's father. Sandra's father is managing things."

"Oh, Sandra's father hired me," Ryder said. "I take it he hasn't met you yet."

"I met him earlier tonight."

"And he still wants to hire us?"

"I'm guessing he's paying to get me out of Sandra's life. Either that or it's a plan to make me look bad."

"Don't quite follow your logic. I mean, the client will pay me, not you, and you look bad already, especially to a lawyer. If he wants you to look bad, there would be easier ways."

"I suppose."

"You said the kid asked to hire us as a graduation present. My guess is our new client is a spoiled rich kid and his dad is giving him the present to shut him up. Sandra's dad, though, probably knows it's a silly idea."

"Harry implied he doesn't expect anything from us other than to try."

"No expectations? That's good, since it's realistic."

"He said our client would send you a letter with background on the case. I get twenty-five percent as we agreed, right?"

"Yes, but time spent on the case goes against the twenty-five percent. I'm not just giving you a bongo bonus."

"Yeah, yeah, yeah, we've been through this. Harry said they would fax the contract over tomorrow. You sign it and send it to Harry along with an invoice."

"I love the word *invoice*," Ryder said. "I'll create our felony rate sheet tonight. Tomorrow morning, I'll run to Carroll Street to find out who at the Madison Police Department is running the investigation, and hopefully, I'll be able to review their files. The case may be cold, but it's only two years old, so whoever was in charge in '96 is probably still in charge. There will be tons of documentation, interviews, and persons of interest. Getting access to files will either go quick, slow, or not at all, depending mostly on who is running the investigation and how desperate they are. Hopefully I can get in tomorrow. If not, I'll wait until Monday. Are you okay coming in tomorrow even though it'll be Sunday?"

"Yeah, I'm short on hours these last few weeks."

"Go into the office and I'll meet you in the afternoon. If you're up early," he laughed, "run to the downtown library and see what articles you find in the *Wisconsin State Journal* and *The Capital Times*. There should be plenty since the disappearance and the murder got lots of coverage. Make copies of the first articles and later ones if they add information.

Don't bother copying twenty articles with the same information. The central library opens at eleven on Sundays. If I leave the office during the day, I'll leave an office key in the mailbox."

"Okay," O'Neill replied, surprised he might get access to an office key.

"If I remember this case correctly, we will find nothing new without a miracle. The woman was running through the woods and she got mugged, raped, and killed. Perhaps he just meant to rape her and the killing was an accident. Either way, we will need new witnesses or fresh evidence. I can't imagine finding something new, but we'll talk more tomorrow. This should keep us busy for a few weeks, yet there's no pressure. Can't ask for more."

O'Neill hung up the phone and took another sip of Scotch, staring blankly at the flask. Rather than walking home, he found his way back to Frances Street and stopped at the Red Shed. He spent a lot of time in downtown bars, but the Red Shed was one of his regulars, partially because it was close to his apartment. The building sat near the corner of Frances Street and University Avenue. A red and white striped awning partially hid its front façade; a wooden wagon with a matching red and white cover sat on the roof.

The inside of the Red Shed was dark. Thick wooden beams boxed in the bar counter. The beams, along with a shingle-roofed brick oven, aimed to give customers the sense of being inside a shed rather than an urban college dive bar. Lighted beer signs and dim lighting added to the ambiance. A pool table sat toward the back and wooden booths lined one wall. The floor felt less sticky than usual.

The bartender handed O'Neill a pint of Berghoff. The glass felt cold in O'Neill's hand.

"What's up, O'Neill?" the bartender said. "I thought you were going to New York. That, at least, is what I read."

"Screw that; I'm staying in Madtown."

"Glad you're staying. There ain't many good bands here, and we can use the business."

The bartender drifted away, refilling a blonde woman's glass. O'Neill took one of the remaining empty stools lining the bar. He preferred to be near the taps, giving him access to the bartenders and allowing him to smell fresh beer. The crowd was college-aged — most crowds near campus were — with older patrons mixed in, some drunk and some on their way. O'Neill recognized several people, but no one he wanted to talk to.

"Have you seen The Johnson around?" O'Neill said.

The Johnson's given name was Tim Johnson. O'Neill had given him the nickname "The Johnson" because, at one time, there were several Johnsons on the Madison music scene. Even though it was stupid, it had stuck.

"He was in last night. I think he said he's playing the Union tomorrow night."

"You got any newspapers?"

The bartender pulled a stack of newspapers from behind the counter. O'Neill perused through two local papers: *Isthmus* and *The Onion*. The only date he found for The Johnson's band, Shifts in Turmoil, was for Sunday night at the Union Terrace.

"You were right; it's tomorrow night," O'Neill said after finishing the search. "He'll probably be out tonight. I think I told him I would sit in with the band, but I'm not sure. Anyway, get me another beer."

"If he comes in, I'll let him know you're looking for him," the bartender said as he poured O'Neill another tap.

"You ever heard of a woman named Andie Sheridan?" O'Neill asked, surprising himself and, apparently, the bartender.

"The murdered runner, right? It was all over the news my freshman year. Was she a friend of yours?"

"No," O'Neill said, not expecting anyone to ask *him* questions about Andie Sheridan. "There aren't many murders in Madison, so when a student gets murdered, it gets press. Someone mentioned it to me, and it got me thinking about how strange it was that someone attacked a runner in a group."

"I didn't know her either, but when I saw her picture on the news, I recognized her from parties or class or something. She was hot."

He drifted along the bar, taking an order for another customer. When he returned, he seemed to have forgotten about Andie Sheridan.

"Will you guys be playing the Union this year?" the bartender asked, referring to O'Neill's band, Sea City Chaos.

"Nah, we broke up."

"That sucks," the bartender said without conviction.

"You were in Sea City Chaos?" the woman on the barstool next to O'Neill asked.

He nodded and looked at her. She was thin with lots of hair. She was college-aged, but he didn't think she was a college student.

"I heard they booted the singer. You're the singer, right?"

O'Neill nodded.

"Bummer."

O'Neill didn't have a suitable response, so he sipped his beer and stared forward. When he finished, he ordered another and read through *Isthmus's* entertainment section. Before he finished the Berghoff, there was a tap on his shoulder.

"Hey, Seamus," a woman's voice said.

O'Neill spun around on his stool. "Hey, Amanda."

O'Neill couldn't remember how he met Amanda, but she was a regular at the Red Shed and often attended Shifts in Turmoil and Sea City Chaos shows. She was a brunette with a solid build and an androgynous look. A different Red Shed bartender dated her at some point, but he couldn't remember much else except that she was smart and into music. She was also friends with Sandra.

"What you up to?"

"Out and about," O'Neill answered.

"Where's Sandra?"

"In Chicago visiting her old man."

She itched at her chin. "I got someone for you to meet," she said, her eyes darting about as if she told him a secret. "But I just want her to meet you if you get my meaning? She's my sister, okay? So no hitting on her."

Amanda disappeared, not waiting for a reply, and returned with a shorter, thinner, prettier version of herself. It was, undoubtedly, Amanda's younger sister.

"Seamus, Jane. Jane, Seamus O'Neill who, as you know, was the singer, guitarist, and songwriter in Theoretically Trashed."

Jane flashed an attractive but oversized smile. Her eyes were bright blue, and they sparkled even in the dim light. O'Neill looked into them for far too long.

"I *was* and *am* a huge fan," Jane said. "I got both of the Theoretically Trashed CDs."

Theoretically Trashed was a band O'Neill fronted in the early nineties. The band put out two CDs on a local label, but neither sold more than 2,000 copies. Having both CDs was an accomplishment.

"You're one of the few."

"You guys were awesome."

"She loves the Trashed, but she doesn't like Sea City Chaos," Amanda said with a half chuckle.

"I like them," Jane said, looking embarrassed. "They're more standard than the Trashed and the songs aren't as good, but I like them."

"How old are you? You must've been awfully young when the Trashed were around."

"Twenty-three."

Amanda whispered something to her sister, and Jane whispered her reply. Amanda then walked away and rejoined her group.

"I haven't seen you around before," O'Neill said to Jane. "Least don't think I have."

"I moved to a new apartment for the fall semester. My old apartment was on East Johnson Street, so the Red Shed was not in my neighborhood."

"You want a beer?"

"Sure, a porter if they got one. If not, then something dark."

"Heavy shit for a little one." O'Neill didn't feel like being witty or charming. He would just drink another beer and let life happen. He waved the bartender over.

"So, what music do you listen to?" O'Neill asked.

"I'm picky but eclectic, meaning I like a bit of everything and hate most everything else. Lately, I'm into Richard

Thompson, Dirty Three, and Brinsley Schwarz, which was Nick Lowe's old band."

"Strange trio for anyone to listen to — especially a college girl. I'm a long-time Richard and Linda Thompson fan, and I like Nick Lowe, though I've never heard of Brinsley Schwartz."

"I picked the band up from a friend who's a foreign exchange student. She's from Nottingham but going to college in Madison."

Hearing "college" brought O'Neill's mind back to the dead runner.

"You are a student, aren't you?" he asked.

"Yep, I'll be out in December."

"Did you know that cross-country team runner who was murdered a couple of years ago?"

Her expression changed. "I remember it happening, of course, and all the publicity, but I never met her."

"Oh," O'Neill said.

She bit her lip, seeming to sense his disappointment.

"I know the woman who was her roommate when it happened. Her name is Mary Gleason and we've been in classes together, including one this session."

"You know the murdered girl's roommate?"

"Yeah, we're both in the School of Nursing. Why are you asking?"

He was acting stupidly. It was probably the drink. What could he learn by asking random people questions about a murder? People would wonder why he was asking. It wouldn't go anywhere, he told himself, yet he couldn't stop.

"I met a friend of the girl's," O'Neill said. He got out his notepad. "His name is Staley, Myles Staley. He told me he thinks the cops screwed up investigating her killing, and I got interested since I sometimes write articles for newspapers and magazines. I thought it might be an interesting story."

"I believe I met Myles before," she said, accepting his story with wide-eyed innocence. "They used to date."

"Who used to date?"

"Myles Staley dated Mary Gleason."

O'Neill's eyebrows lifted, surprised he had learned something relevant. "So, your friend was the murdered woman's roommate *and* Myles Staley's girlfriend? Could you give me her address?"

"I don't know her address, but I could find it in the phone book."

"Uh, well, what she doing tonight?"

Jane smiled, and her eyes tightened as if she might laugh at him.

"It's almost midnight, so either she went out, stayed home, or is at her boyfriend's. Talk to her in the daytime." She stopped talking and her smile turned into a self-satisfied grin. "Come to think of it, I've seen her out at the Razor's Edge a few times. We could check if she's there. Do you want to go look for Mary Gleason?"

Chapter 4

The Razor's Edge was east of the capitol, and it was late. They needed a car, and O'Neill didn't have enough money for a cab. Yet he was curious about Andie Sheridan, and he was enjoying Jane's company.

"Let's go," O'Neill said to Jane. "But is it okay to drop this on your friend? It might feel weird bringing up murder out of the blue."

"You did it with me," Jane said.

"But I didn't really expect you to know her. Your friend lived with a murder victim. It will be personal for her."

"She's always been very open about it. I don't know her that well and she's talked to me about it a few times. I think she likes to talk about things that happen to her."

"Let's go then," O'Neill said.

"Just a sec while I tell Amanda where we're going."

O'Neill slammed his beer. The bartender stopped over as soon as the glass emptied, but O'Neill waved him off, muttering about making another stop. The bartender nodded and O'Neill waited a long minute before Amanda grabbed him by the elbow, pulling him toward the exit.

"Listen," Amanda said, glancing backward before continuing, "I introduced my sister to you because I figured she'd get a thrill from it, but don't screw around with her. She's clueless, and she doesn't need to be stupid with you. Remember, you have Sandra."

"I'm not doing anything," O'Neill replied.

"She said you told her you're a reporter, which is bullshit. What else am I to think? I mean, you are half in the bag. She's a pretty college student, and your girlfriend is in Chicago."

"Okay," he said. "I told her I'm interested in the case and might write about it. Never said I'm a reporter, and I didn't figure you introducing us if you weren't cool with me talking with her. Either way, I won't touch her. I just got to meet this girl Jane knows."

She looked at him with a stern expression. "Okay, I believe you. But keep in mind that Jane's had a crush on you since she was sixteen. She still has a Theoretically Trashed T-shirt, believe it or not. I introduced her to you because she's been asking to meet you since she's been old enough to go to bars, and I'm sick of it. Now she'll think you got the hots for her. Don't do anything stupid."

"Won't touch her."

"And if you don't keep your word, I'll tell Sandra faster than you can drink a beer." She glanced sideways. "Here she comes. And remember, I got my eye on you."

"Let's go," Jane said to O'Neill, "it's late."

Jane volunteered to drive, which was a relief to O'Neill. They hurried across University Avenue's four lanes, going toward the Kohl Center. It was late, so traffic across the one-way street was sparse but moving far above the thirty-mile-per-hour limit. They walked several blocks before Jane pointed to a blue, two-story house that looked like a smaller version of O'Neill's apartment building. The wooden stairs creaked as they stepped onto the porch. Jane turned the key and pushed the door open. They stepped into a large living room. A light was on in the kitchen, and White Zombie's "More Human than Human" played upstairs.

"Just a sec. I'll grab my key fob," she said before rushing up the stairs.

"What's a key fob?" O'Neill said to himself.

Jane returned, running down the stairs. O'Neill followed as she pulled the front door shut and got into a two-door Mazda. An evergreen air freshener hung from the car's rearview mirror and swung from side to side as they pulled out of the parking spot.

"What about this murder caught your interest?" Jane asked. "There was a ton of publicity when she disappeared and they found her body, but you don't hear about it anymore. Are you interested because she was a runner on the cross-country team?"

O'Neill considered the question before answering. He remembered coverage of the murder but had paid little attention to it at the time since Sea City Chaos was on their first and longest Midwest tour.

"Who would attack someone running in a group?" O'Neill said. "It makes no sense, which is what interests me. Also, we're almost at the two-year anniversary, so it's a milestone."

"I remember some of it from the news coverage. The team was running along Monroe Street when she got," Jane glanced sideways at O'Neill, "attacked."

"The attacker may not have known she was running in a group," O'Neill said. "Maybe he watched these women run past, he got excited, and another one comes by and she's a looker."

"You're scaring me," she said.

"It is a scary thing."

They drove the rest of the way in silence. O'Neill wanted to drink from his flask, but he held off. Once on Williamson Street, Jane took a lap around the block before parking.

The Razor's Edge looked much as O'Neill remembered it, though the crowd seemed younger. He viewed it as a student bar, but it had a different vibe than those closer to campus. There were still television sets tuned to ESPN, but it felt less university focused and more chaotic. A rectangular bar with five beer taps on each side dominated the room. The floor was higher outside the rectangular bar, leaving the brass footrail even with the floor, creating the city's grossest rail. The space was filled with tables and chairs, but a few were empty.

"Why don't we grab a drink," O'Neill said as a Smokey Robinson song played in the background.

"There she is," Jane said, pointing. "Mary Gleason *is* here."

O'Neill couldn't believe it had worked.

Jane stood still, staring at Mary Gleason. O'Neill grabbed Jane's hand, and she moved forward. He let her pass him, following as she maneuvered through the crowd. A few students pulled their drinks close to their bodies as Jane and O'Neill squeezed through. Jane stopped in front of a group of women at a corner table. One woman whispered in another's ear while the other two watched Jane and O'Neill approach. Four empty plastic beer glasses and a nearly empty pitcher covered the circular table.

"What's up, Jane?" a curly haired woman said.

"Not much, Mare," Jane said, crouching in front of the table. "How did your 304 test go?"

"The last part threw me. I took a stab, but I'm worried I whiffed on that one."

"The last one was a trick question," Jane said. "It was glandular, but he threw in language about methodologies to screw people up. At least, I hope that's what he did."

"That's what I thought too," the woman sitting nearest Mary Gleason said.

"Then I fucked it up," Mary said, chuckling as she shook her head.

"By the way, my friend here, Seamus, is a journalist," Jane said, leaning closer. Her voice fell to a whisper. "This is awkward. Hopefully it's not bad timing. He's writing an article about your old roommate's murder."

Mary looked at O'Neill. She was an attractive woman with a small nose and perfect teeth. A batch of rings were in each ear, and she wore jeans and a white shirt.

"He looks wasted," a woman whispered to Mary.

O'Neill pretended to not hear the comment.

"I talked to Myles Staley," O'Neill said, doing his best to not slur his words, "and he raised questions about how the police handled the, uh, the investigation into Andie Sheridan's death." He swallowed hard and tried to sound as competent as possible. "The time might not be ideal, but since Jane pointed you out..."

"I hope I'm not being a pain," Jane said.

Mary waved the comment off, keeping her attention on O'Neill. "Myles said the cops were clueless, but I never figured out why he was so belligerent about it. He talked and talked, but never explained why he thought they screwed up. I remember him mentioning a condom and a shovel, but nothing else. I didn't understand why Myles thought the cops screwed up, but I assumed he had a feeling."

O'Neill crouched in front of her so his head was even with the tabletop. He wanted to kneel, but the ground was sticky. His thoughts, however, were suddenly very clear. "Surprising the cops connected a condom with an attack in a city's wooded area."

"Is it odd for a rapist to wear a condom?" Mary replied as she shrugged her shoulders. "Doesn't that happen? The cops must have concluded it was the attacker's condom. Either way, it was not hers. The cops asked me whether Andie carried a condom with her when she ran. Who carries a condom when running?"

"That seems like an odd question for the cops to ask."

"Perhaps that was what led Myles to assume the cops were incompetent. As for the shovel, I remember him talking about one, but he never gave me details. I assumed the police found one."

O'Neill nodded, but his thoughts lost focus. As he looked at Mary, he realized she had known both the victim and the client at the time of the murder.

"You were dating Myles when all this happened, in August of '96?"

"Yeah," Mary said, "but it feels longer than two years ago."

"Are you still dating?"

"No, we broke up that winter before Christmas. We remained friendly, though I haven't talked to him since he graduated this spring and moved home to Chicago."

"How about Andie Sheridan? She ran cross-country, but I'm wondering about her as a person. What was she like?"

"Everyone will start by saying she was beautiful, or they'll say she was an awesome runner. Both were true, but her personality was harder to define. She was a partier and a loner, which seemed an odd match. It started with her hanging out with our group during her freshman year, which was my sophomore year. We'd see her out, and she was friendly. She always had guys after her, so she'd sometimes stay with us to dust guys away. By the end of that year, she was kind of in our group. I knew she wanted to move off campus for more freedom and, when one of my roommates transferred, we asked Andie to move in. We only lived together for a few months. It was us two during the summer, with more girls moving in for the fall."

"Was she a good roommate?"

"Sure, but she was quiet and I didn't see her much since she spent so much time at her boyfriend's. She was at his place a lot. I hadn't realized she was an introvert until that summer since I usually ran into her at parties where she was drinking. She was talkative and outgoing when she drank."

"You mentioned the boyfriend."

"Yeah, Larry Marsh, a TA in the business school. He was attractive and usually likable, but he could be intense and controlling. I don't think they would have been together much longer. She worried about how he would react to what she did, but she didn't know how to break up with him."

"Did she say anything about him being violent with her or pushing her around?"

"There were rumors after she died, but I don't know what was true. She never told me anything about him hitting or assaulting her. I think he messed with her head, though nothing too weird."

A woman at Mary's table tapped her shoulder. They spoke briefly before Mary looked back toward O'Neill.

"Did you talk to Andie the morning of the run?" O'Neill asked. "Was she acting strange or anything?"

"No," Mary said. "She was out the night before, but I didn't go. I heard her getting ready in the bathroom the following morning. She was running late, but I remember her waving goodbye as she left. That was the last I saw her. The cops came a few days later and took everything of hers from our apartment."

O'Neill was surprised that he got relevant information. There were probably other questions he should ask, but nothing came to him. "That is what I was wondering. I appreciate your time."

"Good, because I should head home," Mary said, glancing back as her friends prepared to leave.

O'Neill couldn't think of a proper response, so he smiled and walked away. He could feel adrenaline pumping through his body, and he walked toward the bar's exit rather than to a barstool.

"I hope she didn't mind too much," Jane said as they got into her Mazda. "I don't know her well. She probably thinks I shouldn't have introduced you to her."

"You thought it would be fine," O'Neill said as he wrote a few words in his notepad. "Besides, she seemed open about it. Blame me if she's pissed. Tell her I'm a friend of your sister's and I was being pushy."

Jane laughed, leaned sideways and rested her hand on his shoulder. He felt a shiver run through his body and he put the notepad in his pocket. She was pretty, but not quite beautiful, he thought. Yet her eyes drew him in. He wished he were two years younger.

They turned onto John Nolen Drive, heading south. The road brought them into the lit tunnel under the Monona Terrace Convention Center and along the shore of Lake Monona, one of two lakes which created the isthmus of downtown Madison. O'Neill looked at the clear sky and the lake's smell was unmistakable.

"Where do you live?" Jane asked.

"Half a mile from your place, halfway between the Red Shed and the Kohl Center. You can drop me at your place, and I'll walk home. That way, you won't have to double-back."

"Did you learn anything tonight about the murder?"

"The police apparently connected a condom with the attack," O'Neill said. "If that's the case, I get it. Either way, I can't imagine the police suggesting the condom was Andie's. Not sure about the shovel, but Myles knowing about both surprises me. Maybe they came out in the press. Either way, I'll check into it."

"How will you do that?"

"There might be information in newspaper articles from back in '96. If not, I'll ask someone to review the police files." The lies were getting deeper. "A detective agency I work with can access them."

Jane turned the car onto Broom Street, and it was quiet for a few moments. Once on West Dayton Street, she pulled the car into a spot close to her apartment.

"Being an investigative reporter must differ from writing songs and playing music. You're quite talented."

He almost told her the truth. Instead, he settled for parts of the truth he thought mattered most: "If I am, no one has noticed."

"I have."

He wanted to laugh at her innocence, and at himself. "It doesn't seem to be enough. I'm not going anywhere in music. I've been playing in bands for more than fifteen years and never made over ten thousand a year. Don't think I'm a tortured artist on the fringe of making it big. I'm never going to hit it big. I hope to sell songs and make a few bucks playing gigs around town, but I could make more money painting billboards. I'll keep playing, but I will do other work since there are bills to pay."

"But isn't making it big in music your dream?"

"Making music is what I do. I never expected to *make it big*."

O'Neill opened the car door and stepped out as a pair of motorcycles flew past, going much faster than the thirty-mile-per-hour speed limit. Jane jumped out and followed him.

"I didn't mean to make you mad," she said.

"I'm not mad, just a little tight."

Jane grabbed him by the waist and turned him toward her. Before he could react, her lips brushed against his. For an instant, he tried to pull away. Then, he leaned down so his lips were level to hers and they kissed. He inhaled, smelling her skin as his hands slid down her shirt and to the back of her jeans. He could feel the surge go through him.

And then, as quickly as she grabbed him, she pushed him away.

He looked into her eyes, but he didn't pull her back in.

"Why don't you stop by tomorrow?" she said. She walked away but continued to watch him.

"If I do, your sister might deck me," O'Neill yelled as she got to the porch.

She didn't stop.

"I don't think you locked your car," O'Neill commented.

Jane pulled out the key fob and aimed it at the car. There was a thud and she continued up the stairs.

He tried to say something interesting, but nothing came out. She opened the front door and disappeared inside. He waited a moment before pulling his flask out and taking a drink. Then he turned toward his apartment. As he walked, he told himself he should stay away from twenty-three-year-old women.

Yet he felt giddy, undeniably giddy.

Once at his apartment building, he opened the outer door and hurried up the stairs. As he jumped two steps at a time up the second story staircase, his left leg landed wrong and he crashed hard on the wooden steps. O'Neill yelled an expletive, then stood and felt a sharp pain in his left knee.

He took the remaining steps one at a time.

Chapter 5

O'Neill came to shortly after nine o'clock. He was used to waking up hungover, but knee pain was new. He slid off his mattress and hobbled to the bathroom. After relieving himself, he limped into the kitchen area and drank water out of the faucet. Instead of taking a Motrin, he took four.

O'Neill lay in bed for another hour, remembering the night before. His thoughts centered on Andie Sheridan's murder and Jane's blue eyes.

At ten o'clock, he wrapped his knee in an Ace bandage and got dressed. He tried walking, but any weight on the leg brought a sharp pain that he feared would topple him to the ground. Negotiating the stairs took several minutes. As he got to the second floor, he remembered the old couple in his apartment building. He knocked, and after a wait, the door opened.

"Yes?" the gray-haired woman said.

"Hello," O'Neill said. "You may know me from upstairs. I'm the one always playing whistle and guitar and accordion."

"Yes, I know you," she said. The door opened wider revealing a patterned rug and a wood cabinet filled with dishes and nick-nacks.

"I hurt my knee last night and I'm struggling on the stairs. It made me think of your husband."

"Charles?"

"Yes, Charles. He had a cane. He once told me that his cane helped him negotiate the stairs."

"You would like to borrow my husband's cane?" she said.

"If it's not inconvenient," he said in his kindest voice. Charles had died early in the year.

The door closed slightly, then re-opened. The woman held a weathered brown cane in front of him.

"They shot him in the war," she said, her voice hoarse but with a hint of youthfulness.

"I'll return it to you as soon as I'm better," O'Neill said as he took the cane.

"Whenever you're done with it. He's dead and I don't need it."

"Thanks. If there's anything I can do for you, let me know."

"Perhaps less guitar and more accordion," she said.

"Sure," he said, smiling. "I'll try."

She closed the door and O'Neill started down the stairs. He still felt a dull thud, but the cane limited the weight on the bad leg so a sharp pain didn't flare with each step.

O'Neill opened the building door and sunlight burst in. He put on sunglasses and walked to Johnson Street, which was busy with summer pedestrians and Sunday morning traffic. He struggled to walk, and as groups caught up with him, they lined up in single file to pass him.

Once at the library, he sat on the steps and rested. Despite the cane, his knee ached. When he noticed the time, he got to his feet and hobbled up the steps. The automatic doors opened and a librarian at the front desk looked up briefly.

O'Neill pegged the building as 1960s construction with flooring that looked like it belonged in an elementary school and faux-wood paneling along the walls. Newspapers were on one side of the first floor along the wall with periodicals. A half-dozen people sat at tables holding newspapers or magazines. While there were stacks of papers, they were current. O'Neill assumed papers from 1996 would be on microfiche. After a futile search, he approached the information desk. The librarian pointed him to a row of filing cabinets, noting that microfiche machine usage was limited to an hour. He grabbed the fiche for *The Capital Times* since, unlike Madison's other daily newspaper, *The Capital Times* didn't publish on Sundays and, though Sunday papers were as thick as the other six days combined, they had little hard news.

Murder was hard news.

It only took him five minutes before he found an article on page four of the August 26, 1996, issue.

UNIVERSITY RUNNER MISSING
A University women's cross-country team runner has been missing since Wednesday. The woman, Andie Sheridan, was last seen while running in the wooded University Arboretum.

Sheridan, 19, 416 W. Mifflin St., was one of 19 women to enter the Arboretum on a routine practice run. Sheridan did not check in with coaching staff following the run. On Saturday morning, University Police were notified of her disappearance.

According to Officer Patricia Hynes of the University Police, foul play is unlikely. "There is no sign of a struggle along the path, and the runners reported nothing suspicious. The portion of the arboretum which runs along Monroe Street is being searched."

Sheridan, of Janesville, will be a sophomore this fall at the University. She is a white female, 5 feet 10 inches tall, 135 pounds, with blonde hair and brown eyes. She was last seen wearing black shorts, a black tank top shirt, and white running shoes.

Anyone with information on Sheridan's whereabouts should contact the University Police at 267-7787.

The Capital Times credited the article to Brenda Selig. O'Neill printed the article and found a similar piece in the August 27 issue. This article included a photo of a missing person sign pinned to a bridge on campus, but there was no new information. The August 28, 1996, issue, however, included a large picture of Andie on the front page. The accompanying article was also by Brenda Selig.

UNIVERSITY RUNNER FOUND DEAD
The Madison Police Department found the body of a missing University cross-country runner yes-

terday less than a half mile from where she was reported missing.

Andie Sheridan, 19, disappeared on August 21 while running through a wooded area with the University's cross-country team. The University Police were not, however, contacted by university officials until August 24.

According to University Police Chief Donald Reineke, early indications from university officials and the crime scene did not lead the police to suspect foul play, and they made only a preliminary search of the area prior to yesterday.

Tuesday's search, led by a City of Madison police dog unit, was assisted by University Police, University cross-country coach Reggie Lehman, and student and community volunteers.

"It is unbelievable that this happened in broad daylight to someone in a group," Lehman said.

The dead woman was one of 19 university runners who took part in the August 21 run. She was last seen entering the arboretum path. The coaching staff noted her absence after the run finished at Vilas Park.

Lehman said the arboretum path is part of a regular route the runners took, but it will no longer be used by the cross-country team.

Chief Reineke indicated the University Police and City of Madison Police were cooperating in a full-scale investigation of the death. University Police brought the Madison Police Department into the case on August 25. According to the Madison Police Department, this involvement was initially limited to providing crime scene specialists, laboratory work, and a police dog unit.

An autopsy is scheduled to be performed by the Dane County Medical Examiner's Office.

Sheridan, of 416 W. Mifflin Street, was an all-state track and cross-country star at Janesville Craig High School. She was attending the University on a full athletic scholarship and participated in both cross-country and track.

There were multiple articles from later days and weeks, but few offered new information and none mentioned a condom or a shovel. One article from September included an interview with Andie's mother, but the article focused on Andie's high school athletic career, which O'Neill assumed was irrelevant. He loaded a separate reel, hoping to find an article on the anniversary of her death. He found one dated August 27, 1997, and credited to Lauren Hart. A picture of Andie accompanied the story.

UNIVERSITY RUNNER'S MURDER STILL UNSOLVED

One year ago today, the body of a University track and cross-country runner was found in a shallow grave in the University Arboretum.

Andie Sheridan, 19, disappeared on August 21, 1996, while running on a wooded path through the arboretum with the University cross-country team. University Police did not initially suspect foul play, so only a limited search of the arboretum was made.

Sheridan was one of 19 women who took part in the run. Police established that she entered the path, but none of the runners could verify that she exited the path. Police found her body on August 27, 1996, in a shallow grave between the path and Lake Wingra.

The City of Madison Police took the lead in the subsequent investigation and, according to Detective Phil Garcia of the Madison Police Department, the investigation continues. "We hope someone will offer new information. We need help from the public."

The Dane County Medical Examiner's office performed an autopsy, which listed strangulation as the cause of death and concluded the victim had been sexually assaulted.

According to Detective Garcia, police have interviewed "more than 100 people" and spent "thousands of man-hours" on the investigation. University Police Chief Donald Reineke indicated that they continue to cooperate with City of Madison Police in the investigation.

Sheridan was an all-state track star at Janesville Craig High School attending the University on an athletic scholarship.

The newspaper articles only amplified the central question O'Neill already had: how could a killer attack someone running in a group without being seen? There had to be more to the story, so for the first time since he started working for the Ryder Detective Agency, Seamus O'Neill was eager to get to the office. It was almost noon, so he printed the article, returned the microfiche to the librarian, and limped out. He held the three newspaper articles in one hand and reread them as he walked to the bus stop.

Chapter 6

O'Neill arrived at the Ryder Detective Agency shortly before twelve thirty. The office was on the second floor above Charlie's Subs and was larger than the detective agency needed. The only sign was a thin, horizontal board hanging beside the sub shop reading "Ryder Detective Agency" in a gothic font. An arrow pointed to a thin staircase next to the sub shop's entrance.

The sturdy wood door had a brass knocker with "Ryder" written across it. Inside was a step down in furnishings and in elevation. It was a three-inch step, but the change in elevation gave the room an odd perspective, often causing clients to stumble as they stepped into the office. Ryder claimed that clients who fell tended to hire him.

There were three rooms in the office. The outer room was the largest, and it benefited from three windows. Ryder and O'Neill's desks sat on opposite sides of the room with a computer on each. Ryder kept the bathroom and file room doors closed since both rooms stunk and were a mess.

A Windows screensaver was on Ryder's computer monitor and light shone from beneath the bathroom door. O'Neill started his computer and sat down. Soon, there was a flush and the bathroom door opened and shut.

"Afternoon," O'Neill said, as John Ryder approached. O'Neill's computer was starting up and the three newspaper articles were on the desk.

"Just got back a few minutes ago after talking to Phil Garcia from the Madison Police Department," Ryder said, rolling up his sleeves. "Garcia ran the investigation on this dead runner, the case is still active, and it is still his case. The good news is he's being as open with the files as I could hope. The bad news is he doesn't think it will do any good. We'll end up billing our client for the copies, so I had MPD make a ton of copies. I didn't get everything simply because there's too much. Some sheets have information redacted, but not too many." Ryder walked back to his desk and touched a stack of manilla folders. "I focused on their incident reports, investigation notes, the autopsy, the forensic reports, and statements coming from roughly a dozen people. Garcia thought these were most relevant. If we need a note from someone else's interview or statement, we can request it and they'll make copies and send them to us. But Garcia asked us to not make additional copies except for the summary information. When we're done, we need to return everything. The stuff I didn't get included interviews with the victim's teammates and their ex-boyfriends. It seems like they interviewed anyone who ever dated a cross-country runner. There were tons of logs of contacts with the public. I didn't get them."

"What happened?" O'Neill asked. "The newspaper articles make it sound like the woman disappeared into thin air. I remember coverage of it when it happened, but I didn't pay attention to it."

"A teammate saw the victim, Andie Sheridan, enter the path, but no one witnessed the attack. Presumably, someone pulled or lured her off the path then raped and killed her. There was little evidence in '96, and finding fresh evidence is a pipe dream."

"One newspaper article mentions the sexual assault. Was there semen or blood or anything?"

"They found semen in her hair and on her body and clothes. I don't think there was blood."

"Can they use the semen to identify the killer?"

"If they have a suspect, they can compare the semen they found on her with the suspect's DNA. But it's not like with fingerprints where there's a nationwide database of prints from criminals. The technology keeps changing, but until there's a database, the semen probably doesn't do any good besides comparing it with a specific suspect."

"Okay. How do we approach this?"

"We look through the files to determine who they met with and interviewed. We identify key witnesses and suspects without getting too far into the weeds. My guess is much of the files are the MPD going down multiple rabbit holes with everyone's boyfriends and ex-boyfriends. The MPD assumed it was someone she knew that attacked her, but after going down every back alley, Garcia eventually wondered if it was just a stranger or someone she hardly knew who attacked her. The MPD looked hard at the dead woman's boyfriend, but he had an airtight alibi. Then they investigated the coaching staff, but their alibis were also airtight. The third approach involved her teammates, focusing on the two in the back, including the one who saw Andie enter the path. Finally, they looked at her other friends and acquaintances and grilled twenty or twenty-five people and all their relationships. They were thorough but could not find a hot connection with anyone. Like I said,

Garcia is open to the possibility that a stranger killed her. I think they were waiting for more assaults, but another never happened."

"What did you learn about the sexual assault?" O'Neill asked.

"The autopsy brings up the sexual assault, of course, though I don't remember details. Like I said, there was semen in her hair and on her body but not inside her. They assume the attacker used a condom. They found a condom wrapper near the burial site, but no condom."

"Are the cops giving you access to everything?"

"Look at all these files," Ryder said. His hand patted the stack of files. "Garcia's not a genius, but he's not one to guard his butt and will take any help on a dead investigation. I give him credit for that. Wish they were all that way." He scratched at his thinning scalp. "Garcia didn't want to provide copies of the profile they put together, but he showed it to me. Besides that, I got what I asked for. Garcia said the killer buried her clothes with the body, but nothing else. We won't have access to the actual forensic evidence."

"He buried her with all her clothes?"

"Yeah, as far as we know, the killer took nothing with him," Ryder said, "though she was missing a hairband. But that likely got knocked out during the assault."

"Does that tell us anything?"

"If it was random, I might expect him to take a memento."

"Could the hairband have been the memento?"

"Garcia told me that the profiler they worked with thought the hairband was too impersonal. It's basically a rubber band."

"Do we know if the killer buried her right away or whether he came back?" O'Neill asked.

"The MPD spent a lot of time on that question," Ryder said. "Garcia can't imagine someone coming back with a shovel, yet he can't imagine him having a shovel when he attacked her."

The word "shovel" caught O'Neill's attention. "Bringing a shovel to the attack implies pre-meditation."

"Hell yeah," Ryder said, laughing as if it was a stupid comment.

"Do they have the shovel?"

"No," Ryder said. He opened a file and shuffled through several papers. "We're talking very little physical evidence. The killer's semen was in her hair, on her crotch, and on her underwear, yet they didn't find semen in her vagina. They also found the condom wrapper that I mentioned near the burial site. It had the victim's fingerprints on it, so they know it relates to the rape. They never found the actual condom, though. It was enough for the autopsy to assume the rapist climaxed while wearing the condom."

"Her fingerprints were on the wrapper. Does that seem odd?"

"Not really," Ryder said. "He probably had a knife to her throat and made her open it. Besides, she might have seen the advantage of him using a condom and been willing to do it. Either way, the semen they found on her body and clothes didn't lead them anywhere. The victim's boyfriend willingly provided a DNA sample, but it didn't match the DNA from the semen found on her body. That's an example of DNA eliminating a suspect."

"Why would a boyfriend attack his girlfriend while she's running in a group, anyway?" O'Neill asked. "He wouldn't seem like a good suspect."

"Good point," Ryder said. "Yet the vast majority of sexual assaults and murders involve someone who knows the victim. Boyfriends and spouses are always at the top of the suspect list."

"Was she drugged?"

"No. This surprised the MPD since they assumed he chloroformed her to get her off the path. Alcohol was in her system, but no other drugs. She also had no head trauma, so he didn't knock her out."

"How much alcohol was in her system?"

"It would take me a few minutes to find, but Garcia said the blood alcohol content reflected a night of heavy, but not ridiculous, drinking."

"So, the attacker somehow gets her quickly off the path without being seen. He rapes and strangles her then buries her body."

"That's the short of it," Ryder said.

"If the cops never found a shovel, how do they know he used one?"

"Garcia said the killer couldn't have dug the grave without a shovel or a similar tool. The notes say there were striations in the dirt implying a 'digging tool.' Besides, the grave was deep enough that it couldn't be someone digging with his hands. The MPD viewed the shovel as a given."

"Garcia mentioned to you that he couldn't see the killer having a shovel with him, but he couldn't imagine the guy coming back, either. What did the cops conclude? Did the killer have a shovel with him or did he come back later to bury her body?"

"They thought it was likely that the killer came back. I mean, what job requires someone to carry a shovel on a public path other than maintenance workers?" He shuffled through the papers for a few minutes. "I know I saw something. Here it is. It says in their investigation notes that the University had no record of workers in the area that morning, and no witnesses reported seeing maintenance workers or anyone with a shovel."

"The University?"

"Yeah," Ryder replied. "The University owns the arboretum and handles its maintenance. It appears the MPD concluded he came back and buried her. He could have had a shovel in his car, but what idiot would risk someone seeing him opening a trunk in the daytime and pulling out a shovel? It says here that the MPD interviewed nearby businesses, everyone that had been in Wingra Park, and the nearby homeowners and renters. It references a whole page of contacts. They also dug into males living near the path but didn't come up with any suspects. Dozens of witnesses stepped forward, but no one remembered a suspicious maintenance worker or a shovel-toting man. This included teachers from a nursery school. They arrived before ten o'clock that morning for a field trip with the kids. They were on the path for over an hour and didn't see anyone. Finally, the MPD had a group of metal detector geeks go through the area and they didn't come up with a shovel. I'll go through this more thoroughly, but it seems the MPD concluded the killer came back with the shovel to bury her and took the shovel when he left. I think that makes sense."

"Could he have come back later in the day or that night? Could he have come back another night?"

"The autopsy says the body was not exposed long," Ryder said as he shuffled through papers. "Here's a note from Garcia that references the autopsy. It states that the 'body did not show evidence of prolonged exposure.' Garcia's note says the medical examiner thought she had to have been 'buried no later than twenty-four hours after death.'"

"Okay," O'Neill said. "So, he could have buried the body right away or he could have come back later in the day or during the night. Did our client, Myles Staley, come up in your discussions with Garcia?"

"Yeah," Ryder said. "I confided in him that Myles is our client. Garcia said Myles was a person of interest. Apparently, he and his roommate were out the night before with the victim. But he and the roommate had alibis, so he wasn't a serious suspect."

A crooked smile splashed across O'Neill's face. "So, what do you think? Is this case solvable?"

"Not unless we get damn lucky," Ryder said. "The MPD put thousands of hours into it. We won't put more than 160. What are you thinking?"

"Harry Bartholomew is trying to get Sandra to move back home. He wants me out of her life. That's what Sandra told me. She thinks her dad is going to offer her an allowance or a job to stay in Chicago and give me up, so I was expecting him to come up with a way to make me look bad. Instead, he offers us this job. What's he doing? Is he giving me a few dollars so Sandra doesn't worry about leaving me? Or is he setting me up somehow? Is he trying to make me look bad by letting us fail? Perhaps he thinks that would give Sandra another reason to dump me."

"I can't see a big shot like Harry Bartholomew doing anything elaborate to make you look bad. If he wants Sandra to dump you, he will pay someone to plant crack in your room. The next thing you know, cops knock your door down and you're in jail faster than you can put your underwear on. Your Sandy would dump you for sure."

"What if it's the opposite? What if he just wants Sandra to think I'm doing fine and that I don't need her pity? Sandra may have told her daddy that I found something decent to do without giving up music. If this creates a narrative where I'm doing well, he might think she won't feel guilty dumping me."

"You're suggesting he is either making you look good or bad? How about a third possibility: you're losing it?" He stopped when he noticed O'Neill's cane. "What's the idea with the stick? Is it some fashion thing for you artsy folk?"

"I fell down the stairs and banged my knee."

"Drunk?"

"What do you think?"

"You're pitiful," Ryder said with a shake of the head.

"Trying to be like you."

"Yeah. Anyway, whether he's making you look good or bad, it's a goofy way of doing it. I mean, is your Sandra going to care if your boss can't solve her daddy's stupid case? You think too much. Besides, I don't care whether Sandra's daddy hired us to make you look good or bad or whether he hired us to satisfy the whim of a rich client —though that seems the most likely alternative. We have a difficult cold case on our hands, so why should we stress ourselves? Why not just interview people, write notes, and collect our fee? If we see something of interest, we investigate it so long as we're being paid. Busting our asses will not get us any further."

O'Neill glanced at a black-and-white photo on the wall of Ryder wearing a police uniform. He wondered whether Ryder had a full head of hair under the cap. The rest of the photos were of Ryder's father.

"Are you worried about Sandra?" Ryder said. "You don't want her to think you're a bum or something. Is that what's worrying you?"

"Course not. She already dumped me. She hasn't told her dad yet, though. She views me as a bargaining chip. She thinks her dad will give her an allowance or something just to get her away from me."

"Yet she already dumped you?"

"Yeah."

"Cold."

"Don't rub it in. I just want my twenty-five percent cut like you promised. I need the money."

"Gonna buy an amp or something?"

O'Neill ran a hand through his scraggly hair. "Least I don't have to buy hookers like someone I know."

Ryder gave him the finger and tucked his white shirt into his pants, signifying a change of subject. "I'm heading to Janesville in a few minutes to interview the victim's mother. She said today or Monday works. I thought I'd get it out of the way."

"You want me to come along?"

Ryder paused and licked his lips. "Nah. It's nearly two hours round trip and I don't really expect to get anything out of the meeting other than background information. It's not like she'll know what happened on the run. This is basically a PR trip."

"What do you mean by a PR trip?"

"I want the murdered woman's parents to find out from me that I'm asking questions about her murder. I don't want them hearing rumors and getting pissed off. We need them to help us open doors and not to close them. My fear is that I'm going to sit and listen to her talk for twenty minutes about how great a runner her daughter was. It's not something I'm looking forward to."

"I could help you out there," O'Neill said. "I ran cross-country and track in high school. That might be worthwhile in case she wants to talk about Andie's running career."

"You?" Ryder yelled, pointing at O'Neill as if accusing him of a crime. "You were in a sport?" After a momentary pause, he shook his head. "I can't believe it. You would hang out with the freaks, not the jocks."

"And you didn't have anyone to hang out with."

"Screw you. Besides, you can hardly even walk, let alone run."

"Just offering my running expertise. I could read the file during the trip, which I'd be doing anyway if I was at the office."

"Okay," Ryder finally said. "I must admit I don't know jack squat about cross-country running. If she's the type of mom who wants to relive her daughter's athletic success, it might be useful having you. But we need to roll. Bring the MPD's case files along. And no tin whistle playing in the truck."

Chapter 7

O'Neill bundled the manilla folders together with heavy rubber bands. Ryder let O'Neill struggle on the stairs before finally taking the files from him. O'Neill limped down the stairs and over to Ryder's Chevy S-10. The sun was high in the sky and as O'Neill opened the passenger door, a rush of hot air exited the truck's cab. As he sat, O'Neill leaned forward so his neck didn't touch the hot leather. Ryder tossed his sport coat in the back seat and slid into the driver's seat.

"We're going to stop briefly at the path where the victim disappeared," Ryder said as he started the vehicle. "We don't have time to walk the path or to get into too many details since our appointment is at two o'clock, and it's at least a forty-five-minute trip to Janesville. I want a visual on it. There's a sketch in the first file; see if you can find it."

Ryder turned the Chevy S-10 off Regent Street and onto Monroe Street.

"I ran the path many times, but I haven't been there for fifteen years," O'Neil said as he pulled out the first folder. "It will be good to see it."

"How long is the path?"

"Maybe half a mile," O'Neill said as he found a sketch of the path and an aerial photograph. "Here we go."

"Where should we park?" Ryder asked.

"Park before we get to Mallatt's Pharmacy near where Monroe ends. We can see most of the path from there. Unless you want to be on the path itself."

"Across from it is fine. Besides, you're our agency *running expert*," Ryder said with a chuckle.

They continued driving on Monroe Street, going past Edgewood High School and Dudgeon School Park. Ryder slowed the truck as they approached the pharmacy and stopped in front of a street parking sign.

O'Neill stepped onto the curb, holding the map and the aerial photo in one hand and the cane in the other. Ryder was waiting for him behind the truck. They looked across the street. The area closest to the street looked more like a savannah than a wooded path. A small pond sat directly across from them.

"Is this it, right here?" Ryder asked as a pair of cars passed in front of them.

"Yeah. The path is shaped like a curved sword or maybe a smile. It starts on the northeastern side at Arbor Drive and has a gentle curve toward Monroe Street until it gets to where we are and merges with the sidewalk. The path then curves away from where we are, getting more wooded and turning sharply near the end. It goes behind those houses and exits on Nakoma Road just past where Monroe ends. There is a parking area at each end of the path that fits three or four cars each."

"The weather on the morning of the attack was about seventy degrees and mostly sunny."

"Not that different from now," O'Neill said. "Same with traffic. There would have been cars driving past, but not heavy traffic."

A car pulled up behind Ryder's truck.

"The path is more open than I expected," Ryder said. "I expected a heavily wooded trail."

"It's lightly wooded on the northeast side, which would have been where the runners entered it. Most of the middle is open facing Monroe Street, but then it gets thick at the southwestern end. Obviously, it's wooded behind the path, going through brush, trees, and muck until you get to Lake Wingra."

"So, if they were running now, we would see them most of the time they were on the path?"

"Yeah," O'Neill said. "They'd only be hidden at the beginning and end of the path. The part hidden at the beginning is less than a tenth of a mile. The part hidden at the end is less than two-tenths of a mile. My guess is they'd cover the entire path in a little over three minutes."

"This is a pretty short run for a college cross-country team, isn't it?"

O'Neill chuckled. "This path is a small part of the overall run. But she disappeared on this path, and they found her body near it. The rest of the route went through city streets."

"Okay," Ryder said as he looked at the map. "The X appears to be where they found the body. It's at the end of the path where you said the woods are thickest. That makes sense."

"Yeah," O'Neill said. "That is also the most crooked part of the path, and it would give the most cover to an attacker. Yet..."

"Yet what?"

"There are nineteen women on a run. Who would choose to attack someone in a group on this path? It was awfully risky wherever he attacked her. I agree it's smarter than attacking her on an open street, but it's still hard to fathom."

"No one said rapists are geniuses," Ryder said. He looked at his watch. "Let's get moving. We can come back to the path another day. I just wanted a general idea."

⁂

O'Neill read through the file as they drove to Janesville. He pulled out his notepad and made notes about the details of the run. Periodically, he looked up at the Wisconsin countryside that surrounded Highway 14.

"There's something that bothers me about this," O'Neill said. "Our victim, Andie Sheridan, was toward the back of the path as they ran down Arbor Drive, which runs parallel to Monroe and is where they entered the path. One woman, a Tanya Paulus, passed Andie on Arbor Drive. That left only one person behind Andie. That person, a Donna Ritz, saw Andie enter the path, but she didn't see Andie after that."

"Because he attacked her on the path. What bothers you about that?"

"You saw how open that path is. Wouldn't Andie have been within Donna Ritz's line of sight along most of the path?"

Ryder turned off the radio before responding. "You would think so, but there's a load of women running. It might be hard for a runner to keep track of who is where. When you ran, would you always know where a specific runner was?"

"I suppose not," O'Neill said, paging through the files. "One interesting thing is that two men and two women crossed paths with the cross-country team while on the path. The men came across first. Their names are Gary Fano and Lou Kart. The first guy's statement estimates that they saw twenty women, saying there were two groups of eight to ten runners. He noted two 'stragglers' behind the groups. He was unsure whether they were running with the other women. He picked Tanya Paulus and Donna Ritz from a photo lineup, so the implication is they were the stragglers."

"Either these two guys crossed them *after* the killer attacked Andie, or Andie had caught up with the second pack."

"Yeah, I suppose."

"The two male runners," Ryder said. "They were presumably suspects. What can you find on them? Check the back of the binder. Two have indexes."

O'Neill found Gary Fano in the index. It referenced six separate pages. The first reference was an investigator's note.

"It says here that sixteen of the runners on the team remembered seeing the two guys. They got statements from the men and cleared them."

"On what basis?"

"Give me a minute," O'Neill said. "I'm not quite following how this is all organized. Okay, here we go. The two men got to Wingra Park approximately five minutes later, and there were multiple witnesses. This included the two other runners on the path, two women who were approximately a minute behind the two men and saw the men stop running on Arbor Drive at Wingra Park. This was consistent with the men's statements."

"So, they couldn't have attacked her unless it was part of a larger plot, which sounds far-fetched. How about the Ritz woman?" Ryder said. "It sounds like she is the only one who saw Andie on the path. Garcia mentioned that to me and said they vetted her to death. What can you find on her? I'm assuming Garcia gave us her statement."

O'Neill searched for several minutes before finding the statement in the second binder. He skimmed Donna Ritz's statement then referred to several notes.

"She missed the vans that brought the team to Vilas," O'Neill finally said, "because of a school thing that the MPD verified with the instructor. The coaching staff knew she would be late, and their handwritten log noted her leaving two minutes after the rest of the team. The log showed the team starting at four minutes after nine and Donna Ritz starting at six minutes after nine. Her statements were consistent with Tanya Paulus' statement. There are also interview notes for her."

"The MPD obviously dug into her because they realized there was a possibility Donna Ritz saw something but wouldn't admit to what she saw," Ryder said. "She obviously wouldn't be the rapist, but if that was true, she could somehow be part of it."

"There are a few paragraphs on Ritz as a suspect in a note from Garcia. It says they dug heavily into Ritz simply because she was a key witness. She had been on the dean's list every semester, was from a middle-class family, and blah, blah, blah. She was not acquainted with Andie or Andie's boyfriend. The MPD realized that if she was lying, it would blow up everything, so they grilled her. There are multiple references to interviews. Garcia personally interviewed her parents."

"So, Garcia eventually bought that Ritz was telling the truth."

"Looks like it," O'Neill said.

"How about the body? Any information about who found her body and how they found it?"

O'Neill shuffled through papers for several minutes before finding details on the body recovery. "They found the body on Tuesday morning, which would have been six days after she disappeared. Her body was approximately two hundred feet east of the path, southeast of Monroe Street and Nakoma Road. That would be the end of the path, going away from Monroe Street and toward the lake. That's consistent with the map we looked at."

"Who found the body?"

"A Grace Lee. She was a community volunteer. I'm not finding much detail on how she found the body other than that there was an organized search involving numerous people."

"Such as?"

"Police, student volunteers, community volunteers," O'Neill said, skimming through several pages on the search. "The cross-country coaches and support staff searched too. Hey, the whole women's basketball team searched. Is it odd that they don't reference the cross-country team? They mention the coaches, but not the runners. Wouldn't they want to search for their teammate?"

"That may have been deliberate. They certainly weren't suspects, but either the MPD or the University may have wanted to keep them at a distance from the murder scene. It might not be ideal for one of them to find a dead teammate. They wouldn't have wanted the Ritz woman or Tanya Paulus at the murder scene."

There was a long silence as O'Neill read through notes about the body's location and its condition. "Says he buried her with her top, bra, and socks still on her body. Her shoes, shorts and underwear were buried next to her. The underwear was badly torn. The only thing missing was a hairband, which you already mentioned."

"That could have easily fallen or got knocked off."

"Sure," O'Neill said. "Is this what you expect with a sexual assault?"

"Yes, though I only saw one murder victim in my ten years with the MPD who had been raped and dumped. I'm no expert."

"We know Andie was out the night before and had run into our client, Myles Staley."

"Are you suggesting the semen came from the night before?" Ryder said. "Maybe from Myles?"

"I'm just asking," O'Neill said.

"That would be a huge miss by the MPD if the semen was from the prior night. See what you find in the files."

O'Neill flipped through several papers, slowly figuring out the logic of the file's organization. He found a note written by a Detective Langley, which stated that, "no significant trauma to the body was noted." O'Neill was about to read it out loud when he noticed a separate comment from Langley stating that the victim had changed clothes that morning. She left clothes from the previous night on the bathroom floor at her apartment. The police took the clothes as evidence. There was no semen on the underwear.

"I got my answer here," O'Neill said. "The cops tested the underwear she was wearing the previous night. She got changed in the bathroom of her apartment, leaving them on the bathroom floor. So, it was obvious what she had been wearing and that she put on fresh clothes. Either way, there was no semen or other DNA on the underwear she wore the previous day. So, the semen got on her body and underwear in the woods. I can see the logic, unless we've got a roommate switching the clothes or something sinister like that."

"The killer probably had a knife to her neck or something during the attack," Ryder said. "She probably didn't fight back because she was trying to survive. That also explains the condom wrapper."

"I want to see what they say about Myles Staley. Any thoughts on where to find references to him? I didn't see him in the index."

"You've got the fourth binder now. Check the first binder's index. I think the first one relates to two binders. Keep in mind that the indexes might reference documents we don't have."

O'Neill found Myles Staley's name in the first index. It led him to what appeared to be a spreadsheet that listed names and alibis.

"Myles had an alibi, like you said," O'Neill announced. "He was at the library. They got a librarian who remembered him being there at nine-thirty, which was when the library opened. That's a good alibi since they likely came through the path at about nine-fifteen. Also, that afternoon, him and his roommate, a Ralph Warzyn, drove to the Twin Cities. The cops verified a five-thirty check-in at the Courtyard by Marriott hotel in St. Paul. The hotel clerk identified them both from photos, so Myles couldn't have come back at night to bury the body unless he drove five hours back to Madison."

"They cleared Myles. That's not surprising since it would be odd for him to hire us to solve a murder he committed. How many people are on the listing?" Ryder asked.

"Must be fifty or sixty names on this one. Who the hell could these people be?"

"Take a few names you don't know and see what information you find on them."

O'Neill compared the listing to an index. He picked two names that were in both, but also had additional references in the index.

"The two I found were boyfriends of runners," O'Neill said. "One of Andie's from high school and one of Mandy Monfils'. Like you said, they were grilling through Andie's old boyfriends and the relationships of the other runners. Andie's old boyfriend has a five-star alibi."

"What's that?"

"He was at school at UCLA. That's a good distance. We can check him off our list."

"We're going to be in Janesville in another fifteen minutes," Ryder said. "See what you find on Andie Sheridan's parents."

It took five minutes before O'Neill found anything on Andie Sheridan's parents. There were three pages that summarized an interview with Mark Sheridan and Jennifer Reilly; they divorced in 1988. Jennifer Reilly had custody of Andie after the divorce, though Mark Sheridan remained part of her life. Neither had a criminal record.

"I found an interview summary and a short background write-up. There must be more in the other binders. There's also a copy of a newspaper article of interviews with the mother. I saw that at the library but didn't copy it. Why do you want to interview the parents right away?" O'Neill asked. "I'm not sure what we'll learn from them. They weren't even in the city when the attack happened."

"As I told you, it's PR. The mother is the closest we can come to Andie. We want her support for whatever investigation we do. If we want something from a friend of Andie's or from anyone involved in the case, it would be good to have her support. We want her to bring gravity with us. We want people we interview to know that their answers matter terribly to someone. Otherwise, people just look at us as a pain in the ass. I would prefer interviewing both parents, but Mark is in construction and working on a job in southern Illinois. Getting the mother's support is the most important thing. We'll wield her name in every interview we do."

"I buy that," O'Neill said as he read through the police notes. "There is one interesting thing in the summary. It says the mother wanted the police to look closely at Andie's boyfriend, Larry Marsh. During her freshman year, Andie's roommate called Andie's mother and told her that Andie had a bruised eye that looked suspicious. The roommate obviously thought someone had punched her. The mother talked to Andie, but she denied being hit. She said she got hit by a branch while running. Andie told her she would be more careful, and it would not happen again."

"You buy the branch thing?"

"No fucking way," O'Neill replied. "So, she may have had a boyfriend who hit her. But a boyfriend wouldn't be a logical suspect. I mean, why would he attack and rape her out on a path like this? But knowing he's a girl-hitter makes me wonder. Sounds like he deserves attention."

"Yeah, the MPD had him as a prime suspect for a while at least," Ryder said. "But he has an alibi, and he's the one who voluntarily gave a DNA sample. He's in the clear." Ryder clicked on the blinker, and the Chevy turned off the state trunk highway. "Now remember, you're here to observe and add relevant information about running that might come up, or at least use your running background to develop rapport with her. Let me run the interview. I don't need you saying something stupid. Also, Jennifer and I already had a conversation on the phone, so she knows I can't name our client. I did, however, tell her it was a friend of Andie's from the University. I think she appreciated that a friend cared enough to hire us."

O'Neill nodded his agreement. He kept out the three sheets on Andie Sheridan's parents, and he bound the folders back together with rubber bands.

"We're here," Ryder said, nodding toward a blue one-story house. "Lock your door."

Ryder walked past O'Neill and up the two steps that led to the house. As O'Neill caught up with him, the door opened. A blonde woman in her early forties pushed the screen door open and Ryder stepped in. She wore a Milwaukee Brewers jersey and shorts. She looked tired. O'Neill grabbed the screen door with his fist and followed Ryder inside.

The carpet was newly vacuumed, and the smell of freshly baked bread was unmistakable. A sofa sat in front of a bay window with two chairs opposite. At the end of the room, a soap opera was playing on a console television. Jennifer Reilly turned the television off and offered them drinks. Ryder accepted coffee while O'Neill took water.

They both sat on the sofa. O'Neill looked at the walls, which were filled with pictures of Andie Sheridan. There were no pictures of her running, but there was a small plaque covered with ribbons and awards. Jennifer Reilly returned, handing Ryder his coffee and O'Neill ice water.

"What can I do for you gentlemen?" she asked as she sat in a chair opposite Ryder.

"As I mentioned on the phone, we've been hired to look into your daughter's death," Ryder said in a quiet voice. "We first want to offer our condolences. We can't imagine what you've gone through over these last two years."

Jennifer nodded lightly but didn't respond.

"I was hoping you could take five minutes to give us an idea of who Andie was. It will help us better focus the investigation."

"Andie was wonderful," Jennifer said. "She was my only child, and I loved her dearly. She didn't always have it easy being raised by a single mother, but she was resilient. She was painfully shy, so she didn't have many friends, though there were always boys interested in her. She was quite pretty."

"We can see that in the photos on your wall. Is that one her high school graduation photo?"

"Yes," Jennifer said. She turned toward the photo. "Andie liked that photo. She also liked the one in the corner over there. It includes Mark and me. It's the last professional family photo we have."

"She was also quite the runner," O'Neill said.

"Yes, she was," Jennifer agreed. "She was talented."

"Did she get her running ability from you or her father?"

"I'm not sure. I was a good athlete, but Mark was better. Neither of us were runners, but I played soccer and Mark played pretty much every team sport besides soccer."

"Did you enjoy watching her run?" O'Neill asked.

"Yes, since she almost always won throughout high school," she said, laughing. "But Andie wasn't obsessive about running as people sometimes assumed. She was naturally a great runner and wanted to use that to springboard herself to success. But she wasn't someone who ran for running's sake. She only got into it because the middle-school track coach heard she beat everyone in a race they had in gym class. He talked her into joining the team and she ended up as the best runner the school ever had."

O'Neill was about to ask a follow-up question when he noticed Ryder glaring at him. Ryder asked several more questions, and they talked about Andie's high school friends and her experiences in college. Finally, Ryder got to his feet. O'Neill finished his water and used the cane to push himself up.

"Is there anything else you think we should know as we start our investigation?" Ryder asked as they shook hands.

"Just one thing, I guess," Jennifer said. "When she disappeared, I assumed it was her boyfriend, Larry Marsh, who had killed her. Andie never told me anything, but I could tell she lost interest in him. The police tried hard, but they concluded he couldn't have been involved since he had a perfect alibi."

"That's what we heard," O'Neill said. "What was his perfect alibi?"

"He was at the University teaching a class in front of fifty students."

"I guess that's as good of an alibi as you can get," Ryder said.

"Yes," Jennifer said. "Unfortunately."

Chapter 8

Ryder and O'Neill thanked Jennifer Reilly and made their way to Ryder's Chevy S-10. The leather seats were as hot as O'Neill expected, and he returned the three stray sheets to the manilla folder. Ryder started the truck and O'Neill turned on the radio, changing channels until finding something he wanted to hear.

"Thoughts on the meeting?" Ryder asked.

"It surprised me that there wasn't more discussion about Andie's running career," O'Neill said. "This woman was a division one scholarship athlete, yet there was only one plaque on the wall, and mom only talked about it because I brought it up."

"What does that mean?"

"Maybe nothing," O'Neill said. "It just surprised me." He opened the first binder and found the index. "The other interesting thing was that when you asked for a final thought, she told us, in effect, that she thinks Larry Marsh killed her daughter. But she knows he has a perfect alibi. It's worth seeing what vetting the cops did on that alibi."

"Feel free to dig into it, but I'm not sure it matters since mothers often don't like their daughter's boyfriends."

O'Neill found Larry Marsh referenced on more than a dozen pages of the first file's index. The first was a photocopy of Larry's driver's license, which listed him at six foot two and two hundred pounds. The photo showed a handsome, blonde-haired man wearing glasses and a sport coat.

A separate page detailed Larry's alibi. It listed four students and an associate professor who verified the alibi, placing him at Grainger Hall from eight thirty until eleven thirty.

"They only list four students for his alibi," O'Neill said.

"They likely got verbal statements from more than that," Ryder said, "but only got written statements and contact information from those four. At some point, you don't need more support."

O'Neill also found the DNA evidence Ryder had mentioned earlier.

"It says that Larry Marsh submitted a DNA sample to the cops," O'Neill said. "It did not match the DNA from the semen found on Andie. There's a reference to the test, but I don't think we have the test results." He paused and looked at Ryder. "How do they do that comparison? Did Larry submit a semen sample, or do they get DNA from something else? Is it worth getting the actual test results?"

"I don't really know what they're doing nowadays," Ryder said. "I can ask Garcia, but I don't think it makes a difference and I don't think we need to see the test. The MPD knows what they're doing, so we can rely on their conclusion. Eventually, I think there will be a national database that will collect DNA on convicted rapists and criminals. But I don't know how they collect DNA today or how testing works. Everything is in flux."

"Either way, it supports Larry Marsh's innocence." O'Neill tilted the seat back and closed his eyes.

"Before you fall asleep, the last person to talk to Andie transferred to UW-La Crosse, which coincidentally has three newly opened brewpubs." A smile slid onto Ryder's chubby face. "Talking to her would be a logical start, and your Sandra's dad will foot the lodging and the per diem. And since I wouldn't mind someone to tip a beer with, it makes sense for you to come along, my drunken friend. We could run up late tomorrow morning. I would go tonight, but I got a date."

"A date? Which steakhouse you taking her to?"

"None of your business. Review the notes and summarize the timeline." He pointed at the manila file. "Your experience running, especially on the path, makes you relevant to the discussion with the runner in La Crosse. Her name is Tanya Paulus."

"I wouldn't be able to go tonight either," O'Neill said. "I'm playing the Union, sitting in with a friend's band."

"Okay but get the gypsy mind rot shit out of your system. I don't want to hear anything on the drive to La Crosse except Lynyrd Skynyrd."

When O'Neill and Ryder got back to the office, O'Neill made copies of the summary material. He stuck them in a separate file, which he took home. The trip home was brief, but his knee made the walk difficult. At home, he took off the Ace bandage, swallowed four Motrin, and poured a double shot of Grant's.

At six thirty, he put on a cleaner shirt, re-wrapped his knee, and waited. If The Johnson wanted him to sit in tonight, he would pick him up. It was the way they had always done it. O'Neill was getting anxious, as it had been three weeks since he played in front of a live audience, and he missed the excitement, the applause, and the music. Perhaps he even missed the adoration.

The Johnson arrived shortly before seven. O'Neill met him at the door.

"What's the deal with the wheel?" The Johnson asked, pointing at O'Neill's leg.

"Fell on the stairs last night."

"Looks like it hurts."

"Observant."

As they walked down the stairs, The Johnson looked unsure if he should help O'Neill or ignore him.

"What am I playing tonight?" O'Neill asked.

"Bip left town today with his girlfriend, so you're on bass."

The Johnson was six foot two with a solid build. He had a thin, 1930s style mustache, long hair, and a pair of eagle tattoos on his shoulders. His face was flat, and bulging eyes gave him a predatory appearance. The Johnson had been part of Madison's music scene for years and had co-written several songs with O'Neill. In recent years, an informal bartering agreement between Shifts in Turmoil and Sea City Chaos had developed, so if one band was short a player, the other band lent one. O'Neill was usually the one lent by Sea City Chaos.

O'Neill wanted to play partly because he suspected Jane would be in the audience. The thought of seeing her dominated his thoughts. He wondered who she would be with, what she would wear, and whether her hair would be up. He wondered what she would drink, if she would smile when she saw him, or if she would act like last night never happened. And he wondered how he would act when he saw her.

The show would be the first Sunday concert O'Neill could remember playing at the Memorial Union Terrace. Shifts in Turmoil was opening for a band out of San Francisco with a record deal with Reprise and a single getting played on MTV. The plan was for the Shits, as everyone called Shifts in Turmoil, to play twenty-five minutes and the MTV band to play an hour and a half.

O'Neill was thankful for a quick show since his knee was throbbing. When he arrived, he slammed a beer, tuned Bip Crosby's bass, looked over the playlist, and drank more beer.

He leaned back and watched as sailboats weaved across the lake and students in summer clothes walked along the shoreline. A slight breeze blew off the lake and the rancid smell of algae permeated the clear August night. The outdoor stage faced south so the setting sun would be to their right, providing dim natural light lasting past the end of their set. O'Neill expected a large, unruly crowd, at least for a Sunday.

O'Neill was only half buzzed when the show started, but as they launched into Roy Wood's "California Man," the pain disappeared, and when the twenty-five-minute set was over, he left the stage without a thought of his knee or of Jane. It caught him by surprise when he spotted her at a table with a group of women. She waved at him and there was a smile on her face. A surge of adrenaline shot through him.

"Which one you waving to?" The Johnson asked.

O'Neill did not even realize he was waving. "The brunette in the middle; Amanda's sister."

"I'd do her," The Johnson said after looking her over. Then he turned back to O'Neill. "Gimme Bip's bass. He's anal about this thing and will undoubtedly give her a bath since you touched her. Are you hanging around to watch these guys?"

"I got three free drink cards left," O'Neill replied. He started with five, but a roadie had given him four more. "I'll hang long enough to use them."

"They got a table set aside for us back there. Ed is heading out, but KP and I will hang around. We'll put our gear away and be back."

After a few breaths, O'Neill grabbed his cane, limped to the table, and sat on one of the Union's 4,000 sunburst chairs. The band's table was far from the stage, so he couldn't see Jane's table. It relieved him to sit, but he wished he had a beer. The MTV band was getting ready but wouldn't start for another ten minutes.

A long-haired, college-aged kid approached him. "Awesome show, man. You guys totally rock." The kid's head continued to nod.

O'Neill did his best to avoid music fans who used too many adjectives and adverbs, but he needed a beer. "Thanks a lot. Hey, could you do me a favor?"

"Sure," the kid responded with a chuckle.

"Are you old enough to buy a drink?"

The kid nodded, so O'Neill handed him one of his free drink cards. "I hurt my knee and I need a beer. Could you grab me a drink of anything besides light beer?"

The kid took the ticket and headed toward the bar. In a few minutes, he returned with the beer and a girl.

"This is one of the Shits," the kid said to his girl as he handed O'Neill the beer.

She was tall and thin with spiky yellow hair and long false eyelashes. "You guys rock," she said.

O'Neill would have left, but he couldn't walk. Besides, the kid got him a beer. "Take a seat. The chairs are for the band, but they're putting equipment away."

The kids thanked him and took the chairs. They asked him about Shifts in Turmoil and other bands in town. The two never mentioned Sea City Chaos, so O'Neill brought them up.

"They're okay for a wuss band," long hair announced.

"Yeah, but weird," the girl added. "My roomie saw them, and they played the theme from *Hogan's Heroes*, and they played on and on. People were booing, but they kept going like they didn't give a shit."

O'Neill remembered it differently, but KP and The Johnson showed up, saving him from additional conversation. The kid stood, but his girl didn't. The Johnson sat next to her and KP grabbed another chair and sat across from her. Once the girl saw The Johnson, she focused her attention on him.

The kid drifted away after a few minutes.

As O'Neill finished his beer, Angie Pear, one of *Isthmus'* entertainment reporters, approached the table. O'Neill didn't mind talking to her since she was bright and gave crumbles of press to Sea City Chaos. Pear was a tall blonde in her early thirties with thick black eyebrows and a crooked nose.

"Just sitting in tonight?" Pear asked. "Or is this something more permanent?"

"Just sitting in."

"Any plans for it to be more permanent since you're suddenly a free agent?"

"Nope. No plans at all," O'Neill said, staring at his empty glass. "Can I buy you a beer?"

"Sure," she said, her voice showing surprise.

"Tipped my knee though," he said as he handed her two tickets. "Would you mind getting 'em? A micro-beer would be best, but I'll take whatever you decide."

She looked at him doubtfully but took the tickets and trotted away.

"What did the critic want?" asked KP.

"Not sure, but she's getting me a beer."

O'Neill and KP laughed. They talked for a few minutes before The Johnson's gaze settled behind O'Neil.

O'Neill twisted his neck around to see Jane holding two glasses of beer. Her hair was up, but a wisp of dark brown hair escaped, hanging over her blue eyes.

"Glad you made the show," O'Neill said. He got to his feet, ignoring the excruciating pain.

She handed him the lighter-colored beer. "This is for you."

"A woman after my heart." They tapped their plastic glasses together and drank.

"What happened to your leg?" Jane said, pointing at the cane.

"Oh, the leg. I slipped on the stairs."

"Is it your knee or ankle?"

"Knee."

"Have you been to the doctor?"

"No," O'Neill said, knowing he didn't have money to visit a doctor.

"Would you like me to take a gander at it? I'll have my Bachelor of Science in nursing in a couple of months. I interned last semester."

"Well then, I suppose that makes sense." He glanced at The Johnson and KP. A drumbeat played briefly in the background. "Suppose this isn't the place."

Angie Pear approached O'Neill slowly. "You still want this?" she asked.

"Course I do." O'Neill took a sip from the glass Jane had brought him, then grabbed the other from Pear's hand. "Never can have too many, you know."

"Sounds like a line from one of your songs," the reporter said.

"Maybe it is."

"Good to see you," Jane said to O'Neill. "I got to get back to my friends."

O'Neill realized Jane assumed he had something going with Pear. He stood and put a hand up, grazing Jane's shoulder. She paused, so he put one beer on the table and picked up the cane.

"Jane, you can't go. I need you to fix my knee. Don't you have the Hippocratic oath thing to follow?"

Jane looked at him and back at Pear. "If you want me to, I will."

"Course, I want you to look." He finished one beer, picked up the other, and turned to Pear. "Excuse us, but nurse Jane is going to take a gander at my bum knee. Glad to see you."

Jane reluctantly let him put his arm over her shoulder. He nodded goodbye to KP and The Johnson.

"Where we off to?" O'Neill asked Jane.

"We need light," she said, pointing at the Union. The sun had set, and the twilight was dimming. "We'll go inside and see what we can find."

"The Union won't work, since you'll have to take my pants off."

Her expression implied she had not thought of that.

"Your place free?" O'Neill asked. They cut through the crowd.

"Shush, I didn't offer to look at your knee so we could fool around. Should I look at your knee or not?"

"Yeah, whatever you wanna do."

Jane pulled open the door and ushered him inside. They walked into Der Rathskeller, which was a student hangout and indoor event center within the Union. O'Neill had played the room at least a dozen times and he knew it well. Its walls were peppered with designs and murals. Lights hung from the arched ceiling and several pillars punctuated the space. A bar sat on one side of the room.

The pair maneuvered past a gray-haired man holding two pitchers of beer, but the crowd thickened, so they leaned against a wall while dozens of students, most with textbooks or laptops, studied nearby. As traffic cleared, Jane pulled O'Neill forward, and they exited the room and walked down a hallway. They left the Union and slowly negotiated the building's stone steps. Crossing Langdon Street, they ended in front of the Wisconsin State Historical Society.

"There's enough light here between the twilight, the lamp, and the light coming from inside. You are wearing underwear, correct?"

O'Neill nodded, and they went up a flight of stairs before she set him down. He leaned back, closing his eyes. A stone wall facing the street gave them a level of privacy.

"What did I do to it? I'm afraid I ripped cartilage or did something sinister like that."

"I won't know anything until I have a look, but I don't like the swelling. How often have you put ice on it?"

"Ice?"

"You haven't iced it at all, have you?" Jane rolled her eyes and let out a breath. She shook her head at the bandage bulging beneath his ripped jeans. "I can't believe you got these pants over that bandage. We won't get your jeans off without tearing them." She stuck a nail file into a small hole at the knee and pulled. The jeans ripped loudly.

"Hey, what the fuck?" O'Neill said, sitting up.

She pulled again, and the pants ripped further.

"It's the only way you'll get the bandage off. Besides, I'm not taking your pants off. People are staring."

O'Neill grumbled, since they had been his favorite jeans. He looked around and couldn't see anyone watching them. She tugged again and finished the job with nail clippers, leaving a tear that went from seam to seam at the knee and from one seam to the bottom hem. She unwrapped the bandage, her eyes focusing on the knee.

"What do you make of it, Doc?"

"There is a good deal of swelling." She touched the side of the knee. "Does it hurt here?"

"Yeah."

"How about here?"

"Ouch, course it hurts; it's as big as a pumpkin."

"Can you straighten your leg?" She watched as the leg straightened. "When did the accident happen?"

"I was walking up the stairs at my apartment after I left you last night."

"Was there a crack or a pop when you fell?"

O'Neill took a moment before responding, "I don't think so."

She looked the knee over for a few minutes, bending it and asking him to rate the pain. "There is a lot of swelling, but that's not surprising since we're twenty hours in and you haven't put ice on it. You can straighten and bend your knee despite the swelling, you didn't hear or feel a pop, and you're putting weight on the leg. At first, I thought it was worse, but I'm guessing it's only a bad sprain."

"What's a sprain, anyway?" he replied with a shrug of his shoulders. "Sounds stupid, but I don't know."

"Think of it as a tear that should heal, though it could take several weeks or more to feel normal again. There might, however, be damage that won't heal, so have it examined if it doesn't improve."

"Isn't that what I'm doing?"

"If it doesn't improve in the next twenty-four hours, go to urgent care. I'm not suggesting it will feel normal, but it should at least feel better. You can't be sure without x-rays, but I'm putting my money on a sprain, which is the least damage. I think you can wait another twenty-four hours, or until Tuesday morning, provided you're icing."

"And if there was a problem, I'd need x-rays or an operation," he mumbled. He lay back and laughed. "Unless they do x-rays and operations for free, I'm screwed."

"If it doesn't get better, you'll have to do it anyway. They have programs and stuff. You could get it covered somehow."

"Put the bandage on," he said.

Jane's lips opened, but nothing came out. She wrapped the bandage around his knee, pulling it tight and locking it in place with a pin. He pulled himself to his feet, and she handed him the cane.

"Thanks."

O'Neill stood, navigated the steps, and started toward State Street. He only made it a few feet before she caught up with him.

"Where are you going? I was trying to help. You don't need to get peevish. Like I said, I don't think it's too bad, but that doesn't mean you shouldn't have someone look at it if it doesn't progress."

He didn't answer, so she continued. "If you don't have plans, I got something you will want to do," Jane said. She walked backwards in front of him. "I talked to this friend of mine who knew a guy who had searched for Andie Sheridan's body. This guy, Andrew Farina, was one of a bunch of students who volunteered to search the arboretum for her body. He didn't find her, but he was there when someone else in his group found the grave."

O'Neill stopped. He had been near the wooded path earlier, but he wanted to walk the path and he had questions about the burial location.

"This Andrew Farina took me and my friend to the arboretum, explained where they searched, and showed me where they found the body. I thought you might be interested. Do you want me to show you the spot where the attack happened?"

Chapter 9

On August 21, 1996, the University women's cross-country team started their run at Vilas Beach. It was seventy degrees and sunny at nine in the morning. The nineteen women ran along Vilas Park Drive which skirted Lake Wingra, going through Vilas Park against the one-way traffic. O'Neill wanted to follow the exact path Andie Sheridan took, but his knee prohibited anything more than a short walk. Instead, Jane drove her Mazda through the nearby residential neighborhood, arriving near the spot where the women exited the park.

Jane pulled into a parking lot at the park boundary. He gazed down the road that separated the zoo from the beach. The park was closed, but stragglers were along the shore, and a group of teenagers were underneath a park shelter. The lake was still, but its smell was unmistakable. O'Neill rolled the window down and a rush of cool nighttime air surprised him.

"They started at the beach, but as they ran past here, they would have gone up this hill," Jane observed, turning away from the park. "I wouldn't like to run up such a steep hill."

"I've run the hill many a time," O'Neill said.

"You're kidding?"

"Not at all. I ran track and cross-country in high school, and they used to make us run this hill."

"I can't see you on a track team," Jane said, laughing.

"Why not? I got the build for track, don't I?"

"Yeah, but you don't seem like the type to join *any* team. And I can't imagine you going to a preppy school like Edgewood." She giggled before continuing. "Were you any good at track?"

"Course I was, but I got booted my junior year."

"From the team?"

"From school."

She laughed, and he joined in as she put the car in gear and turned onto Edgewood Avenue.

"The cross-country team went up this hill as they exited the path. At the top of the hill, they turned southwest on Monroe Street. Just a couple of blocks past Edgewood is where they entered the path through the arboretum."

Monroe Street was busy and the heart of one of the city's more fashionable neighborhoods. Besides Edgewood High School, the street included a diverse mixture of shops, restaurants, offices, apartments, and single-family homes. O'Neill ran along Monroe Street many times when he was in school. It was a safe street where traffic was a bigger concern than crime. At least, that's what he thought.

They drove a half mile on Monroe Street until Jane turned onto a side street and pulled into the parking lane.

"Would they cut through Wingra Park before the path, or would they stay on Monroe?" Jane asked.

"When I ran in high school, we cut into the park and went up Arbor Avenue and got onto the path. I'm guessing they did the same."

Jane pulled into the traffic lane and drove for five or six hundred feet before finding a parking spot along Arbor Drive.

"We're stuck walking from here," Jane said.

O'Neill got out of the car, looking at the full moon above the treetops. Two trees stood between the sidewalk and the path entrance, but O'Neill didn't think they would impact a runner's view. His cane rattled on the sidewalk, keeping time as they approached the path's entrance. As they entered the path, the trees blocked the moonlight.

"Gloomy," Jane said. She pointed toward Monroe Street. "But the woods aren't thick here."

"It's because there's a parking spot to our right. Three or four cars fit in."

"Do the woods on the Monroe Street side thicken further down?"

"Only toward the end. Here it's semi-thick, but as you pass this bend, the foliage clears. The path curves toward the road, eventually meeting with the sidewalk for a stretch. Like I told my boss, the path is shaped like a smile or a curved sword. It's not that simple, of course, but it curves toward Monroe Street, runs along Monroe, then curves back away. The curve is sharper toward the end, where it exits on Nakoma Road. Toward the end of the path, the woods are thicker and the path bends sharper, but I don't think Andie made it that far. I want to focus on this early part of the path. This is where I think she disappeared."

O'Neill turned so he faced the path's entrance where it connected with Arbor drive. He stood five feet from the bend and fifteen feet from the path's entrance.

"A runner was behind Andie Sheridan when she entered the path," O'Neill said. He walked back toward the path's entrance. "This runner started late, and she saw Andie entering the path."

"This other runner couldn't have been far behind." Jane stepped closer to him. "Kind of scary, eh?"

He peered at the path's entrance. "Someone running down Arbor can see the path's entrance for a quarter mile. I don't know which side of Arbor they ran down." He pulled a notepad from his pocket then flicked on a lighter to see by. "The police report says this woman, Donna Ritz, estimated Andie was seventy feet ahead of her and Andie was twenty feet behind the person in front of her." The lighter turned off. "The person in front of Andie would have been Tanya Paulus. I am going to interview her tomorrow."

"Wouldn't distance be hard to estimate? I mean, if you asked me how far it is to the car, I'm not sure I would be accurate, especially if someone asked me a few days later."

"Don't they cover distances in nursing school?"

"Perhaps that comes this fall," she replied with a smile.

"Cross-country runners get competent at judging distance — least that's how I remember it. I figured I could cover a hundred feet in eight seconds, so if someone was ahead of me, I would time how long I took to pass a point someone passed. These women are faster than me, but it wouldn't be that different. We should be able to estimate how long the woods hid Andie from view. How long would it take to cover ninety feet?"

"No clue," Jane said, smiling.

"I'm thinking seven seconds, but let's double check. Go to the last tree we passed along Arbor Drive. The tree is about seventy feet from the path entrance. I'll go to the bend, and you run toward me, fast but not sprinting. Let's check how long you take to run ninety feet. Yell when you start."

She hesitated before following O'Neill's directions. As she walked away, O'Neill took the last Motrin, washing it down with Scotch from his flask.

O'Neill backed toward the bend. She yelled, then he turned and counted as she approached. He said "six" before she went past him.

"That would be all he had, though we'll add one more second since we're not quite at the bend."

"Doesn't sound like much," Jane said between heavy breaths. "How would someone get her off the path so quickly?"

"Depends on how he attacked her. I think he would either catch her from behind or basically tackle her from the side. The tackle could happen quickly, but she would see him for an instant. So if he didn't get her mouth covered, she would scream. If she screams, the runners in front of her or the runner behind her would hear. Perhaps he got lucky and she fainted, though that is a stretch. If he catches her from behind, he starts as she passes him. He would sprint to catch her, but when he does, he could cover her mouth before she sees him or get a knife on her neck. It would be easier, but I'm not sure he had enough time. I'm still surprised he didn't drug her."

"It could work, but like you said, it would be foolish."

"What if she went willingly?"

Jane's eyebrows crunched together. "Willingly?"

"What if she saw someone she recognized, and he waved her over?"

"Wouldn't the woman following see her talking to someone?"

"Yeah, unless she left the path right away to talk to this person," O'Neill said, "though that seems a stretch. Could be the attacker didn't know another runner was coming. That makes more sense. After all, it was such a brief window. Maybe he thought she was in last place so he thought he had time. He wouldn't see anyone on Arbor unless he was at the wood's edge. If he was further on the path, he wouldn't see who was coming."

She nodded in agreement. "What storyline are you taking on this? You're still writing a story on this, right?"

He had almost forgotten that lie. "I still might write something, but I don't know what angle I'll take. I'll see where my research leads."

She stepped closer to him. Her hands rested on her hips and a smile was on her face. He could hardly see her in the dim light.

"Is there anything else we could do out here?" she whispered.

O'Neill didn't know if it was an invitation, but he dropped his cane, put his hands on her back, and pulled her close. His eyes closed as their lips met. The cane clinked on the asphalt and rolled to the path's edge. Her lips felt warm in the night air.

"Aren't you worried about my sister?" Jane asked as their hands groped at each other's bodies.

"What sister?"

He maneuvered her off the path, and she leaned against a tree. He unbuckled her belt, and his left hand slid along the contours of her bare skin.

Then there was a noise.

They separated as a bicycle with a single headlight whirled past.

"Holy shit," Jane said after a pause. She took several large breaths, and then she laughed. "I think I peed my pants."

O'Neill laughed with her. "You want me to check?"

"Sick," she said. He tried to kiss her again, but she pushed him away. "Should we get going since it's getting late?"

"Yeah, but can you help me find my cane?"

They both laughed again, but O'Neill stopped abruptly. "You mentioned the body. They found it at the other end of the path, right?"

"Yeah. This Andrew Farina said they searched this side of Lake Wingra from Wingra Park to a road running along the golf course. They assigned him to a heavily wooded area near where Monroe forks into Odana and Nakoma at the end of this path. He said he was searching close to where the killer buried the body. He said a woman found it. They gave everyone flags to hold up if they thought they found something. He could see her standing, holding the flag twenty feet away. He waved over a police officer who went to the woman. After another fifteen minutes, it was obvious they had found something, though he kept searching. One of the police officers told him it was two hundred feet east of the path which was going toward the lake. How far back from the path is the lake?"

"The lake is close here, but further away on the part where you say they found the body. It's close to a quarter mile at that point since that's about as far as the lake goes. How did this woman know she found the body? Was it visible?"

"Andrew said this woman stepped on a slight mound of brush and leaves and thought the ground felt different. She jumped up and down on it and thought something was wrong. That's when she raised the flag."

"She told him this?"

"I think he got it secondhand from another volunteer."

They looked about the woods as whistling trees and crickets filled the silence.

"Do you want to go to the other end of the path?" Jane asked.

"No, but I want to see the parking lot at that end."

"The parking lot?" Jane replied. "Okay."

They walked back to the Mazda and Jane drove down Monroe Street, turning onto Nakoma Road and pulling into the parking lot. Like the other lot, it had three or four parking spots.

"This one's paved," O'Neill said.

"Does that matter?"

"I'm just thinking that if I used a car to get here, I'd rather not leave my tire tracks in a dirt parking lot. The other lot was dirt."

"You think he drove his car and parked here? I thought you said he attacked her at the beginning of the path. That doesn't make sense."

"Yeah," O'Neill said. "That's what bothers me."

Chapter 10

The morning came quickly. O'Neill pulled his second and least-favorite jeans over the ace bandage and descended the Proprietary Apartment steps. Ryder's Chevy S-10 was waiting, and they were soon on Highway 14. But rather than going south toward Janesville, they headed northwest to La Crosse.

O'Neill slept for much of the two-and-a-half-hour drive. He awoke as they came into town, driving past the world's largest six-pack of beer and past the G. Heileman Brewing Company's La Crosse brewery. Like similar Midwest towns, La Crosse's downtown was struggling but not dead.

Ryder had addresses, phone numbers, and maps for three La Crosse brewpubs. He said the information was from an online brewery and brewpub listing, and all three were within walking distance of their hotel. But they only had an hour before their meeting, so the tour of La Crosse brewpubs would wait.

After checking in, O'Neill took a mandated shower and met Ryder in the hotel bar. He brought the newspaper articles, and he swapped his spiral notebook for a notepad from the hotel. He also brought a tourist brochure that he found in the hotel lobby.

Two cummerbund-wearing bartenders were manning the bar while a lone waitress was covering a half-dozen tables. "Hotel California" played in the background.

"Did you know that La Crosse was originally called Prairie La Crosse?" O'Neill said, as he sat opposite Ryder. "It's in this brochure I picked up near the front desk."

"No, and why would I care?"

"It's just interesting, is all."

"Put the tourism shit away. We got work to do."

O'Neill rolled his eyes but stuck the flyer in his back pocket.

"The interview with Tanya Paulus is about the run," Ryder said. "I'm not expecting significant new information but trying to get a sense of the crime seems a logical start. We certainly need to talk to Donna Ritz since she was the last person to see Andie, but I prefer having a better sense of the events of that day before talking to the most important witness. I don't want to conduct the most important interviews until I'm immersed in the evidence."

"Makes sense, I guess."

A plump, brown-haired waitress interrupted them. Like the bartenders, she wore a tuxedo shirt. Ryder ordered a brandy old-fashioned and O'Neill a rail vodka martini since rail martinis were on special.

"The run started at roughly nine o'clock in Vilas Park," Ryder said as he opened a manilla folder. They get to the path at roughly nine fifteen. This, uh..." he glanced at the file, "Tanya Paulus says she passed Andie Sheridan while on Arbor Drive before entering the woods. Tanya left the woods less than five minutes later. She says she glanced back shortly after leaving the woods and Andie was not there. She didn't think about it until they got back to Vilas."

"Back to Vilas?"

"Yep, once they were off the path, the women turned onto Seminole and made their way back to Nakoma where it meets Midvale." Ryder laid a highlighted map on the counter. "The route they took meanders through town, but basically, it's an oval that starts and ends at the top of the hill where Monroe Street meets Edgewood Avenue. They then ran the same part of Edgewood Avenue to Vilas Beach, except this time they run down the hill."

O'Neill pulled the map of the overall route closer. It amazed him that these women had to run such long practice runs. "Those women must be in fantastic shape," O'Neill commented.

"The last runner who matters in this, the Ritz woman," Ryder said, ignoring O'Neill's comment, "she started her run two minutes late, and she saw Andie run onto the wooded trail. Donna Ritz caught up with Tanya Paulus when they exited the trail. Tanya Paulus enters the path, followed closely by Andie, who was followed by Donna. Donna passed Tanya after the path, but says she never passed Andie. That is the primary reason the MPD thought the attack happened on the path and why they focused their search for the body in the arboretum."

"The big X is where they found the body," Ryder said.

"But we don't know where he killed her."

"The MPD assumed it was likely near where he buried her."

"That seems like a big assumption," O'Neill said.

"Well, the condom wrapper was, like, twenty feet from the body. That implies it was nearby unless he attacked her and marched her somewhere else before assaulting and killing her."

"Okay. I get the logic," O'Neill said.

"My guess is the attack was a rape gone wrong rather than an intentional murder. One of those bastards that flings girls around, but he overdid it and ended up strangling her."

They leaned back as the waitress put their drinks on the table. Ryder handed her a twenty-dollar bill.

"Why are you assuming it was a rape gone wrong?" O'Neill asked after the waitress had left.

"There are better places to kill someone. The advantage of the woods, so far as I can figure, is they provide a secluded area for a sexual assault. If he meant to kill her, I think he does things in a way that doesn't require him to return."

"Nine fifteen in the morning seems an atypical time of day for sexual assaults."

"It probably is," Ryder said. "Yet sexual assaults can happen anywhere and anytime. It may seem odd, but it doesn't mean it didn't happen."

"I get that. How about the burial? The MPD worked under the assumption that the killer returned later, presumably at night, with a shovel and buried her body. Why would he return and bury the body?"

"To delay or prevent someone finding the body; it's murder 101."

"Returning to the crime scene is murder 101?"

"No, burying a body so no one finds the victim is murder 101."

"At the same location? Wouldn't you move the body rather than putting it in a place where any reasonable search would find it? Or is murder 101 a remedial class?"

"They didn't find her for almost a week, so whether it was smart is irrelevant since it delayed things. Besides, the guy could be an idiot. Lots of criminals are idiots. Or maybe he has a fetish."

"That's a thought," O'Neill said. He played with his glass rather than drinking from it. "Maybe he returned to hide evidence or he felt compelled to return. If he came back anyway, burying the body makes sense."

"Maybe he wanted to bury her but didn't risk carrying the body out of the woods and having someone notice him or his vehicle? Besides, the more walking and movement, the higher the risk of being seen."

"If I came back, it would be at night. I would move the body to a completely different location. I'd bury it off some lonely country road."

"Like I said, some criminals are idiots. What's the deal with you questioning everything?"

"It just doesn't feel right."

"What's that mean?"

"I don't know," O'Neill said. "I just expect things to flow a certain way. Maybe I think of things the same way I think of music. To me at least, music is alive, and you feel and hear and understand the waves, the patterns, the flow. Usually the flow makes sense, even if you don't like the result. You know where the waves are going, or you at least understand why a note or a chord progression or something goes somewhere. When something doesn't make sense, you feel it."

"I should have known you'd bring music into this. And while I agree that everything doesn't make sense, that's the nature of this crazy world we live in. In the real world, we don't have nice little written music to follow with codas and crescendos. Get used to it." He glanced at his watch. "We've got an appointment to make. Let's get this done so we can check out those brewpubs."

Tanya Paulus lived in a house that reminded O'Neill of Madison's college housing. Blue paint was peeling along the southern side of the house, and two dormers stuck nervously from the roof. The house looked to be an early 1900s home of a prosperous businessman that had fallen into disrepair. Like other houses on the street, a property management company divided the house into apartments and populated it with the most transient of renters: college students.

Since there were no open spots near the house, Ryder parked in Tanya's driveway behind a red Fiero.

"Knowing my luck, the guy with the Fiero will have to leave," Ryder said. "Just how life goes."

Tanya stood at the door as they walked up the steps and onto the porch. She was wearing gray jogging shorts and a sleeveless white Wisconsin Badgers T-shirt. She was slender, but not too slender for a runner. And O'Neill thought she had the largest breasts he had seen on a distance runner.

"You don't look like a detective," Tanya said to O'Neil as they stepped into the house.

He had no suitable answer, so he nodded and took in the Korn and Limp Bizkit posters on the opposite wall.

"Can I see your identification?" Tanya said. "I verified your detective agency with the campus police, but they suggested I make sure you're who you say you are. I also gave the police the date and time of our meeting."

Ryder pulled out his identification, and O'Neill held out a business card.

"Okay," Tanya said. "My roomie is out, but she's expecting me to meet her later. Tammy and I are the only ones here for summer session."

"She at class?"

Tanya flashed a toothy smile. "Birthday party."

"And you are stuck talking with us."

She chuckled, but her expression implied that Ryder was right. "Can I grab you water, a soda, or a beer?"

"No, we don't want to keep you from getting on with your day. We'll ask a few questions and be on our way. My name, as I told you over the phone, is John Ryder. My associate here, Seamus O'Neill, and I are investigating the murder of Andie Sheridan."

"Who hired you?"

"Our client asked that he remain confidential."

"A man, huh," she said, seemingly pleased to figure that much out.

"I can tell you, however, that Andie's mother, Jennifer Reilly, is aware of and supporting our investigation. Did you meet her mother?"

"At Andie's service," Tanya said. "She seemed like a pleasant woman. She took it hard."

"Yes," Ryder said, "that's understandable. Can you start by telling us what happened on the day Andie Sheridan disappeared?"

Her elbows rested on her knees, and she looked at the blank television screen for a few moments before answering. "I didn't see Andie until just before practice. I had been a few minutes late, and she was even later. She came into the locker room when I was getting changed. I remember because I pointed out that I didn't see her earlier at the library. She told me she was hungover so she skipped studying. I wouldn't normally remember that type of exchange, but I've been over that entire day so many times."

"Did she mention the previous night?" O'Neill asked.

"Not that I recall. I went to the van, and she followed. The coaches took us to Vilas for a route that gave us a change of scenery."

"This was a regular thing?"

"Usually it was on Friday during the summer, but not always. We probably did it every other week."

"This time it was a Wednesday," Ryder said as he looked at his notes. "Did you talk to her again?"

"I don't recall saying anything to her. She sat next to me in the van, but her eyes were closed and she was leaning back," Tanya said, itching the back of her left calf before continuing. "The drive was only ten minutes, and I don't remember talking to anyone while I stretched out. And once we got running, I didn't talk to her. I doubt anyone did."

"Why not?"

"We run in groups or clusters talking and joking around, but Andie ran alone and rarely talked. That's how she was. On that day, she was running by herself and once we hit the hill, she fell back so she was ahead of Marcia Woodward and me but not in speaking distance of anyone. There were usually two or three packs. This time there were two packs with a few of us behind. Marcia went to catch the closer pack, so she went ahead of me. She probably passed Andie near the top of Crawley hill." She laughed and her brown eyes sparkled. "I'm glad I don't have to run that hill again. But anyway, I was behind Andie until we cut through the park. She slowed down on Arbor Drive enough that I wondered whether something was wrong. I thought about running with her but pushed it and eventually caught Marcia and the rest of that group. I passed Andie maybe a hundred meters before entering the woods. I thought about giving her shit, but I didn't want to rub it in."

"Meaning?"

"Meaning Andie was always getting guff from the coaches. She didn't put effort into running, and the coach wouldn't like Marcia and I beating her, even on a routine run." She itched her calf again. "Andie was a scholarship runner — full, not even partial. She was talented but a screw off. Andie partied too much, didn't eat right, and did nothing extra. She differed from me in that way. I was not on scholarship. I just like running and it keeps me in shape." She leaned forward like she was revealing a secret. "You see, I have a tendency to put on weight."

Ryder waited, apparently expecting O'Neill to ask the next question. O'Neill flipped through his notepad. "Did you guys go out together, you and Andie?"

Tanya looked puzzled. "Do you think I'm a lesbian? I'm not, and neither was Andie. At least I don't think she was. Was she?"

"No, no," O'Neill said with a chuckle. "I meant: did you hang out with her? You mentioned the library, so I'm assuming you were friends."

Tanya looked relieved, and then she laughed. "You had me going," she said before laughing again. "I thought... Oh well, never mind. As to your question, yes we hung out. She was not one of my best friends, but we ran into each other at parties and would bullshit. We studied together since we took some of the same classes and had the same training schedule. I didn't go out much since I was under twenty-one, but whenever I did, it seemed like I saw Andie. She must have had a great fake ID."

"Did she have close friends on the team?"

"No. Thinking back on it, I might have been the person on the team that was closest to her. Andie talked with Lizzie McBride a lot during her freshman year, but that was more of a mentoring thing. Lizzie was a captain. I don't think they spent time together outside of running."

"Getting back to when she disappeared," Ryder said, sounding almost bored. "How close was she behind you when you last noticed her?"

She looked over O'Neill's shoulder. "I felt sure she was close behind me at first. She was going slow when we hit the woods, but while you sense where someone is when you're running, the woods can confuse you, and sometimes you lose where a person or a group is. She could have fallen back quickly, especially if she stopped to tie her shoe or something."

"Is that what you think happened?"

Tanya's facial expression changed and her eyes glossed over. "Yeah, she must have stopped for something." Her voice became more forceful. "And if someone attacked her, even if she wasn't close, I should have heard it." There was a lengthy silence before she continued. "It could have been a shoe, a twisted ankle, or a cramp. She may have gone to pee as far as I know."

"Otherwise, it would be pretty bold," O'Neill said.

Her legs rubbed together like two sticks. Any remnant of a comfortable, confident college student was gone. "Yes, yes, who would do that? It still gives me the creeps, knowing someone was in those woods when we came through. It freaks me out since I was usually the one in last place."

"Another runner was behind both of you, correct?" O'Neill said. "If Andie had slowed down, wouldn't this runner have seen her?"

"Oh yeah, Donna... Donna... Donna Ritz. That was it. She missed the van, I guess, and started a few minutes late. She ended up passing me soon after we came out of the woods."

"Did you know she was behind you?"

"I don't remember. I really wasn't thinking about who was behind me, since I was probably trying to catch the group ahead of me. Donna passed me. I didn't know it was Donna until she was off my shoulder. Donna was also a scholarship runner. She still is. Not a natural like Andie, but a solid runner."

"How far ahead was the first cluster of runners?" O'Neill said.

"I don't recall. They must have been far ahead, as I don't remember them being in my sight."

There was a lengthy silence

"Is this why you left?" O'Neill asked. "Is this why you transferred to La Crosse?"

"Yes," she said with a nod. "I didn't even finish the fall semester. I couldn't shake the idea he was after me."

O'Neill understood what she meant. "Did you suggest that to the police?"

"Yes. They didn't think so, though they interviewed every boyfriend I ever had, so I know they considered it. And I'm sure they are right that he was not after me, but it's hard to forget about it."

Tanya looked at her watch.

Ryder stood. "We're sorry to have brought this all up again."

"I don't mean to be rushing you off," Tanya said as she stood. If it relieved her, it didn't show on her face. "I hope this was not a waste of your time. I mean, I hope you learned something to nail the bastard."

"I hope so too, Miss Paulus," Ryder said. "We appreciate your help."

"One other thing," O'Neill said as they stopped at the front door. Ryder gave him a dirty look, but O'Neill continued. "Any reason someone would have wanted Andie Sheridan killed? Did you suspect anyone?"

She seemed relieved by the question since it took her away from the woods. "Her boyfriend was a major asshole. Everyone thought he was cute and he thought he could charm everyone, but the way he looked at me gave me the creeps. He's one of those jerks that finds excuses to rub up against you. I would have bet that jerk did it, since I know she was afraid of him. She wanted to break it off, but she never could get the nerve to do it. At first I assumed it was him, but he had the perfect alibi."

"Yes, we heard," Ryder said. "He was teaching class."

"Any chance you can break that alibi?" Tanya said.

"There's a chance," O'Neill replied.

Tanya looked O'Neill in the eye as if she was trying to figure out if he was serious. "Then God bless you and go nail the bastard."

Chapter 11

Ryder was visibly upset as he backed the Chevy S-10 out of the driveway. O'Neill scribbled in his notepad.

"Don't go riffing to interview subjects," Ryder said once the truck got moving. "Who knows who she talks to in Madison? We don't need her telling people that we're going to break Larry Marsh's alibi, especially since we won't be able to. That comment might bite us in the ass. Our role in interviews is to get information *from* them; not to give information *to* them. Get it?"

"Yeah," O'Neill said. "It was nice getting blessed, though."

"Seamus, don't push it."

They drove to the hotel and stuck with their plan by walking to the nearest brewpub. The knee felt better, but O'Neill still needed the cane and he struggled to keep up with his boss. The streetlight was red and the "No Walk" light was lit. But there wasn't a car in sight, so they crossed the road.

"What did you get from the interview?" Ryder said as they walked along Jay Street with the smell of the Mississippi River behind them.

"She's damaged and still freaked out. She had to tell us that the cops knew we were meeting with her. It's hard to blame her for being paranoid."

"Yeah, quite sad. Anything else?"

"We've talked to two people, and both originally thought Larry Marsh was the killer."

"Madison PD focused effort and time on Larry Marsh, but his alibi is airtight. You need to get that through your head. Maybe Larry Marsh is a dick, but that doesn't make him a killer."

"Doesn't make him innocent either," O'Neill said.

"Yeah, but the alibi and the DNA sample prove he didn't kill Andie."

"Then who do we look at?"

"Well, the MPD did the same thing we're currently doing. They looked heavily into Tanya and the other runners, especially the Ritz woman since she was the only one to see Andie Sheridan enter the path and claims she never passed Andie. They dug and dug but concluded that none of the runners were involved. Nothing about today's meeting makes me think differently. Her line about the dead girl stopping to piss had a ring of truth. It's as good an explanation as you need and is probably what happened. Her leaving the path explains why the killer would jump someone in a group, which bothered me. I like the piss idea because it would get her to leave the path voluntarily, whereas if she stopped to tie her shoe, Ritz would pass her. If she's taking a piss, she goes off the path voluntarily, and while she does her duty, this Ritz girl runs past." Ryder stopped walking and pointed across the street. "There be our brewpub."

"Babylon Brew" was displayed in white letters over a black backdrop. The new lettering stuck out in the downtown area. The buildings to the side of Babylon Brew appeared to be abandoned, though one light showed through a second-floor window.

"Dark in there," Ryder said as they crossed the street. "Looks like the brewpub is closed."

O'Neill pulled the door, but it was locked. He had been looking forward to sitting and resting his knee.

"What brewpub closes on a Monday? Should be a crime."

"Looks like they're out of business or they're not open yet," Ryder said. He turned to O'Neill. "Jeez, I got that list off the internet today. Let's go to the next one." He pulled the map out of his pocket. "It's around the corner."

They saw two cars on their walk to the La Crosse Pub, but both were parked. The pub had fifty feet of window space but was only twenty feet deep. It was the smallest brewpub O'Neill could recall seeing and seemed even smaller since the bar nearly ran the length of the pub, leaving only fifteen feet for customers. The bar counter outclassed the chairs and tables surrounding it. There was one bartender and one customer, a man wearing a windbreaker and a Montreal Expos baseball cap.

"What beers do ya got?" O'Neill asked the bartender, as they sat at the bar.

"Taps are here," the bartender said, pointing at a line of four microbrew taps. He chewed tobacco, and his lips didn't move when he spoke.

"Don't you guys make your own beer?"

"We're brewing now," he said. He gestured toward a door behind the bar where a fermenting vessel sat behind a round window. "The batch is not ready yet."

"You brew one batch at a time?" Ryder said.

"We're still in start-up mode," he said as proudly as his static lips would allow.

"Pour me a Lakefront," O'Neill said. Ryder ordered the same.

The bartender took his time getting the beers, spilling Ryder's on the bar and wiping up with paper towels. O'Neill smelled the ale before taking a first sip.

"Smells and tastes good to me," O'Neill said. Then he looked to the ground, noticing the brass foot rail. It connected to the counter which ran nearly the length of the room. O'Neill slid off his stool, running his fingers down the front of the mahogany counter.

"Cool bar furniture." O'Neill said to the bartender. "Brunswick was the big player in bar furniture, though the name was different when they made this. It's the same company that makes pool tables nowadays. I'm guessing the bar is a hundred years old and built for this building. Could be worth something, but there's no matching back mirror or furniture, which puzzles me. Was this building a bar before it was a brewpub?"

"Jeez," Ryder said, "can we work on one mystery at a time? Ideally one we're getting paid to solve?"

"Sorry about that," O'Neill replied.

The bartender walked away, looking relieved to avoid discussing bar furniture.

"You don't seem to buy the piss theory that Tanya suggested," Ryder said. "You're stuck on Larry Marsh somehow raping and killing his own girlfriend."

"It isn't a matter of buying the pissing idea. It simply doesn't get us anywhere and only points to a random attacker. Besides, Tanya mentioned Andie going to the locker room before they took the van to Vilas Park. If she needed to pee, why skip the bathroom and instead do a nature trip? I hardly remember anyone in cross-country pulling off the course to pee, even in practice."

"Not everything we do makes sense. Hell, this morning, I put on a shirt and, just as I was ready to leave the house, I decided I wanted to wear a different shirt."

"Is this going somewhere?"

"I'm just saying we sometimes do things that make no sense."

"Your belief in this theory is an example."

"Screw you," Ryder said.

"And even if she stops to pee, what are the odds this guy's waiting in the woods, and one woman pulls off the path to piss or puke or whatever? He's got to be close to her, but moving through the brush, she would sense him coming and she would scream. It's possible and could work, but I don't like it. The other option is that peeing separated her from the group. Donna Ritz runs past as Andie pees. Once finished, she runs again and gets mugged at that point. Yet both options point to a random attack, since no one could rely on her stopping to pee. Puking would be another possibility since you're absorbed in it and wouldn't be as conscious of what's around you. And you naturally get secluded before puking."

"You would know."

They both sipped their beers.

"We're both acting uncharacteristically by letting the hopelessness of this get to us," Ryder said as he patted his stomach. "I'm the last person to be persistent in a hopeless cause. It sounds bad, but it isn't. Everyone thinks the bulldog detective who doesn't give up is the hero, but that is bullshit. Those guys get paid for two hundred hours and end up working four hundred. They may solve something I wouldn't, but we get paid for two hundred hours on other jobs." He shook his head. "A few of the Milwaukee and Chicago agencies are that way, working their butts off, effectively making minimum wage. Detectives get away with that on the government's dime, but it doesn't work in private business. I'm serious when I say we should give up on a hopeless case."

"You think we should give up?"

"Not when we're getting paid. There's always hope when you are getting paid. Besides, you got me interested in this thing too, I guess. You bring up ideas. I mean, shit, if you hadn't wasted your life playing shitty music, you might be good at something. Too late now, I suppose."

"And if you stopped eating two Tombstone pizzas a day, you could lose fifty pounds."

"I didn't mean to sound like an ass. I was just saying I'm happy I hired you. No one believed you would work out, but I needed someone who could do routine tasks and computer geek stuff without being a computer geek. And besides being able to do computer stuff, you're an underachiever. Successful detectives have a combination of talent, experience, and conviction. Conviction is boring, and I ain't going to pay for experience, so I wanted talent. The only talent I could afford is cheap talent and underachievers equal cheap talent."

"You're making me feel underpaid."

"Oh, screw that. If I fired your ass, you wouldn't get another job like this. You would sit in a concrete park playing your guitar and collecting quarters."

"Nothing wrong with that."

"Bunch of doped up lazy asses."

O'Neill knew many of those "doped up lazy asses."

A group of college-aged men came into the brewpub, sitting several spots away from O'Neill and Ryder.

"Getting back to this case," O'Neill said. "Could Andie Sheridan's boyfriend have hired someone to kill her? I don't know anything about hired killers."

Ryder's skinny black eyebrows pushed together. He seemed puzzled that O'Neill asked the question.

"Hired killers don't rape women and don't take unnecessary chances. A hired killer would not attack someone running in a group. Shit," Ryder said, shaking his head. "We're not going anywhere on this. We need to find something the MPD missed."

The bartender stood nearby, pouring beers for the new arrivals.

"The cops missed the location of the murder," O'Neill said. "And they haven't explained why he buried the body where it was."

"What do you mean? You lost me."

"I couldn't find anywhere in the notes that the cops determined where on the path the attack occurred. They didn't seem to think it mattered and assumed it happened at the end of the path near where they found the body and the condom wrapper."

"Isn't that a logical assumption?"

"By itself, yes. But it doesn't fit the details. The two male runners, Gary Fano and Lou Kart, ran down Odana, cut to Nakoma and onto the path. Nearly every woman on the team remembered them."

"So what?"

"The first and the last of the runners were on the half-mile path with the two guys. We know that since the men came from Odana to the path while the women went from the path and up Nakoma. So, these two guys enter the path going the opposite direction of the women. Let's assume the first runner was just leaving the path at that point. Tanya said the first cluster was far head, meaning the lead runner was hundreds of meters ahead of Tanya, Andie, and Donna Ritz. The wooded part at the end of the path is less than two hundred meters. If the front runner was over four hundred meters ahead, the two male runners would have seen Tanya and Donna toward the middle of the path."

"You sound like a damn math problem. What does it mean?"

"The attack happened on the first part of the path."

"You're sure?"

"Yeah. Even discounting the crossing runners, Donna and Tanya's statements imply that the attack came early on the path. When they entered the path, Donna was seventy feet behind Andie, who was twenty feet behind Tanya. Donna caught up with Tanya as they left the woods. At the start of the path, Tanya was perhaps two seconds ahead of Andie. Going with Donna's estimates, that would put Donna seven seconds behind Tanya when Tanya entered the woods. The path is half a mile, and it took Donna that length, about three minutes, to catch Tanya. We know Andie never passed Tanya, so Donna should have caught Andie about three-fourths of the way down the path before the woods thicken. Even if Andie sped up, Donna could see several hundred meters ahead once she was past the first bend. After Donna was past that first bend, she *should have* seen Andie, Tanya, and the back cluster of runners. Unless all the runners were wrong about these two guy runners and Donna got things wrong or lied, the attack happened early on the path."

"Interesting," Ryder said, "though I won't pretend I processed all that math."

"The question isn't where she disappeared. The question is, why did he attack her at one end of the path and bury her at the other end?"

Ryder finished his beer. "If you weren't such a lush, I might feel threatened."

Chapter 12

Ryder and O'Neill hoped the third and final La Crosse brewpub sold its own beer, but it didn't. The Big Boar Pub opened on July 1 and would not serve their own beer for another month. The brewpub felt upscale, and pints cost a dollar more than at the La Crosse Pub. There were at least a dozen customers at the brewpub. Ryder and O'Neill ordered their beers and walked upstairs.

"We'll receive a memo from our client soon," Ryder said. He took a seat at a booth just as O'Neill got to the top of the stairs. "Hopefully, it will either be there when we get back or will arrive tomorrow."

"Is the memo coming from the Staley dad or the Staley kid?" O'Neill asked as he got to the booth.

"The kid, I assume. The contract said they would send an engagement letter. Perhaps the letter will clear things up."

"So, what's our next step?"

"You found a hole in the Madison Police Department's theory," Ryder said. "That's good, and it could be a selling point to Harry. But I'm not sure it changes what we do. The MPD likely assumed the attack happened near where they found the body, and the condom wrapper reinforced that assumption. Yet it didn't really impact anything they did since they searched the entire length of the path, and it probably won't impact what we do. Even if Garcia had the wrong attack location, we're interviewing the same people and asking the same questions. We need a theory or an angle leading us somewhere beyond the steps the MPD took. Ideally, we find a suspect or suspects to sell this to Harry. This all assumes Donna Ritz and Tanya Paulus are telling the truth. As we saw from Garcia's notes, they believed both were telling the truth. I bought Tanya, but we still need to talk to Donna."

"I don't get why the MPD took the condom wrapper evidence over such significant witness evidence."

"Witness evidence is always questionable. Besides, their primary concern was whether Andie entered the path, and Donna was sure she did. They probably weren't lining up their slide rulers like you did."

"They had twenty witnesses saying the same thing about the crossing runners. That, in combination with Donna's statement, should have clinched it. They seem to have glossed over Donna's statement. I mean, Andie was five foot ten. She had to be the team's tallest runner. She would have been easy to spot."

"Is five foot ten tall for a woman distance runner?" Ryder said.

"Yeah. I'm five foot ten, and I always felt at least average height when I ran among the boys. Course, I was shorter when I ran in high school, but everyone was growing. For college women, I would guess five foot four as being average for distance runners."

"You're saying Andie was a giant."

"Wouldn't go that far."

A waitress interrupted them, sliding two bar napkins on the table. They ordered another round.

"One thing to keep in mind about Donna Ritz is that the MPD initially viewed her as a suspect," Ryder said. "They obviously knew that she was not the rapist, but they strongly considered whether someone was intimidating her or buying her off to keep her from revealing what she saw. They may have questioned everything she said. In the end, her statement set the location of the disappearance, leading the MPD to find the body, and her statement was consistent with everyone else's statements. I would argue that the MPD spent so much effort trying to determine whether Donna was involved in the attack that they ignored some of the other details in her statement. But I'm still not convinced the attack location matters."

"I think it's huge."

"Why? Couldn't the killer simply be trying to confuse the police? Maybe he didn't want the police poking around the area where the attack happened, so he buried her down the path and left the condom wrapper nearby. The police would focus on an area half a mile from where he attacked her."

They both finished their drinks and pushed the empty pint glasses toward the edge of the table. The waitress came by, setting out fresh pints and taking the empties.

"You're suggesting the killer carried a one hundred-and-thirty-five-pound dead body half a mile in the darkness, carrying her shoes, underwear, and shorts," O'Neill said. "Assuming he's going two miles per hour, that would be a fifteen-minute walk."

"Not more math."

"That would be risky even at night, since the path gets bike traffic, and a bike coming at you doesn't give you time to react.

If he stayed off the path when carrying the body, it would be less risky, but it would slow him down. A half mile off a path through the arboretum would probably take twenty minutes and could leave evidence with each step through the woods. He'd be totally bushed by then, yet he goes two hundred meters off the path and has the energy to dig a grave."

"I agree it would be hard work, but maybe the killer was in shape. Perhaps he thought it was worth it to get the body far from where the attack happened."

"Yeah, but the cops searched everywhere along the path. It was only after they found the body that they focused completely on the path's southeastern end. If there was damning evidence early on the path, as you suggested, wouldn't the killer worry about the cops stumbling on it?"

"Sure," Ryder said.

"Then why bury the body? Why not make it easier to find? Once they find the body, they focus on the burial area."

There was a long pause.

"All you do is ask questions," Ryder said. "We need to go to the crime scene to find answers. We should check out the path and the burial location while not discounting the possibility that someone helped the killer. Maybe this helper didn't attack her, but he helped the killer bury the body."

"You think so, huh?"

"Okay, probably not," Ryder said.

"One other question: Tanya mentioned she got changed before getting in the van. Did Andie get changed as well? Did she leave anything in her locker?"

"Thought I saw something in the files on that," Ryder said, flipping open the folder. "Ah, here it is. She left a purse in her locker which had several items, including her identification, keys, gum, tampons, tissue paper, and four dollars. It's detailed here." He slid the listing in front of O'Neill. "They eventually returned everything to Andie's mother."

"There's no change of clothing listed. She partied the night before, right? That's when she saw Myles Staley. If she showed up at the locker room wearing her running clothes, she likely went to the locker room from her apartment or her boyfriend's apartment."

"That was no mystery. Her roommate, I don't remember her name, said she left their apartment that morning. I don't remember the time."

"That's right, I'd forgotten that Andie made it home that night."

"Yes. And speaking of getting home, we should head to the hotel. We have a busy week of interviews. There is the dead girl's boyfriend, her roommate, her friends, her coach, and, of course, Donna Ritz."

O'Neill already talked to Andie Sheridan's roommate, but still hadn't told Ryder.

"You want me to talk to all of them?"

"Nah, I wanna be there. You can talk to the roommate or the cross-country coach. The coach is a guy, and he's still at the University. His name is in the file. I want to talk to Donna Ritz and Larry Marsh."

"I don't understand why the coach didn't report her missing sooner. What do you think he will know?"

"Probably nothing, which is why I'm okay with you talking to him by yourself. He'll explain why he didn't go to the police earlier. Before you talk to him, review what the file says about the delay. My guess is the coach simply couldn't get hold of

Andie, since she split her time between her own apartment and Larry's."

"That would explain a day's delay, but it was three days before the cops got tipped."

"It's weird, so see what you can find out. The coach may also have heard gossip, so find out what he's heard. Also, I have no clue how a cross-country team works, so get background. I mean, are there multiple coaches? Do the men's and women's teams run together, and who sets the runs? Luckily, I have an investigator with a running background. Finally, remember that the MPD initially viewed Reggie Lehman as a suspect, but they cleared him. He did not get along with Andie, but there's no reason to think he would rape and kill her. Besides, he has as good an alibi as anyone."

O'Neill felt nervous. The idea of walking into an office and interviewing someone older than him was stressful. He had now done two formal, in-person interviews, but Ryder had run both. Otherwise, he had only done phone interviews, and those usually were verifying someone's employment status or salary. Interviewing a suspect about a murder was frightening. He would feel different if he ran into the guy at a bar.

The waitress returned. Ryder slid her a bill, waved her off, and she drifted away.

"How do I find the coach?" O'Neill asked between gulps of beer. "And I can't say I'm a detective, can I?"

"It's no different from when you're on the phone. Just tell him you work for the Ryder Detective Agency. Tell him the agency is investigating Andie Sheridan's murder and you're getting background information. And wear something decent. That shirt is acceptable so long as you wash it. And dump the earring, it makes you look like a street musician. And comb your hair for once."

"Right, mom."

"Just trying to make your job easier."

"So, your theory is that combed hair is the key to detective work?"

"Don't look like a bum."

"Or a slob."

Ryder gave him a dirty look.

"When do we talk to our number one suspect, Larry Marsh?" O'Neill asked.

"Seamus, even if the boyfriend is a jerk, he didn't kill Andie Sheridan. He couldn't have, unless you come up with a bright idea that explains how a teacher could kill someone in the woods while teaching miles away at Grainger Hall."

"If I have an idea, I will let you know," O'Neill said. "And if you have an idea, I'll be surprised."

For an instant, Ryder looked angry. Then a wide smile slid across his fat face.

"I'd be surprised too."

Chapter 13

Ryder and O'Neill returned to the hotel before ten o'clock. O'Neill suggested stopping at the hotel bar for a drink, but Ryder declined, reminding him that the free continental breakfast ended at nine in the morning.

O'Neill went to his room, sat on the bed, and switched between television stations. He didn't own a television, so the programs felt unfamiliar. As ten thirty approached, he turned the television off and pulled out his tin whistle. He played a few songs before hearing pounding on the wall. It was only Ryder, but he assumed his playing was audible in the other rooms.

He set the whistle inside the duffle bag, pulled out his wallet, and emptied his pockets. Ten dollars and sixty cents might get him three drinks at the hotel bar. He grabbed his key card and headed downstairs.

The bar was empty except for a lone bartender with blonde hair and a thick mustache. O'Neill sat in front of the taps and set his money on the counter.

"Here's what I got," O'Neill said. "Can I get three beers with this, assuming a fifteen percent tip?"

"Old Style taps are two bucks, so you could get four. They're twelve-ounce glasses. Other taps are three bucks. Bottles are three to five bucks, depending on what you're getting. Rail drinks are three bucks."

"I'll stick with the Old Style tap," O'Neill said as he reviewed the four options.

"You staying at the hotel?" the bartender asked as he filled the glass.

"Here on business, believe it or not."

"Most are on a Monday. Sunday night through Wednesday night is busy with business travelers."

O'Neill nodded as a pair of middle-aged women entered the bar. The bartender set them up with wine, and they settled on a table near the bar.

"You ever run track or cross-country?" O'Neill said, surprising himself as the bartender returned.

"Me? Nah, I was in wresting and football in high school."

"Were you any good?"

"I was decent in wrestling but didn't go out my senior year since I put on weight and knew I would either need to move up a class or do major dieting. I didn't want to do either, so I said adios to wrestling. Played football all four years."

"What was playing football like? I ran cross-country in high school, so I couldn't have played football even if I wanted to."

"I loved football," the bartender said as he dried glasses. "I played fullback on offense and linebacker on defense starting at fullback both my junior and senior years and at inside line-backer my senior year."

"Did you think about playing college football?"

"I wasn't big or fast enough to play college. I got letters from division three schools like Mankato State and UW-La Crosse, but I had no plans for school. Even if I did, I preferred working part time rather than being a scrub at Mankato State."

"Was high school football hard? Did they make you run a lot and condition?"

"Yeah, sophomore year was the hardest. Freshman year was hard in that everything was new, but our sophomore coach was a hard ass, and we were running and drilling and doing whatever. Junior and senior years were better since it was varsity, so people cared more. I was a hard worker, and I was used to training from wrestling, so it was not a big deal. But sophomore year was tough."

O'Neill emptied his glass and slid it forward. "Did you ever skip out of practice or skip drills or anything?"

"I dogged it on sprints but did what I had to do," the bartender said as he refilled O'Neill's glass. "One exception was my sophomore year when I was physically beat up from two-a-days. School had started, and I needed a mental and physical break, so I faked a cold, stayed home, and skipped practice. I figured I could get away with it since we didn't have enough depth for the coaches to play someone in my spot. Varsity was different. If I missed practice my junior year because of anything, I didn't start that week. It was a pisser since I was physically beat up. How about you? You said you ran in high school."

"Track and cross-country are different since you're running to get better at running, unlike in football where you're lifting and running to get into shape so you get better at football. I ran two years of track and three of cross-country. The first years were cool, but in the last year they started having you lift weights and sprinting and wearing funny things on your legs while running uphill and stuff. I preferred to run rather than the training bullshit. Running sprints and weightlifting got old quick."

"I could never run that much. You still run?"

"Running relaxed me, but I don't run anymore."

"Maybe you should."

"Maybe I should."

"Why did you quit track?" the bartender asked.

Before O'Neill answered, the bartender glanced up and moved toward the two women. They had a brief conversation, and he returned with two empty glasses. He filled the glasses with white wine and returned to the table. O'Neill finished his second beer and slid the empty to the bar's edge.

"Sorry about that," he said as he grabbed O'Neill's glass and refilled the glass with Old Style. "What were you saying about quitting track?" he asked.

O'Neill smiled. "I got kicked out of school during my junior year, so I never quit."

"Kicked out?"

"Yeah, I was a bit of a screwup. I was a dumb shit and brought gin to school one day and got caught. Me and another guy were in the blue room at school, bullshitting and taking turns nipping the gin. It was a bathroom. They called it the blue room because the walls were blue. Everyone else is in there smoking and a nun comes in. She's there to bust the smokers, but she catches Jimmy McPherson and me drinking gin."

"A nun came in?"

"Yeah, I forgot to mention it was a Catholic school. Anyway, I was already on probation since getting cited by the cops a few weeks earlier, so they kicked me out of school and, of course, there's no track and field if there's no school."

"That sucks. You run at your next school?"

"No," O'Neill replied. "I had to show that I was cooperative before I could join. Guess I was uncooperative."

"Seamus, what the hell are you doing here?" John Ryder asked as he walked into the bar. The detective was wearing a white T-shirt and gray sweats. "You should get a good night's sleep."

"Sorry about that," O'Neill said. "You look ridiculous dressed like a normal person."

"I was walking on the treadmill before bed, and it occurred to me I should check on you."

O'Neill turned to the bartender. "I'm still uncooperative."

Ryder sat down next to O'Neill, leaning his right elbow on the bar. The bartender asked whether he wanted a drink, but Ryder waved him off.

"Seamus, finish your beer and go to bed. It's midnight, and I'm expecting you ready to check-out by eight thirty in the morning. That way, we can get the free continental breakfast before heading back to Madison. Remember, we should have our client engagement letter."

"This free breakfast is a big deal to you, isn't it?"

"Sure. You should eat, you know. Either way, I thought you might be here since you could buy drinks using your room key."

"Hey, it didn't occur to me that charges would go against your credit card. I should have thought of that. Guess I'm not much of a detective."

Ryder looked at the ten dollars and sixty cents on the countertop. "Finish your beer and go to sleep."

"I got enough cash for one more. The Old Style taps are only two bucks, which I figure isn't bad for a hotel bar."

"Cash him out," Ryder said to the bartender before turning back to O'Neill. "Now finish your beer and go to bed."

O'Neill took a few gulps, leaving the empty glass and seven dollars and sixty cents on the bar.

"Thanks," O'Neill said to the bartender.

"Thank you," he replied. "And remember to run again."

O'Neill nodded and gave him a wave.

"Why does he want you to run?" Ryder asked as they left the bar. "Can't he see you can hardly walk?"

Chapter 14

O'Neill and Ryder were back at the office at eleven thirty in the morning. O'Neill carried his duffel bag inside and called Sandra at her father's house. He got Harry's answering machine, allowing him to avoid speaking with her. He checked the spot in his desk where he had kept emergency cash. He left one dollar, sticking the rest in his wallet.

Ryder was reading through files to prepare for his appointment with Garcia. He put his papers together and jotted notes while O'Neill searched for the name, address, and phone number of the University cross-country coach. As O'Neill finished recording contact information, he heard footsteps and the swish of the mailman's bag rubbing against the front door. There was a "clunk" as the daily mail fell into Ryder's mailbox. O'Neill popped up, walking easier than he had in days. He expected to find Myles Staley's letter, and he was not disappointed.

The return address on the letter appeared to be Adam Staley's home. He handed the envelope to Ryder, who used a handkerchief to pull out two sheets. He made photocopies, returning the originals to the envelope and giving a copy to O'Neill.

"Looks like I was wrong. We got engagement letters from both the Staley kid *and* the Staley dad."

Ryder handed O'Neill the photocopies. He read Adam Staley's letter first.

August 3, 1998

Mr. John Ryder and Mr. Seamus O'Neill
Ryder Detective Agency

Dear Sirs:
Enclosed is a letter from my son explaining his interest in the August 1996 murder of Andie Sheridan. As Mr. Bartholomew already explained, I do not share my son's concerns with the police investigation into this unfortunate event. Nevertheless, I am honoring my son's wishes by requesting your assistance in the matter.

As required in the contract, your firm, or its representatives, are prohibited from contacting my son, Myles Staley, without my permission or the permission of my attorney, Harry Bartholomew. I also prohibit you from disclosing Myles and me as your clients. While this may be an unusual stipulation, it is part of my commitment to helping my son stay focused on his career.

I appreciate your assistance and cooperation.

Sincerely,

Adam Staley

O'Neill thought it a strange letter, almost a disclaimer. He hoped the second letter would be more informative.

August 3, 1998

Dear Sir:

Late in the morning of August 21, 1996, someone murdered a woman named Andie Sheridan. Andie was a friend of mine. Resulting from this tragedy was a police investigation that was woefully inadequate and ultimately unsuccessful. Re-opening an additional, independent investigation is my wish. Yet to succeed, this investigation must ignore the basic premise which the police relied upon in their investigation. My belief is an independent, intelligent investigation can solve this case.

Andie Sheridan was a friend of mine who I miss greatly. Remarkable, she was, and strong willed, energetic, and vibrant. Sadly, killers seem to take the lives of those who enjoy it, but we can't let this killer succeed. History shows that people need to be held accountable.

Sincerely,

Myles Staley

O'Neill's first impression was that Myles Staley wrote poorly. He referred to Andie Sheridan as a friend twice in the brief letter and he stated that "re-opening an additional, independent investigation" was his wish. It was a silly letter for a university graduate. He laid Myles Staley's letter on his desk and read it again.

"Doesn't tell us jack squat," Ryder said as he sat on O'Neill's desk. He took a breath and shook his head. "I hoped this would give us an understanding of why Myles Staley thought the MPD bungled the investigation."

O'Neill stared at the letter from Myles. The redundancies struck him, and one phrase should have been a separate sentence. It only took a minute before he figured it out.

"There is a hidden message in Myles' letter," O'Neill said.

"You're shitting me," Ryder said, snatching the letter from O'Neill's hands. He held the photocopy in the air.

O'Neill snatched the sheet back and sat it on his desk. He pulled a marker from his desk and highlighted the first letter of each sentence in yellow. The highlighted letters spelled L-A-R-R-Y-M-A-R-S-H. "Andie's boyfriend, the professor. The man who should be our number one suspect."

Ryder returned to his desk. "Very interesting."

"What do you think?" O'Neill said. "Does Myles know Larry Marsh killed her? And if so, why use a cipher or code or whatever this would be called?"

"Who gives a shit? It's a secret message. This is getting good."

"Someone is leading us to Larry Marsh, there is no doubt about that. But, as you have said repeatedly, Larry Marsh couldn't have killed Andie."

"Yeah, but this makes even me wonder."

O'Neill's fingers ran over his two-day beard. "You gonna get prints off those letters?"

"Don't you think Myles wrote his?"

"I'm wondering if Harry's fingerprints are on it."

"What would Sandy's daddy have to do with this? You still think there's trickery going on, and he's trying to make you look good or bad? You're paranoid, my poorly named friend. Even if his prints are on the letter, it means nothing. Daddy Staley may have wanted Harry to review the letters before they went out."

"Why the easy cloak and dagger message?"

"How would I know?" said Ryder. He let out a puff of air. "Once again, our clients pay us to answer questions. All you do is ask them. Either way, I need to get ready for my meeting with Garcia, so leave me alone. It shouldn't take long. I'll ask him about the location stuff, but this is really him checking in on us."

"I could come," O'Neill said as he tucked the copies in his wallet.

"Shit no, Garcia wouldn't like you."

O'Neill didn't bother to ask why. "Go ahead, and I'll see you tomorrow. I'll try to talk with this cross-country coach and the roommate, Mary Gleason. Make sure you pump Garcia on Larry Marsh and his alibi."

"Myles Staley's letter makes me interested in Larry Marsh. It also makes his interview more important. Keep away from the Scotch. If you look more hungover than usual, you won't be coming with me to interview Larry Marsh."

All summer, O'Neill had walked home from work, and since his knee was feeling better, he saw no reason to change the practice. The walk took him past the Tango Club. In the early '90s, when he was in Theoretically Trashed, the Tango Club was the biggest local venue they played, and he hated it.

Remembering his days in Theoretically Trashed made him think of Jane, and as he made his way toward Johnson Street, he realized he was only a few blocks from her apartment. He continued, not for a reason but because he couldn't stop himself.

When he got to her driveway, he paused, staring at her Mazda. Before he could talk himself out of it, he walked up the steps and rang the doorbell. A tall brunette wearing black answered the door. Two rings were in her nose, and her shirt said "Humpty Dumpty was pushed."

"Is Jane home?" He didn't even know her last name.

"You must be Seamus." Her smile turned into a giggle that didn't fit her look. "She's at the Shell playing basketball. She should be back soon, though. You could wait for her, or if you want to leave a message, you're welcome to."

"No, I got to go," he said, backpedaling while holding his cane and duffel bag. "Tell her I stopped by."

Rather than walking straight home, he stopped at Peacock Liquor. The man behind the counter greeted him by name and gave him a wave. O'Neill grabbed a liter of Grant's, a six-pack of Point Pale Ale, and a two-liter of Diet Mountain Dew.

Once home, O'Neill poured the last few ounces of his old bottle of Grant's into a tumbler and set the empty in the trash. He pulled out his Yamaha acoustic guitar and played a few chords. Then he put a Theoretically Trashed disk in his CD player titled *Not All is Well*. It was Theoretically Trashed's first CD. He played along on his guitar as he listened to the music, ignoring the rush of memories the music brought. Instead, he thought about the songs and about Jane listening to them. He wondered which songs were her favorites and why.

A knock on the door interrupted his thoughts.

He turned the CD off and picked dirty socks off the floor in case it was Jane. He set the guitar on its stand and opened the door.

"Seamus, let me in," a woman said.

The woman pushed past him and into his apartment. He knew her name, but it escaped him. She was a junkie he hung with when he was on the edge of being one himself. She'd been pretty, or at least she seemed pretty. She pushed the door closed and shoved herself close to him.

"I need a favor, Seamus."

She took his right hand and placed it underneath her skirt. Her eyes were vacant, and her skin was as pale as the sidewalk. She slid her leg along his hips and her tongue wet his ear.

O'Neill knew she wanted something, and she was desperate. She should know he was off dope, so she probably had nowhere to go.

"I don't got any shit."

"Sure, you do," she said. She pulled the buttons open on his pants. "I'll do you whatever you want, anything."

Her hand slid along his hardening penis.

"I don't fucking have anything!" he cried.

She didn't stop, so he grabbed her shoulders and pushed her away. She tripped, falling backwards onto his mattress. Her eyes hardened as she pulled her skirt down and stood up. O'Neill opened the door, and she walked out without a word. He closed and bolted the door. Then he fell back on the mattress and closed his eyes.

He lay still until another knock came. He assumed she was back, so he pulled himself to his feet.

Then he thought of Harry, and it hit him between the eyes: it was a setup, like Ryder suggested. The girl planted drugs in his room, and cops were at his door. He searched the bed, the rug, and the bare floor. If he could find whatever she planted, he'd flush it down the toilet before the cops searched his room.

Another knock.

A bead of sweat slid down his forehead. He felt inside his pant pockets, inside his underwear, underneath the mattress. Nothing. He looked through the peephole, but instead of seeing two uniformed policemen, he saw Jane.

O'Neill let out a large breath, undid the lock, and pulled the door open. He laughed as Jane stepped into his apartment.

"What's so funny?"

"Oh God," he said as he fell on the bed. "I'm so damn paranoid."

"I hear you stopped by my place," Jane said. She didn't close the door and was staring blankly into his apartment with her hands in her pockets.

"Not too impressive," O'Neill said, crashing out of his giddiness.

"It's home, though," she said with a forced smile.

Her nose flared, and O'Neill wondered whether she was smelling Scotch, beer, or just the mustiness of the place. He hoped she couldn't smell the woman who had just left his apartment.

"Your fly is down."

He buttoned his fly. Then he got off the mattress and pulled out his only chair. He used the chair when he worked on the computer and sometimes when he practiced or wrote music. Usually, he laid on the mattress.

She sat in the chair.

"I wish it was more impressive, but this is it," he said, waving his hand across his body. He returned to the mattress. "I got a bathroom with a shower. The microwave and the two-foot refrigerator are my kitchen, and this mattress is my bedroom."

She was staring at the mattress rather than at him. "You don't have a regular bed?"

"Always meant to get one, but that's rock & roll. Besides, I'm used to it, so I don't want one anymore." He went into the bathroom and opened the shade, hoping light would reduce the dreariness. "The best thing about the place is the lady below me doesn't mind my playing and the guy across the hall is almost deaf. The other lady on the second floor enjoys hearing music for background. She lent me the cane. I got two guitars, a banjo, an accordion, a tin whistle, and this beauty." He reached over the side of his mattress.

"Bagpipes?"

"Uilleann pipes. They don't work, but I hope to fix them. My old man used to play. I guess they're worth more than everything else I have even though they're broken. Either way, it is family tradition. My dad and his dad called them elbow pipes, but I guess uilleann pipes are what you're supposed to call them."

"You come from a family of musicians?"

A hint of a smile approached his lips. "They all played, I suppose, as did my grandpa's mom, but none of them were professional musicians."

They were quiet again. O'Neill put his uilleann pipes back on the floor.

"Amanda says you have a girlfriend," Jane said.

O'Neill didn't want to have this conversation, but he should have expected Amanda to warn her sister about him. "I do, but it's over. Or it will be over the next time I talk to her."

"You're breaking up with her?"

"She's dumping me. It's a long story, but if she doesn't, I'll break up with her."

Jane bit at her lip, and her arms wrapped tightly around her body. "What's her name?"

"Sandra Bartholomew."

"What does she do for a living, or is she a student?"

"She's in marketing for the cheese board or something like that."

"Why do you think she will dump you?"

O'Neill considered the question before answering. "She already dumped me, but her father brought her home to Chicago for an intervention. She thinks he'll give her an allowance or something to stay away from me. So, she doesn't want me to announce it yet. Guess that doesn't make me sound that good. I mean, her dad is going to pay her to leave me."

"Why did she break up with you?"

"She knows this is it, and it's not enough. She realized there's a difference between dating someone who plays rock & roll in a band and dating a rock star. And I'm no rock star.

He rolled off the bed and opened the refrigerator, pulling out a Point Pale Ale. "I'm sorry about the self-pity. I'm in a black mood. You want one?"

"Amanda says you're an alcoholic," Jane said, ignoring his question.

He opened the beer for himself. "What's an alcoholic? I drink too much, yeah, but I don't get in fights or beat women or drive a car after drinking. So, what's an alcoholic?"

"Someone who drinks too much and can't stop."

"I don't know if I could, but I don't want to stop. That would make me a dipsomaniac instead of an alcoholic."

"That sounds like the alcohol talking."

"If the alcohol was talking, I wouldn't have offered you my beer." He laughed, but only for a moment. "I drink a lot. That is how it is. I used to do drugs too. Shit, there was a time I was bad news with drugs, drinking, anything. I've cut the shit out, and I cut down on the booze. Now I'm where I wanna be. I have fun, but I'm not so blitzed that I can't enjoy it. Some don't like it, but it's how I want to live."

"They say alcoholics have to quit drinking and cutting down isn't an option."

He didn't answer.

"What are you thinking with... me? I mean, Amanda acts like you're a leper or something."

"I always thought she liked me."

"She likes your music and you as someone to talk to, but not as someone to date her sister. She says she's seen you with tons of women over the years."

He ran a hand through his hair. "I don't know what to say, except the past doesn't matter. This is about you and me."

Jane stood. Her hands were shaking.

"Amanda says I like you because I remember you from Theoretically Trashed."

"She's probably right. I would be a lonely man if I never picked up a guitar."

"But you're not lonely now?"

"Not when I'm with you." He put his hand on his forehead, covering his eyes, embarrassed by his sappiness.

She started walking in place. "I got to go. We'll talk again."

He stood. She backed up to the door and waved goodbye. When the door closed, he fell on the bed, covering his head. He was sure Jane was done with him. She had seen his bad side early, which was just as well. It would save her from wasting time on him and would stop him from hoping too much.

Chapter 15

O'Neill played a few melodies on his Sweetone tin whistle. He tried playing a Sharon Shannon song he recently heard on public radio, but he couldn't remember enough to make a go at it. He switched to his button accordion with no better result, then decided to create a melody. After moving back to the tin whistle, he landed on something he liked and switched to guitar. He kept the melody, created a hook, and found a chord progression to run with it. Humming along, he incorporated a few words and landed on a line of, "It don't shine."

He turned on his tape recorder and, after twenty minutes, he had the framework for a song. There wasn't a title yet, but he stopped. He put his guitar aside and poured a double shot of Scotch.

The song, of course, was about him and Jane and was sad and sappy. Playing music only kept her in his thoughts. He got out his notepad and tried focusing on Andie Sheridan and her murder, but thoughts came back to Jane.

He figured he needed a change of scenery, so he decided to stop at Topper's. Although they saw little of each other in recent years, O'Neill had known Topper since the mid-eighties when they busked for change on State Street. They moved to Chicago and put a band together, intending to take the country by storm. The band had O'Neill on guitar, Topper on vocals and bass, and a guy from Northwestern University on drums. They were a punkabilly band, but they did nothing but busk on the street. Within a year, the drummer got hit by a car while on an acid trip, and Topper descended into heavy drugs.

O'Neill responded by taking his dad's old uilleann pipes to Chicago's Irish district. In Madison, no one could touch him on the pipes, but Chicago had plenty of musicians playing Irish music with Irish instruments. It took a week for him to concede that he was no musical prodigy.

On January 2, 1987 — the day after his twentieth birthday — he pawned his dad's old pipes and came back to Madison on a Greyhound bus. Topper came back in 1996 driving a BMW. Word was, he got himself off junk and had been dealing and running books. Topper bought a pipe shop and the apartment above and had been a player in Madison's underground scene ever since.

O'Neill filled his flask and trudged to Howard Johnson's. He tried Topper's number but hung up when he got an answering machine. Next, he tried the pipe shop. A female voice answered the phone, but eventually Topper was on the line.

"Seamus, what's up?"

"Same old, same old. Anything up tonight?"

"Whatever you want. Come to the shop and we can jam, shoot the shit, and catch up. It has been months since we've talked."

O'Neill stopped home and picked up his cane. He no longer needed it for quick trips, but he figured he might make a few stops. By the time he got to Topper's shop, his knee needed rest.

"You look like shit," Topper said. "What's the deal with the stick?"

The door closed behind O'Neill. Topper stood behind a long glass case filled with pipe and smoking paraphernalia. Topper looked as pale as O'Neill remembered. The only difference was the size of his mustache, which expanded with age.

"How's business at the head shop?"

Topper laughed but didn't answer. A woman was behind the counter helping high school kids choose a bong. Topper waved O'Neill forward, and they went to a back room. Topper flipped on a light and locked the door. Chairs and two acoustic guitars sat in the middle of the windowless room.

"You want something to drink?" Topper opened a counter, revealing a line of bottles and glasses. "You still drink Scotch, right? Is Cutty Sark okay?"

"Course."

Topper set two glasses on a tray atop the counter. He filled both glasses with the golden amber fluid and handed one to O'Neill. Then he opened another compartment and pulled out what appeared to O'Neill to be crack cocaine.

"Keep that shit away from me," O'Neill said, laughing nervously.

Topper put the bag back and closed the compartment. "You can't tell me you're clean."

"Try to be. I'm definitely steering clear of crack and smack."

"I get your issue. I got a little too into it last year and it nearly whacked me out again."

O'Neill looked over the guitars and picked up a Warrant. He strummed the guitar, tuned it, and sat on a stool as Topper picked up the other guitar.

"What's going on with your band? I hear you got canned."

"They wanted to go on tour, while I didn't. We voted, and I told 'em I wasn't going. They voted to throw me out." He strummed an E chord. "I voted with them on that one."

"Looking to start a new band?"

"No. At least not right away."

"What you up to, then? You're not here to play guitar with me. You, of all people, know I can't play worth shit."

O'Neill strummed a few cords before answering. "I'm a little down, I guess. Woman troubles."

"Did that yuppy one with the long black hair dump you?" He snapped his fingers. "Ah, Sara... Sandy..."

"Sandra, yeah. She dumped me, though not officially. But she's not the reason I'm down. There is this other woman, you see."

"You're getting dumped by two women at once? The trick is you don't date 'em, you keep it to sex so when they leave you, you're not dumped."

O'Neill switched the topic to music. Topper was far from an accomplished musician, but he could jam and their common background meant they enjoyed much of the same music. They talked for a while, played a Hank Williams song, a few Steve Earle songs, and slid into "Off to Dublin in the Green." A knock on the door interrupted them. They stopped playing and Topper got to his feet.

"It's me, Janice," a voice said. "I'm closing the till."

Topper looked through the peephole. "Give me a couple of minutes since she's new. Once I'm done, we can take a cab to the Essen Haus, if that works for you. I'll line up dates and we can drink boots and have a beer at The Great Dane. The night is on me."

O'Neill didn't have time to answer, but it all sounded fine to him. The Essen Haus was a German restaurant with draft German beer, pretzels, and polka music, while the Great Dane was a local brewpub with a Scotch ale O'Neill had taken a shine to. If the night was on Topper, O'Neill's nearly empty wallet didn't matter.

He drank three stiff glasses of Cutty Sark before Topper came back. Topper called a cab, and they brought the nearly empty bottle of Cutty Sark with them.

The Essen Haus was northeast of the Wisconsin State Capitol within a quarter mile of Lake Monona. The original owners of the property had built part of the building during the American Civil War as a hotel for German immigrants. Various restaurants and businesses operated at the site, but to O'Neill, it was always the Essen Haus.

O'Neill and Topper stepped inside and pulled up to the bar. Beer steins hung above the counter, and the male bartenders and waiters wore lederhosen while the women wore dresses with aprons.

The square mahogany counter was once in the Fauerbach Brewery, which closed in 1966. But O'Neill didn't mention the bar to Topper. Instead, they ate pretzels and reminisced about old times. O'Neill's old friend seemed to enjoy his role as the successful one. It was apparent in the way he dressed and acted. When the dates arrived shortly before seven o'clock, O'Neill knew he was getting the full charity treatment. Topper had the younger one sit next to him and the other sat next to O'Neill.

"This is Tammy," the older one said, "and I'm Cara."

Tammy had a tongue ring, a nose ring, several tattoos, and an assortment of earrings. Both wore short skirts and O'Neill noted their dirty fingernails.

"This is Seamus O'Neill, he's a musician," Topper said. "A damn good one, I might add."

"What kind of music do you play?" Tammy asked.

"Most call it rock & roll, but some might not."

Tammy and Cara exchanged glances.

"I think you have a head start on us," Cara said to O'Neill.

"Seamus always looks and sounds that way," Topper said. "If he doesn't, he's hungover."

Cara ran her fingers down O'Neill's leg. He thought he saw a hint of revulsion in her expression. He glanced at Topper's watch, and a thought clicked.

"Just a second," O'Neill said as he stood up. "I got to make a phone call."

He meandered through the thickening crowd, past the bouncer, and to the pay phone near the entrance. He had Harry Bartholomew's number in his notepad. His eyes had trouble focusing, but he finally read the number. He dialed collect and Sandra answered.

"Seamus?" she said, her voice tentative. She accepted the charges. "I'm glad you called. How are you?"

"Just peachy."

"Just what?"

A group of young women walked past him and into the bar.

"Peachy."

"Oh."

"How's the week going with Harry?"

"We've had a wonderful visit, and something exciting happened," Sandra said. There was a tasteful pause. "I have a job offer from Rupert and Crowley Publishers doing marketing and publicity for a new magazine they are launching."

"Rupert and Crowley? Never heard of them," O'Neill said. "They based in Chicago?"

"Yeah, that is the bad part." There was another tasteful pause. "The position would be here in Chicago. I know it's awful, but you have to answer when opportunity knocks."

O'Neill assumed Harry could hear their conversation, so he played along. "You gotta take 'em where you can get 'em."

"I'm starting a week from Monday. Tomorrow I'm going to start apartment hunting and I need to decorate and do a complete load of planning. Daddy will help with rent, which is great."

She went on for a while longer, but O'Neill hardly paid attention. He instead reflected on how Sandra had pulled things off. She got a respectable job in Chicago in a field she was interested in and got Harry to pay her rent. O'Neill decided that the job Harry gave him must have been more a peace offering than a bribe. As Sandra was saying goodbye, O'Neill interrupted her.

"Can I talk to your dad once?"

"Why do you want to talk to my dad?"

"I got a question for him about this case he's given us. It's nothing about you and I."

"Just a minute, I'll check."

After a long minute, Sandra returned. "He went to pick up today's Chicago Tribune, so he's not here."

"Okay then, I'll call back in fifteen minutes."

"No, I'll have him call you."

"Sandra, you know I don't have a phone, and I know he's there otherwise you wouldn't have talked the way you did. Let me talk to him. I did a favor for you, so you can at least get him on the phone."

She gave in, muttering something O'Neill didn't understand.

"Seamus," Harry said in his rustic, good-natured tone. "What can I do for you?"

"About this case you gave us. I'll be straight up with you, and I would appreciate it if you were straight up with me. When you gave me this job, I assumed it was a bribe or a peace offering so Sandra didn't feel guilty dumping me."

"Seamus, I assure you..."

"Is Myles Staley really our client?"

"Technically, Myles' father is your client since he hired you, while I am his agent. Why wouldn't Myles and Adam be your clients? What's this about?"

"I know who the killer is," O'Neill said.

There was silence. Even the noise in the bar seemed to subside.

"You know what?"

"I know who killed Andie Sheridan."

"Who do you think killed her?" Harry asked, his voice trailing away.

"Andie Sheridan's former boyfriend, Larry Marsh."

"Why do you think he's the killer?"

"It's too complicated to get into on a public pay phone."

"Seamus," Harry said in a firmer tone, "I want you to listen to me. I need to talk to my client before we talk further. Can I call you tonight, or can you call me back?"

"I can call you back."

"In two hours, I want you to call me. I have seven fifteen, so I'll be expecting the call at nine fifteen." He cleared his throat. "Does anyone besides you and your boss know this?"

"No, just me and Ryder."

"Leave it that way, at least until I call you back."

"I'll be calling you."

"That's what I meant."

O'Neill hung up, then put change in the machine and dialed Ryder's home phone. He told Ryder about the call.

"Why the hell did you tell him Larry Marsh is the killer?" Ryder said. "All we have is a new murder location and a stupid-looking message. You said that the damn message looked too simplistic. We need more than secret codes. We need evidence."

"I wanted to hear Harry's reaction."

Ryder let out a breath of disgust. "And what did you determine from his reaction, oh mighty one?"

"Screw you," O'Neill said. "He's checking with the client. I still don't know if Myles Staley is our client or if his daddy is."

"Shit, you're going to get us in trouble. You're accusing someone who couldn't have been the killer."

"It was a hunch, and what have we got to lose anyway?"

"Remember, we're early in our two-week contract with an option for two more weeks. If you tug at our client — whoever he is — and give him a bullshit story, we could lose any opportunity at an additional two weeks, you drunken lout. I've had enough of your shit. If I had any sense, I would fire your ass."

"Okay, I went a little overboard," O'Neill said after a pause.

"More than a little," Ryder said in a restrained tone. "We'll talk tomorrow."

O'Neill knew he should tell Ryder that he planned to call Harry back, but he didn't. Instead, he hung up the phone and walked to the table. Topper was by himself except for four beer mugs.

"They're in the ladies' room," Topper said. "They needed fortification." He lifted his eyebrows twice, implying that O'Neill was in on the joke.

O'Neill took a gulp of the beer. "What is this stuff?"

"DAB, the strongest stuff they got, not counting a doppelbock. Six-point-six ABV, if I remember correctly."

"Topper, do you remember a murder of a university cross-country runner from back in '96?"

"What about it?" Topper replied.

"Did you know the murdered woman?"

"Nope, don't think I did."

"Do you know a guy who teaches at the University named Larry Marsh?"

"No, I don't. Why are you asking?"

There was no good way to answer. He had spent a few nights pretending to be a detective, hoping someone he ran into would, by any luck, have information about the murder. It might never work again.

"I don't know," O'Neill answered. "Someone told me about the attack, and it seemed strange."

The women returned to the table. They had combed their long hair and thickened their makeup. Cara sat next to O'Neill again, no more relaxed than when they first met.

They talked and drank as a polka band arrived. The band consisted of two guys wearing lederhosen, one with an accordion, and one with a drum set. They set up in front of a large United States flag that had forty-five stars. It took only a few minutes before the band was playing polkas. After two songs, O'Neill tried to convince Cara to polka with him, but she wouldn't. In the end, O'Neill took Tammy to the dance floor.

"I've never done this!" she yelled into O'Neill's ear.

"You've never danced?"

O'Neill knew what she had meant. He was giving her a hard time.

"I've never done a polka."

"You're not from Wisconsin, are you? I thought I might hear an accent. Poland, maybe?"

"I was born in Poland but came to Racine when I was nine. You have a good ear."

O'Neill pulled her close and they danced to "Just Because," but had a difficult time since he was drunk and she didn't know how to polka. They bumped into an older couple, and O'Neill came down hard on his bad knee. And after half a song, they were off the dance floor. When they came back to their table, Topper and Cara were nowhere to be seen and a different group had taken their table.

"Guess he thought you liked me better," Tammy said.

"We should head out," O'Neill said, glad he had finished his beer.

"We going to your place?"

O'Neill didn't like that idea since she would link him with Topper, and he worried she would be at his door someday like the girl earlier in the day. "Topper forgot that I don't have any cash on me. We could go to a club and listen to music, but I'm broke. Topper said the night was on him."

She rolled her eyes. He started walking toward the exit, and she followed. Once outside, he turned up Wilson going toward the capitol.

"Where are we going?" she asked after a few steps.

"I don't got any money," O'Neill said. It was technically true, but saying he had three dollars and change only sounded worse.

"Topper paid, but he said I would have a place to stay," she said as they neared King Street.

He stopped and looked her over. She was pretty and seemed nice enough. It seemed wrong to force anyone onto the street. "We can listen to music and hang at my place, or you can go it alone. Your call."

She itched at her nose ring. "Yeah," she said after a pause. "It's way too early to hang it up, so I'll go out alone. But we might as well walk to State Street together."

"Might as well."

They continued walking toward the Wisconsin State Capitol. Tammy was rubbing her arms together as if trying to generate heat. "What are you to Topper, anyway?"

"We've been friends from way back."

"That why he gets girls for you?"

"First time he's ever done that. I suppose he wanted to play the big shot."

As they approached State Street, another thought came to O'Neill. He tried to stop himself from asking her, but he couldn't.

"You ever heard of a guy named Larry Marsh?"

"Don't know no Larrys,"

"Do you remember a girl named Andie Sheridan? Someone murdered her in Madison back in '96. She was a cross-country runner."

"No, I've only been here since spring."

"Figures," O'Neill said. "It figures."

Chapter 16

O'Neill got home before ten o'clock, turned on the radio, filled a tumbler with Scotch, and read Herman Melville's *Billy Budd*. The book didn't enthrall him, so he put it aside and found the binder of copies he had made. It included Ryder's case summary, Garcia's summary, an accompanying map, and a listing of interviews. Before digging in further, he remembered his promise to call Harry back at nine fifteen. He put his shoes on, walked to Howard Johnson's, and called Harry Bartholomew's residence. Sandra answered the phone.

"Seamus, you should have called hours ago."

"I got caught up in something. Is your father around?"

He could hear her whisper, "He sounds drunk."

"Seamus, I was wondering whether you would call," Harry said, pausing. "You think this Larry Marsh killed the girl from the University? According to our client, he was the murdered girl's boyfriend. Can you prove he killed her?"

"Not yet, but we'll get there."

"I want more information but prefer coming to Madison rather than reviewing a written report. You and Mr. Ryder can explain your theory, and we can decide what to do next. Until then, I want you to hold off on sharing information with the police. I'm busy tomorrow and Thursday but could make a

Friday meeting. You and Mr. Ryder could familiarize me with your ideas on the case. We could meet at your office at, say, noon?"

O'Neill mumbled his agreement and hung up. He paused for a moment, considering whether he should head home or walk by Jane's house. "Don't be an idiot," he said, and he started home. He considered spending his remaining three dollars at the Nitty Gritty bar, but he needed the money for laundry, so he made a second wise decision and continued home.

A knock at the door awoke O'Neill. Light coming in through the bathroom told him it was daytime. He crawled off the mattress, stood, and stared into the peephole. It was Ryder. He was wearing a yellow shirt and a red tie. O'Neill let him in.

"What time is it?"

"Time for you to drag your drunken ass out of bed," Ryder said as he pushed his way past O'Neill and into the room. "I hope you realize you've got me exceedingly pissed off."

"Then it was worth it," O'Neill said as he closed the door.

"What a dump," Ryder said before pointing at the mattress. "You sleep there?"

"Very observant. You must be a detective."

Ryder's head was shaking. "Now I understand why you're not worried about being homeless. Is this the only room?"

"You never heard of an efficiency? I have a bathroom," he said, motioning with his head, "and that is my kitchen area."

"How can this place make code?" he said. "This explains how you survive on what I pay you. There isn't even a window.

Can you put a shirt on? Looking at you reminds me of middle school gym class."

O'Neill took a newly washed T-shirt out of his dresser and pulled it over head.

"What you want?"

"I got an email this morning from Sandy's daddy. He says he'll be meeting with us on Friday at noon regarding our findings in the Sheridan murder investigation." His teeth ground together. "What findings is he referring to?"

"We'll come up with some, I guess."

"You guess?"

"Oh, screw you, I got you this job. If I mess up, then who's the worse for it? Let me go back to sleep."

"Don't give me that crap. This is my reputation we're talking about."

"It's not like you're waiting for Chicago-area clients, and, like I told you last night, I wanted to cut through the bullshit and see Harry's reaction."

Ryder let out a breath of air. "This job should be a cakewalk. We interview a few people, and they pay us two weeks at full rates. Instead, you're turning it into a pain in the ass. That is fine if you get us extra weeks, but otherwise it is not fine and will piss me off."

O'Neill stepped into the kitchen area and drank a few gulps of water from the kitchen faucet. "You came over to tell me you're pissed?"

"No, that's a bonus. If you were a normal human being, you would have a phone so I wouldn't be at your dump apartment. Shit, I should get you a beeper or a cell phone or something. No, you would lose it. But I got to meet with a potential client, so I need you setting an additional interview today. I had planned on us going together, but we've got a lot of territory to cover before Friday so you may need to go alone."

O'Neill smiled. "Who do I talk to besides the cross-country coach?"

"Him plus Andie's roommate, Mary Gleason, and the runner who was behind Andie in the race, Donna Ritz. She is an important interview, so don't screw it up. If she wants to meet tomorrow, that's fine. If you have time, read the file. They are in the office but keep them there. Three interviews may not sound bad, but it's hard to contact people and schedule meetings on short notice. Be sure to mention Jennifer Reilly if people are hesitant to meet, but don't expect perfect recollection from anyone. Set your interviews as early as you can for today or tomorrow. If I can make them, I'll join you. You can try to interview the male runners if you can't get the others. Names and contact information are on the sheets I threw on the floor, but some are out-of-date."

O'Neill already interviewed the roommate, meaning one of the three interviews was already complete, and he didn't see any reason to interview the male runners.

"How did the meeting with Garcia go?" O'Neill asked. "Did you learn anything new about Larry Marsh's alibi?"

"Nothing except that Garcia worked hard to break it and couldn't. His gut told him that Marsh was the guy, but the facts simply don't support that. Otherwise, I didn't learn much. He got interrupted, so we only talked for about ten minutes."

"There's one problem," O'Neill said, as Ryder prepared to leave. "I don't get paid until tomorrow, and I, uh..."

"Let me guess," Ryder said, putting his hands on his hips. "You drank all your money last night and you want an advance."

"You hit the nail on the head."

Ryder let out a disgusted sigh and pulled out his wallet. "Thirty bucks as an advance."

O'Neill put a ten in his wallet and the rest under his mattress. "What about you? What will you be doing?"

"I'll be meeting with this potential client for reoccurring work. It's out in Stoughton. I will, however, meet with Larry Marsh, and I am going to Janesville to interview Andie's father. I wasn't planning on meeting the father, but he called and wants to talk. I don't think he has any important information; I just think he wants to be part of it. I'll be in the office tomorrow at noon. If you're not there, you're fired. If we have nothing new, we'll work on the bullshit story you gave Harry about Larry Marsh."

"Don't you want me to come with you when you meet with Larry Marsh?"

"You'll be busy enough. He's got classes at ten fifteen, one, and three at Grainger Hall. I'm going to catch him between the first two classes. We might get another chance to meet with him." Ryder glanced at his watch. "Shit, I got to roll."

O'Neill locked the door and wrote Larry Marsh's class times on his notepad.

Chapter 17

At ten o'clock, O'Neill was at Grainger Hall, which was the base of the University's School of Business. Grainger Hall was new with modern conveniences, considerable computer wiring, and enormous bathrooms. Unlike other university buildings he had been at, the building wasn't a box with classrooms. Instead, there was open space, large windows, and carpeted floors.

O'Neill was too early for Ryder's meeting with Larry Marsh, but he decided that was okay. He wanted to see the man. He wanted to look into his eyes and see whether Larry Marsh could be a killer. Ryder would say it was silly and unprofessional, but O'Neill didn't care.

He found an information booth and got directions to Larry Marsh's Accounting Systems 315 class. As students switched classes, the decibel level in the halls increased. O'Neill found an elevator and exited on the third floor. He got lost twice before finding the room. He stood outside the door and listened to the students chattering. At ten fifteen, he went inside.

O'Neill expected a lecture room filled with sleeping students and a teacher at a podium. He stepped forward, and the door swooshed closed behind him. The classroom of students looked at him, and everyone stopped talking. O'Neill's eyes darted among the twenty-five or thirty students before landing on the teacher, who O'Neill recognized as Larry Marsh. He was a tall man with brown eyes, blonde hair, and a powerful build.

"Can I help you?" Larry Marsh asked.

It was dead quiet as fifty eyes stared at O'Neill.

"I got an interview with Mr. Schwartz," O'Neill said. "He said it was in room 351."

"This is 355," Larry Marsh said. "The number is on the door."

Larry Marsh didn't move or speak until O'Neill left the room. The door closed, but O'Neill waited outside.

"Let's hope he's not a candidate for the chancellor position," O'Neill heard Larry Marsh say to his class. The students laughed.

O'Neill straightened up and walked toward the stairs.

O'Neill found the cross-country coach's office location in the campus directory. Reggie Lehman was head coach of the women's cross-country team and an assistant women's track coach. O'Neill stepped in, holding a business card, but Reggie Lehman's secretary said Coach Lehman was out. She took the card and stuck it atop a pile of notes. O'Neill left the office feeling disappointed. As the door closed behind him, a short, dark-haired woman approached the door. O'Neill thought she looked like a runner.

"Hey, aren't you on the cross-country team?" he said. "Um..."

"Yes, Lisa Pederson," she said, seemingly surprised and excited about being recognized.

"I thought that was you. Looking forward to a great season. Anyway, I was looking for Coach Lehman, but he's out. Do you know where he is?"

"You'll rarely catch Coach Lehman in his office during the summer," Lisa said. "If we're not running, he's usually at the Memorial Union Terrace. It's where he does his paperwork during the summer. And if it's raining, he's in the Rathskeller."

"Great, it's much appreciated. But before I go, Coach Lehman's picture on the website isn't ideal." O'Neill said, remembering the black-and-white photo showing women running past a sweatsuit-clad man. "Could you give me a description so I can recognize him?"

"What's this about?" Lisa asked, pulling her backpack strap tighter.

O'Neill handed her one of his business cards. "It's about one of his former runners, Andie Sheridan."

She looked at the business card before replying. "Yeah, I heard about that. I'm only a sophomore, so it happened before my time. Coach Lehman is tall, thin, and balding. He's in his late forties and has a long scar on his left cheek. He mentions the scar to people so they can recognize him, so I'm not out of line pointing it out."

"Course not," O'Neill said.

⁂

The Union Terrace was busy even though it was summer session. Groups of kids ran along the shoreline, giving a different mood than a few nights before when O'Neill played with Shifts in Turmoil. The atmosphere was also different from the one that would dominate during the fall semester.

O'Neill found Reggie Lehman almost immediately, as the scar didn't disappoint. He was a gaunt, black-haired man with a receding hairline. Notebooks, a glass, and a laptop were on the table.

"Coach Lehman?" O'Neill said. Lehman nodded but didn't speak. "My name is Seamus O'Neill," he said, handing the coach a business card. "I'm with the Ryder Detective Agency."

"A detective?" Lehman said, examining the card.

"My agency is investigating the murder of a woman who ran for you back in '96, Andie Sheridan."

Lehman looked relieved. "Yes, Andie. It was quite..." his head shook, "a shock. Are you working for her family?"

"I can't divulge who our client is, but I will say that Andie's mother is aware of and supporting our investigation. Can I sit?"

"You are welcome to sit, but I'm not sure I can help you beyond what I already told the police."

"I have seen the police files, but I have a few questions about Andie as a person. First off, how well did you know her?"

His head bobbed side to side. "Not too well. I'm afraid we never hit it off personally or professionally. She had talent but no commitment to running." His lips pushed together. "I knew that when she arrived."

"Why did you give her a scholarship if she had no commitment to running?"

The coach seemed taken aback by the frankness of the question. He licked his lips before speaking.

"I'm afraid we should have known when we recruited her, but we made an evaluation error. She had flawless form which we credited to her high school coaching staff. Coaching only works when the athlete is coachable, but, in retrospect, I don't know how Andie got her form. Was it her natural style, or had she been coachable when she was younger? Whatever it was, when I knew her, she was not coachable. We were after her for both track and cross-country, so offering her a scholarship was not wholly my decision. I had concerns, but I bought too much into her form. Once she signed the letter of intent, my concerns amplified. She was at Janesville Parker and once she had her scholarship, she claimed a back injury that forced her to miss the end of the cross-country season. The injury limited her in track that spring, yet she competed in most meets. When she came here as a freshman, I had an uphill battle."

"Did you make progress?"

"No. She got by on her talent in track but only minimally in cross-country. At this level, we expect a lot of mileage out of our athletes. Running is a daily grind and talent isn't enough. But running was not one of her priorities which sounds ridiculous for a college cross-country athlete. She was smart, so her grades were good, which is something the University looks at when evaluating athletes. Before the season started, I considered dismissing her from the team, but that is hard to do when someone's grades are strong."

"Did she have positives beyond grades and her form?"

"I'll admit she was gutsy, competitive, and talented. She held her own in meets despite being more focused on partying than running. She should have been a 5K All-American, but she settled for mediocrity."

"You said she ran track, too. I didn't realize that. Was she on scholarship for cross-country, track, or both? Could she have wanted to get canned from cross-country so she could just run track?"

"Scholarships for track and cross-country are complicated, but I suspect she needed to stay on both teams for financial reasons. She came from a family with limited means, so I don't think she would have been able to stay enrolled without her scholarship. Quitting cross-country would have left her with a fractional scholarship, and they allocated a bigger portion to cross-country. I think she needed a full scholarship."

"What about negatives for her, beyond her lack of commitment?"

Lehman rubbed his hands together and his head shook from side to side. "I couldn't figure her out. She was shy and didn't fit in with her teammates. Whenever I talked to her, she would stare at the ground. I don't remember her ever looking me in the eye. When she was running, she certainly cared about winning, yet she didn't care about running. That might sound strange, but that was Andie. Even more frustrating was that she wanted to be woodwork, meaning she didn't want to be noticed. But she was so talented and so beautiful. She naturally stood out. I hate to be an amateur psychiatrist, but I don't think Andie was comfortable being Andie."

"Did you know her boyfriend, Larry Marsh?"

"No, but I heard about their relationship. Mr. Marsh was a teacher's assistant, making the relationship improper, and there was a minor scandal when news of the relationship broke."

O'Neill was unfamiliar with the workings of a university, so it had not occurred to him that an affair between a student and a teacher's assistant might be controversial.

"Was the relationship a secret at the time?"

"They apparently kept the relationship quiet, but her teammates knew. The University reviewed his actions but decided after her death that the relationship did not violate ethics rules since she was not in the School of Business and had no classes with Mr. Marsh. He's now an assistant professor, so apparently they concluded it was not an issue."

O'Neill leaned back and tried to put his next question together. He wished he had a drink, since he thought better with a drink in his hand. "On the morning of the attack, you drove the women to Vilas for their run."

"The run was an oddity we did sometimes. Not everyone liked the route since part of the distance was on sidewalks and they got stuck at streetlights, but I believe runners benefit from variety. We started and finished on the beach near the Henry Vilas Zoo. We took that route four or five times each summer. It was the week's easiest workout, going over 12K if I recall correctly. Usually, we ran it on Fridays, but this was a Wednesday, I believe. We took two vans. I drove the first. Andie was in the second van."

"My understanding is you didn't publish any sort of weekly or monthly schedule, correct?"

"Correct. On most days, the women come to our rally point and after stretching, we go through workouts, sprints, lifting, different routines. When they run, me or my assistant send them on one of several regular routes on trails or paths. This Vilas route was an oddity, but it allowed the women to go to the beach after running, so they liked it."

"The women knew they would run through the arboretum that day."

"Yes. They needed to know so they could catch the vans or go directly to Vilas Beach."

O'Neill cleared his throat, struggling for a line of questioning. "Must admit, while I ran in high school, I don't know how college cross-country works. 12k is over seven miles. A seven-plus mile practice run has got to be a killer when you're training for 5K or 6K."

"That's the difference between high school and D-1 college. Besides, they're running easy, maybe six thirty per mile. It's not a stressful run."

"When I ran, the coach would sometimes drive along to watch over us. Does that happen in college? Do you watch their practice runs?"

"You can't watch collegiate cross-country practice the same way coaches in other sports watch practice. On the Vilas run, we walked to the bridge as they hit the hill, but other than checking their times, that's it. Cross-country is not like other sports where the athletes are constantly in front of the coaches. I'm there for lifting, stretching, and sprint workouts, but the nature of cross-country is unique. That usually isn't a problem as we don't need to babysit our women. Maybe Andie needed babysitting, but I didn't have time to waste on her. I felt she could sink or swim on her own."

"Makes sense. How many coaches and support staff were involved on the day Andie was killed?"

"My assistant coach, Fred Doerpinghaus, was on vacation that week. He was in Florida in case you're wondering. So, it was just me and the training staff. That would be our trainer, Marv LaHaye, and our student manager, Brianna Michael."

"Was Andie under the weather the morning of August twenty-first?"

His shoulders shrugged. "I got used to seeing her that way, but I don't specifically remember."

"But she always made practice?"

"I didn't say that," he replied, his lower lip quivering. "I disciplined her for missing practice, and don't forget, it was still summer. In her freshman year, she'd been sick or injured for a half-dozen practices before I required her to provide an excuse from our trainer. That reduced but didn't end skipped practices."

"She was near the back during that day's run. Was that unusual?"

"No. She usually came on and ended in front of the second cluster. These are practice runs and not mini races, but for Andie Sheridan, everything was a race. She may not have cared about running, but once she started running, she couldn't stop herself. She couldn't separate a run from a race, so she wanted to win. She never finished running with a group. She either came in running strong or ran herself ragged earlier and dragged herself in. Part of the problem was that she couldn't win a 12K or a 15K race. 5K worked best for her in cross-country. She did the 5K in track and field, but 3K was her best track distance."

"She never finished the run on August twenty-first. What did you do when that happened? You mentioned you checked them off as they finished."

"We noted she did not finish. Our student manager, Brianna Michael, had seen her out that night, so I assumed she dropped out and would let us know later, claiming injury. Brianna drove the route in case Andie was injured and waiting for help but didn't see her. I called Andie's apartment later that day and was told she was at the doctor's office."

"Did you believe that story?"

"The back is an evil thing, but I didn't believe Andie anymore. I figured she would come in the next morning with a doctor's note. Later, I learned Andie told the roommate to tell me that story if I called."

"And when she didn't show the subsequent morning?"

"I called and she, of course, was unavailable. I told her roommate that Andie should read my email which said I would suspend Andie from the team unless she provided a doctor's note and checked in with our trainer — something along that line. The email laid out the riot act, but I expected some sucker with a medical degree would write her a note. When she didn't show on Friday morning, we went through our protocols, contacting the University and Andie's parents. We checked in with the University Police but waited until Saturday morning before formally requesting they locate her."

"It still seems odd, though, that she disappeared on a Wednesday, yet no one filed a missing person's report until Saturday."

"I went over and over this with the police. Perhaps it makes me look suspicious to you, but I had absolutely nothing to do with Andie's murder."

"I understand. But we need to look Andie's mother in the eye and tell her we took reasonable steps in this investigation. We can see what you did in the police files, but I want to understand why you did what you did."

"Yes. Well, in retrospect, I took administrative steps later than I should have. It was my fault, but I was sure her absence was nothing more than Andie being Andie. My focus was on disciplining her. I thought this might get her off my team. It might sound bad but kicking someone off a team is hard to do in a public university, so my focus was on documenting her skipping practice and taking the required disciplinary steps. The idea of an attack during a run was not on my radar."

"I think I get it," O'Neill said. "That helps. Earlier, you mentioned a student manager. What was her name again?"

"Brianna Michael."

"I don't recall seeing her name in the files," O'Neill said.

"We call her Brianna Michael, but her name is actually Brianna Michael Schladweiler."

"That is a mouthful."

Lehman nodded his agreement.

"Is she still with the team?"

"No, she graduated in May, though I believe she had a course yet this summer. She's got a job lined up with Northern Illinois University in sports medicine starting this fall."

O'Neill had the coach spell out the name, then changed his line of questioning. "What about rumors? Did you hear rumors about Andie's killing or who attacked her?"

"Rumors were flying around, but I don't know if I should spread rumors at this point."

"We're trying to find an angle the police overlooked," O'Neill said. "The police may not ask that question, but we do."

The coach shrugged his shoulders, apparently feeling the answer was good enough. "Most everyone assumed it was a stranger or a psychopath, but if the killer was someone she knew, most would guess Mr. Marsh killed her."

"Why Larry Marsh?"

The coach fidgeted uncomfortably. "Andie told one of her teammates that Mr. Marsh hit her at some point her freshman year. She said he would hold her down and not let her move. I don't know details and I can't say if the stories were true. The police would have details and presumably investigated the stories."

"Sounds like there was reason to be suspicious," O'Neill said. "What made people change their minds and stop suspecting Larry Marsh?"

"When we heard she was sexually assaulted, we figured it wasn't him. And then at some point, the six o'clock news ran a story saying the police cleared Mr. Marsh since he was in class until lunchtime, hours after the murder. He obviously couldn't have killed her, right?"

"So it seems," O'Neill replied. "So it seems."

Chapter 18

O'Neill called Donna Ritz on a payphone, exhausting his change but only getting her answering machine. He then tried to get her schedule from a university information desk at the Memorial Union, but they only gave student schedules out with University Police Department permission. O'Neill knew the police would not give him permission, so he didn't ask.

He bought a bottle of Diet Mountain Dew at the Memorial Union, breaking his ten-dollar bill. He went to the information desk and the woman at the counter searched the directory online after he spelled out Brianna Michael Schladweiler's name. It did not surprise him that only one name came up. She lived off campus, so he wrote the phone number down and returned to the pay phone.

To his surprise, Brianna answered the phone. He explained who he was and asked if she had two minutes for questions.

"Anything to help."

"My understanding from Coach Lehman is you had seen Andie Sheridan out on State Street the night before her disappearance. Can you give me any details?"

"It has been a few years, but I remember it well since everyone talked about Andie and her disappearance. I was at a bar called Mondays on State Street with a few friends. She was with a group of maybe three guys and six girls. She caught my eye and waved to me, which surprised me since I didn't think she even knew who I was."

"You were not close?"

"Not at all. She wasn't mean or anything, but she was quiet and standoffish. At some point soon after that, she stopped by my table, said 'Hi,' and gave me a hug, which surprised me. She left, and the guys at my table spent the rest of the night trying to convince me to bring her back."

"Because she was attractive."

"She was breathtaking. They were slobbering on the table."

"Anything else you recall about Andie or her group?"

"She was flirting with one guy. At one point, we caught eyes again, and I mouthed 'He's hot,' to her. We left before nine thirty. I remember because I had a rule to get home before ten o'clock on a work or school night. I don't remember if they left before my group."

"You mentioned this to the coach when Andie didn't finish her run, correct?"

"Yeah, when she didn't show at the beach, I assumed she was out late and couldn't finish the run. I took the van and drove the route in case she was waiting for someone to pick her up. When I got back, Coach Lehman said he was done waiting. He said he'd send her an email, so I finished cleaning up, loaded up the van, and went home."

"Were you with Coach Lehman during the run?"

"Yeah. Me and Marv LaHaye, who was the trainer, went through updates on treatments each runner was receiving, and we updated notes and so forth at Vilas. Coach Lehman and I cleaned up and got ready for the women to return. The three of us were together the whole time. I remember that because the police were trying to verify our alibis."

O'Neill was writing notes. "Reggie Lehman...*Coach* Lehman mentioned an incident between Andie and her boyfriend, Larry Marsh. Do you know anything about the incident or their relationship?"

"I never met him, but during Andie's freshman year, Lizzie McBride asked my advice about whom to approach about concerns that a man had hit Andie. Lizzie was unsure if she should tell the coach, her advisor, or whoever. Lizzie told me, and we talked to Marv who talked to Andie about being hit. I don't know what came of the allegation or even if it was her boyfriend who hit her, but I told the police when they interviewed me. My guess is Andie didn't push the complaint and let it go away."

"Lizzie McBride was a team captain, right?"

"Yeah. She graduated in '97 and lives in California, I think."

"Her and Andie were close?"

"I wouldn't go that far. Lizzie tried to mentor her, so it was more of a big sister relationship. You could talk to Lizzie to clarify. She's a good egg."

O'Neill wrote "good egg" next to Lizzie's name. "Which teammates were close to Andie?"

"Tanya was probably closest to Andie. That's Tanya Paulus. But I don't even know if they were great friends. I don't think Andie really wanted to be friends with her teammates or with us. That's why it was so weird when she gave me a hug on that night. It was like she was a different person."

"One last question, then I'll let you go. The night before Andie disappeared, who was she flirting with?"

"I didn't recognize him. I just remember he had sandy blonde or brown hair and was handsome in a hunky way."

O'Neill didn't write "hunky." Instead, he thanked her and wished her luck in her new position.

O'Neill thought about going back to the office, but rather than pondering his predicament, he meandered down State Street, figuring he would grab a beer and give Donna Ritz another call. If she didn't answer, he would go to the office, take a nap, and read the police file.

State Street was Madison's "outdoor mall" and was both a tourist attraction and a troubled spot. The street started at the Wisconsin State Capitol Square and ended at the University's edge. Foot traffic was heavy since the city limited motorized State Street traffic to buses, business deliveries, taxis, and confused tourists.

O'Neill spent a lot of time on State, mostly in bars. But his early days were on the street since he was underage, and State Street was the best place in town for musicians to busk. And though O'Neill had not been a regular street musician since his days in Chicago, he continued to busk periodically for beer money. On good nights, he could make twenty bucks an hour. On other nights it would rain, and he pulled in a few dollars before giving up.

As he walked through the Library Mall and up State Street, he passed hundreds of students, dozens of tourists, and a score of people he knew or assumed were homeless. He knew some of the homeless by name and gave one of them, an old guy from Nova Scotia named Red, two quarters.

O'Neill stopped at the Irish Pub and sat in front of the long line of taps. The bartender was a guitar player, so they talked about instruments and guitar heroes while O'Neill drank three Garten Braus. He used the Irish Pub's phone to call Donna Ritz's number, but there was no answer. It was a five-minute walk to her apartment on Langdon Street, so he left the pub, limped past Concrete Park, and turned toward Lake Mendota at Frances Street.

He found Donna's address and "Ann Emery Hall" molded into the apartment's ornate stone entryway. The wooden double doors were ten feet high, including windows, and were surrounded by various designs, including an assortment of rounded nuts and foods. O'Neill surveyed the designs for a few moments, as he had never seen nuts and baked goods in stone.

The large door creaked open, and O'Neill slipped into the foyer, finding a panel of buttons with room numbers. He pushed Donna's room number, and there was a buzz. He counted to fifteen and pushed the button again. The inner door opened, and a young redhead stepped out.

"Hello, my name is Seamus O'Neill. I am looking for Donna Ritz."

The woman smiled, stepping fully into the foyer and allowed the door to close behind her.

"Seamus O'Neill? You're the singer in Sea City Chaos, aren't you?"

"Yeah. You a fan?"

"You bet I'm a fan," she said, extending a hand. "My name is Bernice Torkelson, but everyone calls me Niece. I've seen you play several times. I almost bought one of your CDs a few months ago when you played the Rathskeller."

"Great to meet you."

"Sorry, you're here to talk to Donna, not me. Give me a minute and I'll bring her down." She unlocked the inner door and disappeared.

O'Neill took a sip of Scotch from his flask and waited. After a few minutes, Niece returned with her roommate.

"Seamus, this is Donna Ritz," Niece said. "Donna, this is Seamus O'Neill, the singer in Sea City Chaos."

A smirk was on Donna's face. "Listen, I don't know you or Sea City Chaos. What do you want?"

"I work for the Ryder Detective Agency," he said as he handed Donna a business card. "We're investigating Andie Sheridan's murder, and I was hoping to ask you a few questions."

"You're a detective and a rocker," Niece said. "That's the coolest."

"Yeah, the coolest," Donna said without conviction. She looked at her roommate, mouthed "thanks," and turned toward O'Neill. "Let's step outside and talk."

O'Neill waved to Niece and backed into one of the immense doors. The door creaked open, and he followed the elusive Donna Ritz out of Ann Emery Hall. Donna sat on a stone hand railing which flanked the doors. She had a short afro and was wearing long, silver earrings. O'Neill leaned against a black iron fence, trying to stay far enough away so Donna wouldn't smell his breath.

"What do you want to know?" Donna asked. "I gave multiple statements to the Madison Police Department. Isn't that enough?"

"I read your statement, as well as notes on several interviews, but there are things I was hoping you could clarify. First, I'm trying to verify a theory we have that Andie disappeared early on the path rather than late in the path, which is what the police seem to have concluded. I'm basing this on a few things, including on how close you were behind her when you entered the path at Arbor Drive."

"I agree with you," Donna said. "I saw Andie enter the path and I should have seen her again once I got past that first turn, but I didn't."

"Are you sure it was Andie who entered the path and not someone else?"

"It was Andie. She was tall, and she had this distinctive running form that never varied. She was grooved in with her movements. The police thought I was saying she was graceful, but that was not quite right. She was more robotic than anything, wasting no energy."

"At the time it happened, did it strike you as odd that you didn't see her beyond the path's first bend? You just said that you *should have* seen her."

"I probably assumed she put the guns on, ripped past the La Crosse woman and caught up with the back group. I only saw the La Crosse woman and the group in front of her. It didn't strike me as odd at the time because I focused on the person in front of me and not on other runners."

"You mean Tanya Paulus?"

"Yeah, once I got past the first part of the path, Tanya was in my sights and she was my focus. I could see the back group about twenty meters further ahead. Tanya was always last, so I did not like being behind her. I told the police I didn't see Andie on the path, and I told them her gait was so distinctive you couldn't help but notice her. I might miss her in a group, but not on her own. They seemed to dismiss me. One detective pointed out that I was the only Black runner on the team. I think he assumed I couldn't differentiate one white woman from the rest of the white women. That might have been true for some of them, but not for Andie."

"I don't think the detectives were runners," O'Neill said.

"That's exactly what I thought. They didn't appreciate how unique she looked out there. Not only her size, but her gait. Lizzy used to call her Cyborg. Her running style was the one thing about her I admired."

"You didn't like her?"

"Oh, I didn't mean it that way. Truth is, I didn't know her. But she was so apathetic it frustrated me. She had as much talent as anyone on the entire cross-country team. Yet she didn't seem to care about the team, and that annoyed me because she wasted her talent."

"The police files say two male runners crossed the team on the path. Their names were Gary Fano and Lou Kart," he said, referring to his notebook. "Do you remember them?"

"I vaguely remember two guys followed a little later by two women, but I couldn't identify any of them. Even back when the police interviewed me, they put in a bunch of photos, and I couldn't identify them. Just two white guys, one tall and one muscular. I couldn't even tell you that much about the women. I remember the men crossing, but don't remember where on the path."

O'Neill leaned back, trying to remember what else he wanted to ask. She lifted herself off the stone railing, looking toward him. It was clear she was ready to leave.

"Last thing," O'Neill said. "Anything unusual about Andie or the August twenty-first run?"

"It was an unusual run for me. I was late because of school, which left me running from behind. I don't like running from behind, though I caught the second group and stayed with them." She stood and opened the door but paused. "There is one thing I had forgotten," she said, holding the door. "When we were on Arbor, Andie broke form, and glanced backward. She was probably ten meters from the woods. After the disappearance, I wondered whether she was looking for someone or was worried someone was following her."

"Did she see you?" O'Neill asked.

"I don't think so since I was so far back, but I'm not sure."

"Could she have been looking to see if any runners were behind her?"

"She could have," Donna said with a shrug of her shoulders, "but I don't know why."

"Thanks."

She waved to O'Neill and the wooden door closed behind her.

O'Neill walked toward State Street, but his eyes were heavy and he only had thirty cents. The walk home was less than half a mile, but his knee was unhappy, so he stopped at Concrete Park and curled up on a shaded spot along the curb. They called the area a park, but it was a wide alley with no thru traffic. There were bushes, trees, and often homeless people. Steps ascended on one side. Half a dozen kids dressed in late '70s punker outfits were hanging out in the small outdoor space. O'Neill paid no attention to them, but one kid pushed him, saying it was his spot.

"Bugger off," O'Neill mumbled. His eyes creaked open to see a kid with a green mohawk and a tattoo on his forehead that said, "Shove Me."

"Didn't you hear me, old man?" the kid said.

"Bugger off," O'Neill said again, closing his eyes.

To O'Neill's surprise, the kid did just that. When he opened his eyes, the park was empty and the sun had crossed the sky. He pulled himself off the bench and felt for his wallet. He was surprised it was gone, but he was not worried since there was no money in it. But there were telephone numbers, coupons, and pictures of his mother and his sister.

He walked around the area, searching the sidewalk, the trash, and the grass. There was a green Shifts in Turmoil flier taped to the ground which said they were playing tonight at the Lamp Light. O'Neill kneeled beside the flier, which had a picture of The Johnson peeking from under his sunglasses. KP, Bip, and the other guy whose name O'Neill couldn't recall were a few feet behind their leader. The photo looked ordinary, but cool enough, O'Neill thought.

As he stared at the flyer, he wondered whether leaving Sea City Chaos was a mistake. He considered it for a short while before his thoughts cleared, as he needed time to reflect. After a few weeks or months he would decide whether he would join or start another band.

O'Neill pulled the flier off the sidewalk and stuck it into his pocket. Perhaps Jane would be at the show, he thought. It was foolish, but screw everything else.

He continued to search and found his leather wallet near the Wine and Hop Shop. His coupons and phone numbers were gone, but the pictures were inside. He put the wallet back in his pocket.

Chapter 19

O'Neill was glad KP recognized him at the Lamp Light's entrance. The guitar player whispered something to a bouncer who waved O'Neill in. KP took O'Neill to the back bar, joining Bip, The Johnson, and two women. A separate group of women were downing shots of Dr. McGillicuddy's while a lone man typed on a laptop.

"I take it the knee's better?" The Johnson said as O'Neill approached.

"Still sore but getting better."

"Cane's gone," KP observed.

"I lost it. Or rather, I left it at Topper's head shop."

"He'll sell the thing back to you," The Johnson said with a chuckle. "I feel quite honored having Seamus O'Neill show up at one of our shows. Grab a beer and sit. We don't go on for another half hour."

"Can you spot me five bucks? I get paid tomorrow."

The Johnson pulled out his wallet and handed O'Neill a five-dollar bill.

"That makes it an even twenty-five," The Johnson said.

"Twenty-five is odd," O'Neill said as he took the bill. The Johnson rolled his eyes.

O'Neill went to the bar and returned with a Sprecher Amber.

"You ever heard of Sea City Chaos?" The Johnson asked the women sitting at their table. One woman had straight, semi-greasy strawberry blonde hair, the other straight, semi-greasy black hair.

"Local party band, right?" the strawberry blonde responded.

"Yeah, they opened for someone here before, maybe Paul Westerberg," said the black-haired woman. Her eyes locked onto O'Neill's. "You're the singer, aren't you?"

"You bet he is," The Johnson said.

She smiled at O'Neill and twirled her hair. "You guys are not quite my thing, but you're interesting." She talked in quick bursts as if she was trying to get words in between puffs of a cigarette. "I remember you played a fast version of a Raffi song. Weird, ya know, but cool since it was unexpected. I was probably the only one in the crowd who knew it was a Raffi song and not some rock song."

"Doesn't Raffi do kid songs?" KP said with a laugh.

"Yeah, but he's a tunesmith to six-year-olds," O'Neill replied. "I learned a few songs for my nephew."

"No wonder they gave you the boot," KP said.

"They booted you for that?" the strawberry blonde said.

"Not for that," O'Neill replied. "They were used to going along with me on a few songs." He took a gulp of his beer. "The main issue was the tour. They wanted to go east and tour, setting a home base near New York City."

"And Seamus didn't," The Johnson said. "It would hamper his drinking routine."

"Did the rest of the band go?" the strawberry blonde asked.

"No idea," O'Neill said. "No idea what they're doing."

"They're looking for a new singer," The Johnson said, "saying they'll be more straight-out hard rock."

"Not surprised," O'Neill said.

Someone waved The Johnson to the event room. Bip followed, but KP and the women stayed.

"My name's Stacie," the black-haired woman said to O'Neill.

O'Neill shook her hand. He liked that she knew Raffi, but he wasn't in the mood to talk to anyone new.

"I'm going to grab another beer," O'Neill said. "Can I get anyone else one?"

All their drinks were full, which was the reason he asked. As the bartender handed him another Sprecher, Jane's sister, Amanda, came in and a bolt of adrenaline pumped through him. He took a generous gulp and watched her and the people with her. Jane was not one of them. Amanda and her group sat on the opposite side of the bar.

When Amanda saw him, she crinkled her lip and gave him the finger. It didn't surprise him since he had broken his promise even if he had not meant to. He wanted to grab her by the shoulders and tell her he had fallen for her sister. It would sound like bullshit, and perhaps it would be bullshit, but it felt true. He took another gulp, leaving the cup half empty.

He walked around the bar. She was wearing a black sweater and jeans and her hair was in a tight bun. Her back was toward him.

"Hey Amanda," he said.

"Hey asshole," she said as she turned to face him. "You've got nerve, coming over here after the way you went after my sister after you told me you wouldn't."

"This is the guy?" asked one of her friends.

"Yep, this is the guy. Pretty pitiful, eh?"

"Hey, I'm sorry about your sister," O'Neill said. "I wasn't after her. I told you the truth. Things just happened, but literally nothing happened."

"What do you want from me?"

"I wanted to explain."

"You're saying you're sorry you hit on my sister when you told me you wouldn't. Okay, forget it." She licked her lips before turning away.

"Did she say anything about me?"

Amanda turned back toward him. Her eyes were wide. "Don't tell me you got a crush on her?"

O'Neill backed up a few steps. "I'm thirty-one years old; I don't get crushes."

"She's twenty-three years old; she does. Remember that. And next time, remember when you've got a girlfriend. I already texted Sandra." Amanda got off the bar stool, implying the conversation was over.

Amanda and her two friends walked past him into the event area. O'Neill finished his drink and put the empty on the bar. He looked toward the table where he had been sitting. The women were gone and KP waved to O'Neill, mouthing something about the show. O'Neill walked past the bar, through the event hall, and out the front door.

On his way home, O'Neill found himself at the Red Shed. Though he didn't have any cash, he went inside. If he could sponge a beer off someone, he could hang around. Either that or the bartender would pour him a drink without asking for cash up-front. The bartender might give him a free beer, or worst case, he would pay the next time he came in.

Inside, there were two regulars at the bar and three students playing pool. The air was musty so he got close to the taps. The muscular bartender spotted him and filled a mug of Berghoff.

"What is up with you, O'Neill?" the bartender asked.

"Same old, same old," he said. He nodded at a regular and took a barstool.

O'Neill noticed the bartender was wearing a gray "Houdini Museum" sweatshirt. On the front of the shirt, a muscular Harry Houdini was standing with arms held high next to a water tank. In one hand he was holding handcuffs, in the other, an untied rope.

"You into magic?" O'Neill said, pointing at the sweatshirt.

"Not more than the next guy, I guess, but Houdini was from my hometown, Appleton. My ma got this from someone who works at the Houdini Museum." He paused as he passed out a beer. "The Houdini stuff, like the water chamber thing, is cool. He was in chains and dropped upside down into this water torture chamber for like fifteen minutes. People thought he was dead because no one could hold their breath that long. Even nowadays, I guess no one can go much past ten minutes."

"And then he pops out," O'Neill interrupted, "all wet and breathing hard, free of the chains."

"Yeah, no one besides a few magicians figured out how he did it."

"It's a trick."

"Sure, it's a trick, but how did he pull the trick off?"

O'Neill finished his beer. "I know how he did it."

"Sure, you do," the bartender said.

"I figured out the solution when I was a kid. I watched a TV show with something on the water torture chamber trick talking about how people couldn't figure it out. My sister and I watched, and the answer came to me."

"You're yanking me."

"No, I'm serious. I'm not saying it's the way Houdini pulled it off, but it would work." O'Neill felt his empty wallet. "I'll tell you what. You give me the beer I just drank and one more on the house, and I'll tell you how Houdini got out of the water torture chamber."

"You tell me your idea. If it's good, your beer's on the house."

"Good enough," O'Neill said without hesitation. "The trick is he made you concentrate on the wrong problem. They start out with this big tank of water. The tank is on four stubby legs. The crowd can see the legs and the bottom of the tank the whole time. They drop Houdini in upside down, chained, and handcuffed. The works. Then they put a curtain in front of the tank and the audience waits. Everyone holds their breath, and after a few minutes, everyone in the audience has taken another breath since most people can't hold their breath for over two minutes. They can see the tank legs and the floor below the tank, so they know Houdini has not escaped since the water would spill. So, they sit and wait and are amazed, because even Houdini shouldn't be able to hold his breath that long. Houdini set everything up to convince the audience that he either must hold his breath the entire time or he escaped from the tank. They know he has not escaped, so the issue becomes how long can anyone hold their breath? When everyone assumes he's toast, he bursts through the curtain, soaked and puffing."

"You're not telling me anything new."

"The trick is they focused the audience on how long he can hold his breath, yet Houdini isn't holding his breath the whole time."

"I don't get it."

"They built a hose into one leg of the water torture chamber. After the curtain goes over the tank, someone from below pushes the hose upward to an agreed-upon length. The curtain covers this. Keep in mind, Houdini could hold his breath for a long time. All he needs is to exhale every five minutes and then he gets his mouth around the hose and gets air. The hose is hooked to an oxygen tank and pump below the stage. Houdini must take the handcuffs and chains off, but he's not limited to one breath. Once he's out, they pull the hose down and Houdini jumps out of the tank and amazes everyone."

There was a long silence.

"Sounds good to me," said the regular sitting next to O'Neill. "I assume there is enough pressure to keep the hose from filling with water."

"A misdirection, wouldn't you say?" the bartender said, his head nodding. "I say you earned your two beers." He stepped over to the tap, filled the empty glass with Berghoff, and slid it across the bar.

O'Neill smiled at his own trick. And then it came to him. It was not a fully formed theory, but in that instant, he realized where he went wrong in the Andie Sheridan case. Suddenly, he breathed clearer. He heard every sound in the bar and smelled every drink. He gulped his beer, pushed his chair back, and got to his feet.

"Where are you going?" asked the bartender.

"I gotta go," he said, pushing the chair back up to the bar.

"What about your free beer?"

O'Neill already had two free beers, but if the kid wanted to give him a third, he would take it. He raised his finger and waited. Not even solving a murder would stop him from drinking a free beer.

Chapter 20

Before pouring a glass of Scotch, O'Neill looked for his copy of Myles Staley's letter. He checked in the pockets in both of his pants, in the laundry bag, and inside his desk. He even looked under his mattress. Finally, he let out a loud explicative and poured a Scotch. As he sipped the Grant's, it came to him: he put his copy of the letter in his wallet.

He swore again, then opened his wallet. As he expected, the letter was not in the wallet.

O'Neill sat for a moment, took ten dollars from under his bed, filled his flask, and headed to Howard Johnson's. The phone was being used by two teenagers, so O'Neill waited. Once the phone was free, he dialed Ryder's home number. After four rings, he heard the answering machine pick up. He hung up, got his change, and dialed the Ryder Detective Agency.

"What the hell you doing at the office at night?" O'Neill asked after Ryder answered the phone.

"What the hell you doing calling the office at night?"

"Wanted to talk to you."

"Then calling was a good idea," Ryder said. "Do you have any new information, or have you come up with a theory to save your ass by supporting the bullshit story you told Sandy's daddy?"

"Give me a minute while I decipher that sentence."

The detective let out a loud sigh. "Theory or no theory?"

"Maybe, but there is something else."

"Yeah," the detective said, sounding tired.

"I stuck a copy of Myles Staley's letter in my wallet. I was on State Street, and someone lifted my wallet."

"You put a letter in your wallet? Who would take your wallet? Any idiot would realize you don't have jack squat."

"That is why it's strange."

"Okay, it's strange. What can I do?"

"Coincidental, me getting mugged when that letter was in my wallet, isn't it?"

"Are you saying someone somehow knew you had a copy of the letter on you, so they lifted your wallet? If your theory is someone doesn't want us to see the letter, please remember you have a Xerox. The original is here in the office. I was looking at it a few minutes ago. Also, who besides you would put a letter in a wallet? You're getting more paranoid every day."

"And you're getting fatter every day."

"What of it?"

"Let's get back to my point. Who would want that letter?"

Ryder let out a large breath. "Maybe the killer wants to find out who hired us to investigate Andie Sheridan's murder. But isn't it more likely that you got mugged? Where were you when you were mugged?"

This time, O'Neill took a large breath. "I suppose you're right and it's nothing. But it is disconcerting. I got this feeling someone is leading us around."

"Seamus, creativity is good but can divert into fantasy. Myles Staley obviously wants us to consider Larry Marsh as a suspect. Why turn this into a grand conspiracy?"

O'Neill decided his boss was right. "This came up because I wanted to read Myles' letter. It relates to an idea I'm working on. Could you read the letter to me?"

"It should help you sleep," Ryder said. After a moment, he read the letter to O'Neill.

"Thanks," O'Neill said after Ryder finished.

"That's all you needed?"

"Yeah. I wanted to hear that basic *premise line* again, for one."

"Okay. But just so you know, Larry Marsh pushed me off until Friday morning, so maybe you can go with me. Nothing interesting from my interview with Mark Sheridan. What about your idea?"

"I'm going to let it ferment overnight. I'll lay it out tomorrow."

"Did you get any interviews in?"

"Yeah. I talked with the cross-country coach. He was forthcoming about things, and I bought his answer about why it took so long to file a missing person's report. My sense was he thought Andie was a lazy ass. He should have reported her disappearance earlier, but he assumed she was partying and wanted her kicked off the team. He also talked about Andie, though nothing eye-popping. I talked to the roommate, Mary Gleason, as well." O'Neill didn't admit that he had talked to Mary Gleason on Saturday night at the Razor's Edge. "Did you know she dated Myles Staley?"

"No, I didn't, but guess that tells us how Myles knew our victim."

"Mary Gleason talked a bit about Andie and what type of person she was. Andie was a loner and Mary Gleason thought that odd for a partier."

"Do you think that is odd?" Ryder said.

"Course not. Everyone sees this beautiful, talented woman and thinks she's got it made, but she's fucked up like the rest of us."

"How about the Ritz girl?"

"Yeah, I finally caught her," O'Neill said as he pulled out his notepad. "She confirmed details about the run. Donna agreed with me that Andie disappeared early on the path."

"Sounds like progress, but no giant steps. Harry's going to be here Friday, so we need giant steps tomorrow."

"Like I told you, I got an idea but it has not coalesced yet."

"Coalesced? You're getting quite the vocabulary for a high school dropout."

"Screw you," O'Neill said.

"Hey, you called me, so quit bothering me and coalesce your theory. I just got back from Janesville and I'm bushed and need to sleep. So, like I told you this morning, we'll meet at the office at noon. If you're not there, I'll dock you a day's pay so don't get too blasted tonight."

"I almost forgot my other interview. Brianna Michael Schladweiler."

"Who is she?"

"She was the cross-country manager who saw Andie out the night before she disappeared. Reggie Lehman mentioned her."

"I vaguely remember seeing her name in the files. Anything interesting?"

"She said Andie was flirting with a guy that night. Do you remember who was out with her?"

"Myles Staley," Ryder said. "I'm not sure that tells us anything. Andie undoubtedly had guys hitting on her wherever she went. Myles had an airtight alibi. He was at the library, I think. And Reggie Lehman. He was with the two trainers at Vilas Park. Everyone has airtight alibis."

"Not anymore," O'Neill said. "Andie wasn't killed at nine thirty. I'll tell you more tomorrow."

Ryder muttered something in response, but O'Neill hung up the phone.

Chapter 21

O'Neill walked alone on the sidewalk, sensing his theory ferment. It wouldn't answer every question, but the theory would show that Larry Marsh *could* have killed Andie Sheridan. That alone could force Harry into giving them another two weeks.

As O'Neill considered the practical elements of retaining his ex-girlfriend's father as a client, he realized, or perhaps admitted to himself, that he was walking to Jane's house. The realization made him stop, but only briefly. As he approached her house, he spotted her bronze Mazda in the driveway. He rang the doorbell, and when the door opened, the dread of the event invaded his bones. He put his hands behind his back and shifted into a practiced smile.

Jane was wearing an over-sized, long-sleeve Green Bay Packers shirt that went below her shorts. Her hair was in a ponytail, but bangs hung over her eyes. Her feet were bare, and she wore no makeup. She didn't look beautiful, but he only wanted her more.

"Hello, Seamus," Jane said. She didn't smile, but O'Neill thought he noted a hint of pleasure in her voice. "I'm surprised to see you."

He tottered from one foot to the other. "Do you have a minute?"

She answered by pushing the door open. Jane and O'Neill walked upstairs, ignoring the people in the living room.

"Your knee must be better," she said, closing the door. "I bet icing helped."

He hadn't iced the knee but didn't admit it. "It's getting better. Guess you were right about it being a sprain."

O'Neill followed her up the stairs. They went into her bedroom. It was small but looked and smelled cleaner than his efficiency. The twin bed had pink covers and a single white pillow on one end. Beside the bed was a CD player and a desk with a computer. Concert promotional fliers covered the walls. Some fliers were for name bands like U2 and the Rolling Stones, but most were lesser known and local bands. He found an old flier with Sea City Chaos from April of '98. After a bit of looking, he found one for Theoretically Trashed.

"You make a lot of shows," he commented.

"Not really. I just nick the fliers." She sat at the computer desk and motioned for him to sit on the bed. "Amanda's the one that goes to lots of shows. There aren't many bands I wanna see."

"Is there one for Shifts in Turmoil? Your sister goes to most of their shows."

Her head shook. "They're okay but don't thrill me. I attended the last one because you were playing."

"Wait until I tell The Johnson. Maybe he'll want me to join his band."

"You wouldn't do that?"

"Course not. It's The Johnson's band. If I joined, it would be one big frustration. Besides, they're not my cup — if you get my drift?"

"Do you want to talk about Tuesday night?"

"I do, yeah," he said, running a hand through his hair. "There's something else, too. I got an idea about this murder case, and I wanted to check if you would, uh, help me out."

"You don't want to talk to Mary Gleason again, do you?"

"No, Ryder settled on my interview with her."

"Who's Ryder?"

When saying one lie, he forgot an earlier lie. "He's a private detective I work for. I am not a reporter like I implied. I'm more of a detective."

"Hard to believe."

"That's why I lied when I met you. I was looking into this murder case, and I didn't know how you would react if I told you I was a detective. Didn't think you would believe me but thought you might believe that someone who writes music could also be a journalist. I'm sorry, but I panicked. Everything else I told you though, was true — at least I think it was."

Her eyebrows lifted. "Okay, you're a detective and not a reporter."

"I'm not actually a detective. I just work for a detective agency. Either way, Myles Staley hired the agency I work for to look into Andie Sheridan's murder, and anyway, I know who killed her, but I need transportation to go to the Monroe Street area and a few other places."

"Did you consider a taxi?"

"Okay, so I don't *need* you to help me out. I thought it would be fun if you would come with me."

He expected her to give him a speech about how he's a jerk for lying to her and how she wouldn't get involved with him. Instead, she pulled her purse out of a desk drawer. "Let's get it done. It's almost ten thirty and I've got an eight o'clock class tomorrow morning. The session is almost over, so I shouldn't skip."

O'Neill pulled himself off the bed. She opened the door, then quickly closed it. She flipped around, her eyes flashed wide, and she pushed him to the bed and jumped on him.

He didn't understand this girl.

Their lips locked long and hard, and his hands slid under her shirt and up to her bare breasts. Their mouths separated. She put her arms straight up and he pulled her shirt off. Then his lips attacked her body as he undid the drawstring on her shorts.

"Do you think this is a mistake?" Jane said in his ear.

"Course it is."

"Did I surprise you?" she said afterward.

He laughed, but only lightly since she was lying on top of him, slowly crushing him. His hands were resting on her buttocks. "I was afraid you might tell me to get lost. Not to say you still won't."

"That is not nice to say."

"I'm sorry. I didn't mean it that way." He took a few large breaths while he could. "I was admitting to being afraid, but didn't want to box you in. Should we wait until tomorrow to go to Monroe Street?"

"What would you rather do? Can you stay the night?"

"Not like I have a roast in the oven. Course I can stay." He maneuvered until they were lying side by side. "Besides, it might work better since the shops along Midvale and Mineral Point aren't open now."

"Why do you want to go to shops along Midvale and Mineral Point?"

O'Neill's eyes were already closed. "Andie disappeared on the first part of the path and buried on the second part. That got me thinking about where someone would bury a body. To me, the best place would be out in the country somewhere. But the best place near the path is where she was found."

"Because the area is heavily wooded?"

"Yeah, and because it's near a paved parking lot. If it was me and I could drive, I'd park the car in that lot and carry the body straight back into the woods."

"You're saying you would put the body in the car in one parking lot, then drive it to another parking lot?"

"No, not quite. Part of my idea is that we approached this case the same way the cops did. We assumed Andie Sheridan was raped and killed in the woods."

"I thought that was a given."

"We all did. But something one of the other runners told me got me thinking. This woman, Donna Ritz, was the last person to see Andie alive. She said she glanced back before Andie went onto the path. Perhaps Andie looked to see who was behind her."

"Like she was being followed?"

"That's what Donna suggested. But I'm thinking Andie could have been checking if there were runners behind her."

"Why?"

"I keep thinking I have an idea of who Andie was and, in some ways, she was not so different from me. I was considering what would I do if I was hungover and running a seven- or eight-mile oval route and I didn't give a shit?" O'Neill's eyes opened. "These women were running what was basically an oval route through town. If the coach wouldn't buy bullshit excuses, I would fall back into last place, drop out on the wooded path, and cut the run in half. I would walk to Midvale or Mineral Point. Somewhere along where the return part of the run happens."

"What do you mean by the return part?"

"The women were in the early part of the oval course, of which the wooded path was a small part. I would slip off the path, walk up to Midvale Road and Mineral Point Road, and wait inside a shop or something. Once the last of my teammates ran past, I would wait until she was far enough past, then go after them. I would be fresher, even if I was hungover since it would cut three or four miles from the run. I might even pass some runners before the end of the run."

"You're saying you would cheat by cutting the run in half. But you're a musician; Andie was a world-class athlete. Would a world-class athlete cut a practice run? Isn't she focused on getting better?"

"She was a top athlete, but she was a partier and an underachiever. She was a misfit. Perhaps she wasn't worrying about getting better. Perhaps she simply wanted to get by. I mean, she may not have bought that she needed to run that much anyway. She was a 3,000-meter runner who's running seven, eight, or ten miles at a time. She probably thought it was bullshit, or she rationalized it as bullshit.

"I'm guessing Andie assumed she was in last place when she entered the woods. She probably didn't realize Donna Ritz had started late. Had she realized Donna was behind her, she might have waited until Donna passed before doing her trick. Yet it wouldn't be hard to exit the path in six or seven seconds as we figured. She'd go around the bend, slip off the path, and to the parking lot. Could be she knew Donna was behind her, or maybe she didn't. Either way, Donna didn't see her sneak off the path."

"Did the police consider this at all?"

"Not in that way," O'Neill said, licking his lips. "I don't think they understood her. They viewed her as one of nineteen runners and assumed they were all good little top-flight runners. They assumed she was following directions like the rest of the team and was doing what she was supposed to be doing."

"If he didn't kill her in the woods, where was she killed and when?"

"I'm not that far yet. But it could have been anytime that day and anywhere in Madison."

"If he killed her elsewhere, how did her body get to the woods?"

"Larry Marsh probably knew Andie's trick. He knew she skipped out on the wooded path, or perhaps she told him afterward. I'm guessing Larry Marsh killed her and he figured, if they found her body in the woods, the cops would assume she was attacked and killed there. He brought her back to the wooded path because he wanted her found there. He didn't know where on the path she skipped out and probably thought the end of the path, being secluded, made sense. It gave him a paved lot to park in, reducing the chance of him leaving tire tracks. He took off her shoes and shorts, ripped off her underwear, and left a condom wrapper near her body to make it look like a sexual assault."

"What a dick," she said after a pause.

"Yeah. Does it make sense?"

She turned off the light and kissed him on the cheek.

"I think so," Jane finally said.

"Yeah. But now I've got to prove it. That might be the hardest part."

"You can do it."

"You sound confident," O'Neill said.

"That's because you are amazing."

O'Neill kept his eyes closed and went to sleep, almost believing her.

Chapter 22

O'Neill woke at eight thirty in the morning. Jane was on her side, her mouth slightly open and her right hand resting on his chest. They were both naked and O'Neill was freezing. They weren't underneath the bedspread, so the only things keeping him warm were a thin, blue blanket and Jane's body heat.

He moved and Jane rolled onto her back, taking the blanket with her. There was little room to maneuver on a twin-size bed, but he twisted closer to her, resting his arm on her chest. She popped up, holding the blanket over her. Her eyes locked onto his, as if she didn't recall how he had gotten into her bed.

"Oh, my God," she said.

O'Neill sighed, got off the bed, and slipped on his clothes.

"Where are you going?" Jane asked.

"Midvale and Mineral Point Road, like I told you last night."

They were quiet while he finished getting dressed.

"Do you want me to go with you?" Jane said.

"If you want to."

"Sure, I do."

"Then what's with the reaction? You looked surprised and didn't look... too pleased."

She got out of bed, leaving the blanket. She kissed him, then pivoted to the dresser, pulling out underwear and a bra.

"I told myself I wouldn't do what we did. Amanda made me promise I wouldn't — as stupid as it sounds. When I woke, my reaction was to be pissed at myself, if you understand what I mean? I'm sorry. I can see what you thought, but it was about me rather than you."

"I'm glad, because I got a thing for you."

"I've never had a guy say that to me, at least not that...poorly."

"I won't put that line in a song," O'Neill said as he ran his left hand along her shoulder.

She smiled, but then her mouth dropped open. "Shit, I can't believe I slept until eight thirty!"

"I can't believe I'm up at eight thirty."

"Let's move. I'll have to get away with missing my eight o'clock class, but I have a quiz at eleven. No way I can miss a quiz."

Once dressed, they brushed their teeth and tiptoed down the stairs. The woman who had been wearing the Humpty Dumpty T-shirt was sitting on the couch. She was wearing a Tweety Bird robe and holding a textbook.

"Hi, Seamus," she said without looking away from her book.

"Hello," O'Neill said before slipping out of the apartment and into Jane's Mazda. The sun was out, but the August air was unusually crisp. Jane put the heater on, and they drove to the edge of Vilas Park. At O'Neill's request, they drove slowly up the hill. O'Neill searched through the glove compartment and pulled out a map.

At the top of the hill, they turned left onto Monroe Street, and traffic forced Jane to speed up. O'Neill's attention jumped between the City of Madison map in his hands and the street signs along Monroe Street.

"If she was going to cut the race, the best spots were the woods and the Wingra Park entryway, but Wingra Park wouldn't work since Tanya was behind Andie. She could have stopped running at any point but risked a teammate seeing her stop or go the other direction. It could have made someone suspicious."

"Would the other runners care if she was cutting the run?"

"Most wouldn't, but runners talk amongst each other. I wouldn't trust eighteen other runners with a secret like that. I wouldn't care what others thought, but I wouldn't want my teammates to know I was ditching runs. Assuming I'm right and she was minimizing her risk of being seen, the woods make sense as the place to stop running. I would exit at the beginning of the path, or I would stop on Arbor and not get on the path." He looked toward Jane, and since she didn't reply, he continued. "If I'm correct, she exits after hitting the path, cuts to the parking area, and probably goes northwest up Glenway or Odana. You would cut more going up Glenway, so I'd do that and stop at that tavern across from the golf course or cut to Midvale. I think there's a strip mall on Midvale, though I don't remember where."

They drove south on Seminole Highway. O'Neill didn't know the exact route the runners had taken between Seminole and Midvale Boulevard, so they guessed, finally turning onto Midvale as the road intersected Nakoma. A middle school dominated the early part of Midvale Boulevard, but it was residential until they approached the Midvale Shopping Mall.

That's when O'Neill noticed the sign for Madison Public Library's Sequoya Branch. "There's a library in this mall," O'Neill said. "Pull in."

Jane pulled her Mazda into the Midvale Shopping Center and pulled up to the library.

"I wish I had the files with me," O'Neill said.

"You think she stopped here at the library?" Jane said. "That would make sense. There's a nice front window to look out. Andie could have sat there and watched for her teammates to run by. No one would be suspicious unlike if she went inside the bakery. What are we going to do? I'm assuming we're going to go in and ask if the librarian had seen Andie before. But even if it's the same librarian, we would need a picture of Andie to show them."

"Good point," O'Neill said.

"Was the library open on the morning she was killed?"

They both got out of the Mazda and walked to the "Hours" sign on the door. It showed the library opening at one o'clock in the afternoon on Mondays and Tuesdays and nine thirty in the morning on Wednesday through Saturday.

"What day was it she got killed?" Jane asked.

"August twenty-first."

"What day of the week?"

O'Neill thought it was a Wednesday but was unsure. "We can look it up in the library."

Jane pulled her checkbook out of her purse. O'Neill leaned over her shoulder and pointed at the name written on top of the checkbook. "Your last name is Preston?"

She ignored him. "The twenty-first of August was a Wednesday."

"Then we're in business, assuming the hours haven't changed." O'Neill pulled the door, but it didn't budge. "They're not open until nine thirty. What time is it?"

"Nine fifteen," Jane said. She pointed at a bakery two doors from the library. "Let's go to the bakery. I could eat a horse."

O'Neill had ten dollars in his wallet, so he agreed. They strolled into the Midvale Bakery where she picked out two pastries and he chose a Vienna bread roll. They munched on the baked goods as they waited in the car.

"You play basketball, I hear," O'Neill said.

Jane chewed her pastry before responding, "How did you hear that?"

"When I stopped by one time, your roommate told me you were playing. I didn't imagine you as a basketball player."

"There isn't demand for five-foot-two players who can't shoot. But I can pass, dribble, and play defense. Anything else you want to know since we're killing time?"

"What was your favorite Trashed song?" O'Neill said.

"I wondered when you would ask me that. I always loved 'Lost Pause,' and 'Dutch, Dutch, Dutch,' but I also had a thing for 'Madonna Dumped Sean Penn for Me.'"

"I have not thought of the Madonna song in ages," O'Neill replied. "Don't know how much of it I even remember."

"I know the song by heart," Jane said.

Before he could comment, movement inside the library caught their attention. It was a few minutes before nine thirty, but the treasured library doors were unlocked. O'Neill and Jane finished their breakfast and rushed into the library.

The Sequoya Branch was much smaller than the downtown library. Newspapers and periodicals were in the front next to the large window. A woman was sitting behind the counter. Jane got to her first.

"Excuse me," Jane said.

The librarian was a woman with wide glasses and a wider smile. "Can I help you?" she spoke without looking up.

Jane introduced O'Neill as a private detective. She asked the librarian if she remembered the murder of a cross-country runner in '96.

"Yes, I remember," the librarian said in a hushed voice. "It was a terrible thing."

"I was a friend of Andie Sheridan, the woman who was murdered. Or rather, my friend was Andie's roommate. That is why I'm here with Mr. O'Neill. Anyway, we were wondering whether Andie ever visited this library?"

"Yes, she had."

O'Neill and Jane exchanged glances.

"I never saw her," the librarian continued, "but there was quite a lot of talk about her disappearance and then her murder. One of my co-workers, Carver Stringer, recognized the woman. She was not a regular patron, but Carver remembered her. He says he remembered her because she fell asleep up in front and he woke her. Falling asleep upset her. He says that was why he remembered her, but I suspect her being so striking looking might have helped him remember."

"Was this the day she disappeared?" Jane asked.

"No, both Carver and I worked on the day she disappeared and neither of us recalled seeing her that day."

"When did he see her?" O'Neill asked.

"If I remember, he said it was that summer but several weeks or months before she disappeared."

"A long time to remember a patron."

The librarian's head tilted sideways. "I wouldn't doubt him. It was like when Kathleen Paling was running for county executive. We saw her picture and he told me she had visited the branch years before. Neither of us heard of her, and it seemed unlikely since she was an east-sider. Yet, low and behold, I found out she had lived nearby and moved to the east side in early '95. He was probably right. Like I said, he's got an eye for faces and a splendid memory. When he saw this dead woman's picture in the paper, he recognized her right away. That is what he told me."

It came easier than O'Neill expected. "Did he report this to the police?" he asked.

"No, he saw her well before she disappeared. It was a curiosity rather than something relevant to her attack. I'm sure she visited many places in the weeks before the incident. Yet the police interviewed me the week following the disappearance. I think it was before they even found her body."

"The police interviewed you?"

"Yes, but they weren't asking about the victim. They were asking whether a certain boy was here on that day. I inferred this boy was a suspect in Andie's disappearance who claimed he was at the library that morning. They spoke to both me and Carver since they visited on a Saturday and both of us were here. But I was in before Carver. I remembered this boy being here. They told me his name, though I don't recall it right now."

"What do you remember about him?" O'Neill asked.

"This boy came in about two minutes after I opened, as you two just did, so I knew it was at nine thirty. I knew it was a Wednesday since Wednesday and Saturday are the only days Carver and I work together, and I mentioned it to Carver after he arrived. I remember this boy was looking for a woman. He was tall and good looking. He was twenty to twenty-five years old. I don't remember anything else about him other than that he was dressed casually. I told him he was our first patron for the day. He thanked me and left."

"Does the other librarian, Carver Stringer, work today?" Jane asked.

"He'll be in on Saturday. You can leave your card if you like, and he could get back to you. The main office could get you his contact information if you can't wait until then."

"If it becomes necessary, we'll do that."

"Thank you for your help," Jane said. Then she looked to O'Neill.

"Oh, yeah, thanks," O'Neill added.

"What now?" Jane asked as they walked outside.

O'Neill stretched his arms above his head. He could use a drink to help him think. "The librarian is Myles Staley's alibi."

"Wait," Jane said, "you're saying Myles Staley is the boy the librarian was referring to? He was at this library on the day of the murder?"

"It would seem so. It was a librarian that gave Myles an alibi. I had assumed he had been at one of the university libraries, but it looks like I was wrong. My guess is Myles and Andie met up here, probably outside the library, which is why neither of the librarians saw Andie. I'm also guessing it was Myles' semen that was found on Andie's body."

"But Myles was dating Mary Gleason," Jane said.

"You don't think Myles would have... strayed?"

"I don't know. Does that mean it was Myles who killed Andie?"

"I don't think so. Myles left Madison later that afternoon. If Myles killed her, when did he bring the body to the arboretum path? Theoretically, he could have done it in the daylight, but that seems hard to fathom. Do you remember the librarian's name? Not Carver Stringer but the lady we spoke to? Suppose I should have asked," O'Neill said, shaking his head at his own incompetence. "I can go back in and check, I guess."

She pulled out a notepad from the backseat of her car. She wrote the names and handed the notepad to O'Neill.

"Emily Hawkins. I didn't remember her giving a name."

"It was on her nametag."

"Brilliant. Oh well, it's early for me. Either way, let's go with the idea that Andie met with Myles Staley here in the library parking lot. We have to figure out what happened after that."

"How about Carver Stringer? It seems weird that he remembered Andie months after she was in the library. And what if he already knew she was skipping practice runs? She might have told him earlier. And it could be he knew she ran through the arboretum. Should we look at him as a suspect?"

"We can put him on our list, but let's hold off on following up since he's someone the police don't know about. We'll be better off letting Ryder set the game plan for that. At worst case, having a new suspect might be a selling point for getting our client to keep us investigating. I wish we had proof Andie was at the library on the twenty-first."

"Just as well if we wait before doing anything else," Jane said, glancing at her watch. She got into the car and O'Neill rushed to the passenger side. "It's nine forty-five. It will take me fifteen minutes to get to class, so I'm running out of time to be your Watson."

O'Neill wondered whether she was trying to tell him something. His gaze dropped to her legs. She was wearing cutoff blue sweatpants. He put his left hand on her thigh, and her legs opened slightly. She backed the car out of the parking spot then switched the engine into drive. She put her hand on top of his. When they arrived at O'Neill's apartment, he invited her to his room.

"I don't know how you can stand these steps," she said as they passed the second floor. "I won't have energy by the time I get to your room."

"We'll see about that."

Inside, O'Neill turned the stereo on. "What would you like to hear?"

She leaned over his shoulder as he opened his CD case. She pulled out one of Sea City Chaos's two singles. The CD sold five hundred copies.

"I've never heard this one. I tried to buy it one time, but I couldn't find it."

"I thought you didn't like Sea City Chaos."

"I never said that. I just like Theoretically Trashed better."

O'Neill put the CD in his player. "Only two of the songs are mine. They're the good ones."

"Naturally."

"If you don't believe me, listen. There are only three songs."

"Good, since we're short on time."

They pulled their clothes off and scurried to the mattress.

At ten forty-five, Jane was mumbling expletives as she tied her shoes. O'Neill watched her rush down the steps, then he looked out his bathroom window and imagined her scurrying into her car and driving away. He fell back onto the mattress, pulling a blanket over his head. He thought about Jane, about his bottle of Grant's, about Andie Sheridan, about Myles Staley, and about the person he knew was a killer.

Yet he needed evidence. He had none.

Chapter 23

It was five minutes before noon when O'Neill arrived at the office. Ryder was behind his desk, an unlit cigar in his mouth and a Styrofoam coffee cup in his hand. A front window was open.

"I didn't think you would make it," the burly detective said over the sound of traffic.

"Pure luck I did."

"Hope your theory doesn't disappoint."

O'Neill pulled his chair up to Ryder's desk, laying Jane's Madison map between them. He showed Ryder the route the runners had taken and laid out his theory that Andie Sheridan had left the path voluntarily with the purpose of reducing the length of her run. He explained how the entrance to the woods afforded Andie an opportunity to break away without being seen and reminded his boss that Andie was hungover on the day she disappeared.

Ryder's head was nodding slowly. "I like it. And there's no math involved."

O'Neill paged through one of the manilla folders until he found the table of suspects and alibis.

"Do you remember that Myles Staley has an alibi? It was a librarian." O'Neill held the sheet in front of his boss. "Under

'Alibi Witness #1' it says, 'Emily Hawkins, Librarian.' Emily Hawkins is a librarian at Madison Public Library's Sequoya Branch, which is in the Midvale Shopping Center. If I'm right," O'Neill said, pointing at the map, "Andie cut up Glenway Street to Midvale via Tokay. That put her at the library. The building would be an ideal spot for her to wait. Once her teammates ran past the library, they would go up a slight incline. If Andie waited for them to get over the incline, she could join without fear of being seen. If they saw her after that, they'd think she was running with them the whole time."

"You're saying that both Andie Sheridan and Myles Staley were at the Sequoya library that morning?"

"Yeah. It's about a twenty minute walk from where she stopped running. That would put her at the library at around nine thirty. The library opens at nine thirty on Wednesdays. That's the exact time Myles was at the library. The librarian remembered him because he showed up at opening time looking for a woman. It's in the files."

"Holy shit."

"This moves the time of death past nine thirty in the morning. The police went under the assumption that Larry Marsh had an alibi since he was teaching class until eleven thirty that morning. Basically, this says we only know he murdered her after nine fifteen on August twenty-first. It destroys Larry Marsh's alibi, and it means that the killer brought the body to the path after the murder using a shovel to bury the body."

"You're saying he did not attack her on the wooded path, and she met Myles Staley at the library. I don't get how it explains the shovel or how her body got back to the path."

"I'm assuming Andie told Larry Marsh that she cut this run by walking to the library or somewhere nearby. She could have told him that day or weeks before. Once he kills her, he realizes people might place her disappearance in or near the woods since it was the last place her teammates would have seen her. Larry wanted people to believe someone attacked Andie while she ran through the woods, setting her disappearance before nine thirty when he was teaching class. When the police found her body in the woods, it implied someone killed her there as well and gave Larry Marsh an alibi. Larry Marsh buried her, perhaps because it seemed logical — murder 101, as you said." O'Neil's eyebrows popped up and down. "Yet he didn't know where on the path she dropped out. He guessed the southwestern side of the trail since it was the most heavily wooded part of the path."

"This might sell," Ryder said, chomping at his unlit cigar. "I knew I hired you for a reason." He jumped up and slapped O'Neill on the back. "This is good. Garcia is going to shit his pants when we tell him."

"I talked to one librarian out at the Sequoya branch. She said one of the other librarians, a Carver Stringer, recognized Andie. He didn't see her the day she disappeared, but he remembered seeing her earlier that summer at the library."

"Excellent memory," Ryder said.

"That's what I said. Andie fell asleep in the library and, like you said, she was a looker. This librarian — it was a man — remembered her, though he didn't recall seeing her on the day of her disappearance."

"You're saying she did this before?"

"Apparently. And it sounds like something she'd do, least that's the feeling I got from talking with the coach — Reggie...Reggie...whatever his name is. He told me he came down on her because she was skipping practice and didn't finish runs. He threatened to suspend her. This library trick was a way she slacked off when they used that route. If it was me, I'd drink when the next day's run was easier, which this was."

"Can we put her at the library on the day she disappeared?"

"Not yet. I suspect Myles could verify it."

"What about the DNA? Even if we blow up his alibi, the DNA evidence still shows that Larry is not the rapist. Doesn't this basically prove that Myles Staley is our killer? If we shared this with Garcia, he would bring in Myles and get a court order for a DNA sample. If that sample matches with the DNA in the semen, it ties everything up. It's what we will have to do, but it shoots down any hope for two more weeks from Harry."

"You're still assuming there was a rape. I think Myles met Andie at the library and they went home together and had consensual sex. That's where the semen came from."

"Okay," Ryder said with hesitation.

"Let's take this step by step. We need to place her at or near the library on the twenty-first. We know this was not a one-time event, but we need evidence she did the same thing on the twenty-first."

"Or we need evidence that she was at Myles Staley's apartment."

"We could interview Myles and get his side of things," O'Neill said.

"You think Harry would let us do that?"

"No. But he can't stop the cops from doing it."

"Let's hold off on accusing our client of murder or at least of pissing him off."

"I'm not accusing him of anything. Larry Marsh killed her," O'Neill said. "It's obvious."

"Why is it so obvious?"

"He's an asshole with a history of pushing Andie around, and I don't like him."

"That will hold up in court," Ryder said, his head shaking. He stood up and straightened his tie. "The prosecutor will need the MPD to provide evidence to support any theory, and a musician not liking a professor won't qualify."

"If I have questions on court procedure," O'Neill said, "I will come to you. The point is, he had motive, a history of abuse, and opportunity."

"What about lust as a motive? Who says Myles Staley didn't pick her up at the library and bring her home to rape and kill her? He then brings the body back to the path because, just like you're saying Larry Marsh did, it implies that the attack happened on the path between nine fifteen and nine thirty and he has an alibi for nine thirty."

"But do you remember what Myles did that night?" O'Neill said. "I thought I remembered him going somewhere with his roommate." O'Neill grabbed the first binder. "It was something we found while driving to Janesville."

It took a few minutes before O'Neill found the reference. It stated that Myles and his roommate, Ralph Warzyn, drove to the Twin Cities on the night of August twenty-first. The MPD verified their check-in at a St. Paul hotel, and the hotel clerk identified photos of them.

"Look at this," O'Neill said.

Ryder leaned over the photocopied MPD notes. "If Myles did it, he couldn't have buried her that night unless he drove back to Madison in the middle of the night, which seems unlikely. How long does it take to get to St. Paul from Madison?"

"At least four hours. They checked in at five thirty, meaning they left Madison no later than one thirty."

"Still plenty of time for Myles to kill her and bring her body to the arboretum in the daytime."

"I can't believe anyone would arrive with a dead body during the daytime. There is too much traffic on that path. Remember, there was even a school field trip at ten or ten thirty. It would be crazy to pull in next to a few other cars and pull out a dead body."

"Could Myles have driven back to Madison in the middle of the night?"

"He'd need probably nine hours. Ralph Warzyn should be able to tell us whether they separated for that long. Yet even that would be a stretch."

"Okay," Ryder said with a hint of resignation. "It seems unlikely that anyone would drive the body to the arboretum during the day, park their car in an area with pedestrian traffic, pull out a body, carry it two hundred feet or meters or whatever, and bury it. While it's possible, it's highly unlikely. It would be good to tidy up the timeline and find out exactly when Myles left Madison."

"I agree. We need to talk to Ralph Warzyn."

"If we can verify Myles' alibi with Ralph, it will prove Myles isn't the killer. If that happens, you win."

"Holy shit!" O'Neill yelled. "This has been my day."

"However, we've got to place her at Larry Marsh's apartment or place Larry on the path later that night. At the least, it would be good to place her at the library."

"Do we talk with the librarian, Carver Stringer? I'm not sure if he can give us new information, since we know he saw Myles but did not see Andie on the twenty-first. But it's possible he knew what Andie was doing, since she had been at the library earlier."

"You think the librarian is a suspect?" Ryder asked.

"No, but Jane thinks he is."

"Who is Jane?"

"A friend with a car. The library was too far to walk."

Ryder shook his head. "Okay. Some woman thinks he's a suspect but you don't?"

"I think he's unlikely. Jane thought it was creepy that he remembered Andie, and it's true he might have known that Andie was cutting her run. Imagine a scenario where she falls asleep in the library and he wakes her up since it has happened before. She realizes she's well behind the runners, so he says he'll give her a ride to catch up with the group. She accepts, meaning she's in the car with him and he knows others last saw her in the woods."

"Interesting."

"Course, what's next? He can't have knocked her over the head in his car since the autopsy showed no head trauma. How could this librarian attack her in broad daylight? And he's supposed to be working. Does he drift away from work and no one notices or cares? And even if he does, how does the attack happen and where?"

"I agree he's not a good suspect, but we can do our due diligence on him." Ryder let out a sigh. "I wish you waited three or four more days before bringing Harry here. Oh well, why don't we run somewhere and talk about things over a burger? I can't help but think we can make this work for us so that we get an extension from Harry, but also bring Larry Marsh to Garcia. Let's figure out how we end this."

Chapter 24

Ryder locked the office and drove to the Stadium Bar across from Camp Randall Stadium. The lunchtime traffic in front of the stadium was heavy, and a steady flow of bicyclists flowed along the bike path crossing Monroe and Regent Streets. A cloud passed in front of the sun as they got out of Ryder's Chevy S-10, but the air was warm, so O'Neill left his sweatshirt in the truck.

Because of its proximity to the home of the football team, O'Neill expected the bar to be loaded with Badger paraphernalia, but they kept old football jerseys and beat up programs to a minimum. The walls were not even Badger Red.

Businesspeople dominated the lunchtime crowd joined by two tables of firefighters from the nearby Fire Station 4. O'Neill went to the bar and ordered two pints of beer. He drank two gulps before handing the other beer to Ryder.

"Heavenly," O'Neill said.

"Let's grab a table. I don't want to sit at the bar since we won't be able to talk."

"I prefer to be near the taps."

"You would."

O'Neill followed Ryder to the newer part of the building, which was filled with tables, chairs, and televisions. They sat at a window table with a clear view of the stadium.

"What you gonna eat?" Ryder asked.

"I don't know," O'Neill said as he glanced at the menu. He finished his beer. "I'm gonna grab another beer."

A waitress came to their table. She was wearing a pink shirt and a blue tie. "Something to drink, sir?"

O'Neill sat and ordered another round. Once the waitress drifted away, O'Neill pulled his flask out and snuck a drink.

"What's that for?" Ryder asked.

"Scotch is a rip-off to buy at a bar," he said. He took a large gulp then screwed the cover on. "I'll buy beer at a bar, but if I want spirits, I bring them."

"You'll get us thrown out. These sorts of places don't allow carry-in drinks."

"I didn't know that," O'Neill said facetiously.

"Screw you," Ryder replied, his head shaking in disbelief. "If they kick us out, I'll fire your ass." He looked around the room. "Oh, shit," he finally said. "If you're going to have it, at least give me some." O'Neill passed the flask under the table, and Ryder took a nip. "Tastes like crappy Scotch."

"Even good Scotch in a flask tastes like crappy Scotch," O'Neill replied.

Ryder passed the flask back, and soon enough, the waitress returned.

"There you go, gentlemen," she said, sliding cold tap beers on the table. "Are you ready to order?" She pulled out a notepad and waited.

Ryder didn't bother with the menu. "Gimme the cheese-burger basket."

She noted the order as she turned her attention to O'Neill. He assumed Ryder would buy, but he wasn't sure.

"Grab him a burger too," Ryder said.

"No, I'll take a sandwich. Do you have a turkey sandwich or something?"

"Sure," she said, pointing to an item on the menu.

It cost only two dollars and ninety-five cents, so O'Neill agreed.

"And bring us another round when you have a chance."

"Jeez, you're starting a bender," Ryder said after the waitress left. He laughed heartily and loosened his tie. "You bummed about something?"

"No, I'm fired up and ready to celebrate."

"Because we cracked Larry Marsh's alibi? Or is it something else? Is Sandra not dumping you after all?"

"No change there."

"Oh, sorry to hear that. She had a nice body."

O'Neill laughed.

"What's so funny?" Ryder asked.

"You are."

"If it isn't your Sandra who's got you depressed or excited, what is it?"

"She's not my Sandra. There is another girl I met. Let's leave it at that."

"Tell me about her," Ryder said, leaning forward.

O'Neill took another nip from his flask. "She's no one you have met."

"Come on, what's her name? Is it this Jane girl with the car?"

"Yeah," O'Neill admitted. He thought of the night before when they laid together on her bed and she told him he was amazing.

"Jane what?" Ryder said.

"She didn't tell me her last name," O'Neill said, bending the truth.

"But you've already done her, right?"

"Shut up."

"Come on, you can tell me. I'm your boss."

"No, Jane and I have just kissed."

"What does she look like?"

"Ryder, you need a girlfriend."

"Who says I ain't got one?"

"I do."

Ryder swallowed hard. "I had one until a few weeks ago. She got a job in Mississippi, though."

O'Neill wanted to laugh but held off. "How long were you dating her?"

"Almost a month."

"But she got a job in Mississippi? I don't know many people who move between Wisconsin and Mississippi."

O'Neill still wanted to laugh, but he held off. He told his boss he had to use the restroom. Once inside, he laughed as he relieved himself. Then he took another sip of Scotch and headed to the table.

Two uniformed police officers had joined Ryder. One was sitting in O'Neill's spot, while the other was standing. He recognized one but couldn't quite remember from where he recognized him. O'Neill went to the bar, ordered another beer, and waited.

When his waitress came past, he tapped her on the shoulder. She turned toward him, clearly surprised. "Excuse me," O'Neill said. "I was sitting with the big guy in the ugly suit."

"Yes," she said hesitantly.

"Couple of cops are sitting with him now. They're friends of his. Would you mind telling me when they're gone?"

"Okay," she said, backpedaling away from him.

After two minutes, the waitress tapped his shoulder. "Those policemen moved to another table," she said.

O'Neill grabbed his beer and joined Ryder at the table. Ryder was finishing his burger while O'Neill's sandwich was untouched.

"Who were the cops?"

"Couple of guys I knew from my days on the force," he said between bites. "They were kids when I worked with 'em."

"What they want?"

"Nothing." A small piece of chewed hamburger shot out of Ryder's mouth, landing on the table. "They saw me and said hello. Take it they made you nervous?"

"I've seen the one that was standing. He's an asshole."

"Bullshit. Tom Carpenter's a good cop. What did he do to you?"

"He pushed me on the stairs once," O'Neill said. "He was hurrying me out, and he gave me a shove. Not a big deal, but it is something cops like him do."

"You were probably piss your pants drunk and you fell." He pointed at O'Neill's sandwich. "You gonna eat your sub or not?"

O'Neill took a bite. It was a small sandwich with thick layers of turkey, cheese, lettuce, and mayonnaise. He would have preferred less meat and more bread.

"Is it good?"

O'Neill didn't answer until he finished chewing. "It's a turkey sub."

"I never asked what it was. I asked whether it was good."

"It is marvelous, okay?"

"Give me a taste."

O'Neill rolled his eyes. "You can have the rest." He took one more bite and handed the rest of the sandwich to Ryder.

Ryder looked like he might refuse the gift, but he finally took the basket. "You should eat more." Ryder said. "You're built like a middle-schooler."

"You're certainly not built like a middle-schooler."

"Yeah, I know. But anyway, let's talk about our problem."

"How can we determine where Andie Sheridan went after she left the path on the day of her disappearance?"

A glob of mayonnaise fell on Ryder's blue tie. "Shit!" he said, dumping a napkin into his beer and rubbing the napkin on the tie. "This is brand new, too."

O'Neill was tempted but didn't comment on the spill. "The question is, can we get evidence proving Andie was at the Sequoya Library or somewhere else on August twenty-first?"

"We could request a list of who checked books out on that morning. We could interview them, and one might recognize her, implying they saw Andie that day. Maybe she was there but the librarians didn't see her."

"We can request checkout information from the library?"

"I'm not sure, but we might." Ryder put the napkin down and tried to straighten the wrinkled tie. "I don't know anyone at the Madison Public Library, but I could talk to somebody that would. If we thought it would help, we could request it. Might cost us a few bucks, though."

The waitress slid the bill in front of Ryder. He looked up at her and smiled, and she smiled back before scurrying away. Ryder held the handwritten bill as far away from his eyes as his arm would allow. Then he set the bill back down.

"Things seem obvious," O'Neill said, speaking slowly because he realized his words were slurring. "Myles Staley hired us not because he *thought* the cops were wrong, but because he *knew* the cops were wrong. And how would he know? He knew because he saw Andie alive after the cops said she was dead."

"Why didn't Myles contact the police? And why didn't he just call us instead of sending us a letter that spelled out Larry Marsh's name?"

"Myles probably thought he would be a suspect. If he slept with her after meeting her at the library, he'd know the cops would have his DNA. We know Andie and Myles spent time out the night before. And we know Andie was flirting with someone. That was probably Myles. Why he hasn't contacted us, I have no idea. Maybe his dad is controlling things."

Ryder grabbed the bill. "Let's head out. I'll pay, but your half will come out of your next check."

"Don't forget, I paid cash for the first round. And speaking of which, today is payday. You haven't given me my money yet."

Ryder paid O'Neill weekly. O'Neill didn't have a checking account, so O'Neill wrote the check over to Ryder, who deducted a quarter of O'Neill's monthly rent and gave him the rest in cash. Ryder then paid O'Neill's rent.

"The check is back at work. I'll give it to you there, but I'd be careful with how you're going. You don't want to go crazy on a payday. If you keep sipping Scotch, you'll be on another three-day bender. Why don't I drop you home after I pay you? You take things easy and come with me tomorrow to Larry Marsh's interview."

"We are early in the afternoon, and I'm having a day. Think of the progress we made and don't worry. I'll be in bed at a decent time and be ready to talk with Larry Marsh tomorrow. I won't miss it."

Ryder didn't look convinced.

"Take me to the office." O'Neill said. "I'll walk from there."

The sun left the Chevy S-10's upholstery too hot to touch. O'Neill sat leaning forward, and Ryder laid his coat behind his back.

"Who told you to get black seats?" O'Neill said.

"I didn't buy the thing new. It had black seats when I bought it, so I got black seats." He started the car. "I need to take it easy. I had four drinks, thanks to your Scotch, putting me at my driving limit. You have had five or six drinks by now, so take her easy."

Ryder pulled the S-10 into the parking lot. It was a block walk from the parking lot to the office but was also a block closer to State Street. They walked up the stairs and entered the office. Ryder pulled O'Neill's check out of his locked desk. O'Neill signed and Ryder passed over his cash.

"Why don't you put most of this in your safe spot," Ryder said. "I'm afraid you're going to go on a bender."

"Okay, Dad," O'Neill said. He stuck everything but twelve dollars and change in his desk.

"I'm meeting with Larry Marsh tomorrow at his place at ten thirty in the morning. Do you need me to pick you up or not?"

"Yes, please."

"I'll be at your place at ten fifteen," Ryder continued. "I will not wait for you, so make sure you're ready. Meanwhile, I'll go through the statement and check if I can glean anything from Myles' or Larry's statements. Anything else?"

"Yeah, you forgot to thank me for blowing up the dickhead's alibi."

"Get him arrested or get us two additional two weeks and I'll thank you," Ryder said.

"Will do."

Chapter 25

Scenarios ran through O'Neill's head, each explaining how Andie ended at Larry Marsh's apartment. O'Neill held a newspaper in front of him, but he wasn't reading it. When a female bartender at the Red Shed put his fifth Berghoff in front of him, she leaned close and suggested he "slow down."

When he finished the beer, he left a tip and moved along to Wando's. He tried to read a newspaper that he found lying on the bar, but his eyes struggled to focus. Instead, he stared at the paper, drinking and thinking. After a few more drinks, he found himself outside, drinking Scotch with a fat, worn-looking beggar named Falcon.

When O'Neill's flask was empty, he headed home. He nearly fell on the stairs again but made it inside his apartment. His mind kept coming back to Myles Staley and his alibi for the night of August 21. He thought it a strong alibi, but details in the police file were not definitive, since the interview with Myles only verified that Myles had checked into the hotel that evening. There was nothing proving that Myles didn't drive back home and bury Andie Sheridan's body. He had to know, so he found the name and phone number of Myles Staley's former roommate. He refilled his flask and started for the pay phone.

After a few steps he stopped, realizing the phone number was probably out-of-date, and Howard Johnson's pay phone had no phone book. He stood on the sidewalk for a moment before starting for Jane's apartment.

O'Neill knew that going to Jane's was a mistake. He was tired and far too drunk. When he arrived, he took a sip of Scotch and pounded on the screen door.

There was no answer. He stood on the porch and looked for any sign that someone was home. He stepped off the porch and could see that Jane's upstairs window was dark. Swearing a few more times, he slipped on the porch steps and fell to the floor.

Rather than pulling himself up, he laid on the porch and was soon asleep.

"Seamus, wake up."

O'Neil's eyes opened, and he mumbled something.

"What are you doing here?" Jane asked.

"He's wasted," Jane's roommate said.

"You got a phone book?" O'Neill asked. He wiped drool off his cheek. "I need to call this Ralph Warzyn guy."

"Seamus, it's past nine. Go home and get some sleep. You can call this guy tomorrow."

"I got to call tonight," O'Neill said as he grabbed the porch railing, trying to get to his feet. "It's got to be tonight. I need to verify Myles' alibi."

The two women talked to O'Neill for a few minutes before Jane opened the door and helped him to their sofa.

"His name is Ralph Warzyn," O'Neill said as he handed Jane the sheet of paper that he had used to write Warzyn's phone number. "That one's probably old. I need to know his number now. He lives in Madison."

"Seamus, you're mumbling. I can't understand you."

"I can't understand you either," Jane's roommate said. "And I'm experienced at talking to drunk people."

"Sara, get me the phone book," Jane said to her roommate.

It only took a moment for Jane to find Ralph's phone number.

"Gimme the phone," O'Neill said.

"You can't talk to him," Jane said. "I can hardly understand you. There's no way he'll be able to understand you on the phone. What is it you need to know?"

O'Neill talked in circles for a minute before Jane finally understood what he was trying to do.

"I'll make the call," Jane finally said. "You stay there, but keep in mind that he might not answer."

"Make sure you let him know that Andie's mother is, like, all on board with our investigation. And make sure he knows that we're trying to show that Myles Staley is not a killer. Don't forget to ask whether they owned a shovel."

Jane dialed and waited. The phone picked up. Sara leaned closer to Jane so their heads were touching.

Through the phone, O'Neill could hear a muffled male voice.

"Hello, my name is Jane O'Neill. I work for the Ryder Detective Agency and we're investigating the murder of Andie Sheridan. I recognize it's late," Jane continued, "but we have an interview tomorrow with the Madison Police Department, and I'm hoping to verify a few things with you. Things that will help exonerate your former roommate, Myles Staley, in Andie's murder."

O'Neill heard Ralph Warzyn ask, "Who hired you?"

"Mr. Warzyn, I can't tell you who hired us, but I can tell you we are in close contact with Andie's mother. We think we can prove who killed her daughter, and we want to provide her with closure. I want you to verify a few things. It will only take a few minutes.

The room had an odd smell, and O'Neill felt queasy. He swallowed hard and didn't look up.

"I was hoping you could tell me about the afternoon and evening of August twenty-first, which was the day Andie disappeared. My understanding is that you and Myles drove to the Twin Cities. When were you with Myles during the day? Okay. And when did you leave for the Cities?"

O'Neill could feel vomit fighting its way up his chest. He swallowed hard, and he felt as if the room was wobbling.

"What did you do after you arrived? I'm just trying to verify whether Myles was with you all night."

O'Neill couldn't hear the muffled response.

"Did you wake up during the night?" Jane asked. "Okay. When did you get up in the morning? Okay. Yes. Great. Did you guys just stay the one night? Two nights? Okay. Last question: did you or Myles own a shovel? Yes, that makes sense. Yes, that's what I needed. I appreciate your time. Thank you."

"You're good at that," Sara said after Jane hung up the phone.

"I'm going to write this down," Jane said to O'Neill. "I'm not sure how much you'll remember. The gist of it is, Ralph got home about an hour before they left for the Cities. He thought they left around one o'clock, but he wasn't sure. They checked in at the hotel, went out, and got back to the hotel at one in the morning. They were up probably by ten. He remembered because they got to the hotel restaurant while the breakfast was open. You might need to verify when they stopped breakfast, but he thought it was ten o'clock. That means there wasn't enough time for Myles to drive to Madison and back to St. Paul. They stayed one more night, but I didn't get into details. As to the shovel, Ralph says they never had one."

O'Neill was struggling to listen as the queasiness took over. "I gotta go," O'Neill said. He took a step toward the front entrance but collided with a coffee table.

"Seamus, you can't make it home on your own," Jane said.

O'Neill stumbled to the door. He pushed on the door, but it didn't open. Jane flipped the handle, the door popped open, and he fell out, tripping and falling down the three steps. He crawled onto the grass and vomited.

Chapter 26

A sunny day greeted O'Neill's bleary eyes. He decided the clock said nine twenty-six. He visited the bathroom, closed the door as he left, then drank water from the sink. After falling on the mattress, he pulled covers over his head and tried to remember the previous night.

O'Neill remembered being at Jane's apartment, but he couldn't remember why he felt the need to verify Myles Staley's alibi other than wanting certainty.

Ryder was picking him up at ten fifteen, so his mess of feelings took a back seat to reality.

They would interview a murderer. O'Neill laughed out loud as he thought about it. He wondered how he would feel. For now, a wave of self-confidence won out. It didn't matter that he didn't have ironclad evidence. It didn't matter that Larry Marsh might recognize him from the previous day, and it didn't matter that Ryder would run the interview. All that mattered was they knew Larry Marsh murdered Andie Sheridan.

After showering, he dressed and sipped on a bottle of Diet Mountain Dew. The Dew didn't taste quite right; nothing tasted or felt right. When Ryder arrived, the bottle was empty and he was on the verge of falling asleep.

"Jeez, wouldn't you like to wake up for once rather than coming to? Do you expect me to take you along looking like that? And why do you drink diet soda when you're so skinny?"

"Ryder, what's the phrase about glass houses? Look at you. You got a piece of donut hanging from your lip, and it looks like you pissed in your pants."

Ryder wiped his mouth and looked down at his pants. A wet spot encircled his crotch. "Shit, I must have leaned against the sink and it was wet or something." He wiped fiercely. "It'll dry before we meet with Larry Marsh. But you still look like a United Way poster boy. Don't you ever comb your hair."

"I don't own a comb. I brush my hands through my hair."

"You don't own a comb? Who taught you to avoid combs? They're, like, thirty-nine cents and they're unbreakable."

"Is this leading somewhere?"

Ryder finished drying his crotch. The spot still showed but had faded. "I don't want you to go with me. Larry Marsh is not a big shot, but he is a respected assistant professor. If you come in looking like that, he won't take us seriously."

"What's the problem? These Levi's only have a small hole in one knee, and this is an Eddie Bauer shirt."

"You bought an Eddie Bauer shirt?"

"Sandra gave it to me."

"Either way, it's the hungover look, not the shirt. You stay here while I talk to him. We can meet afterward to talk things over before Harry's arrival."

O'Neill stepped into the bathroom, briefly ducked his head under the shower, and pushed his hair straight back. Ryder followed, leaning into the bathroom. O'Neill found an unopened container of Dep hair gel under the sink and squeezed a glob of the gel into his hand, plastering it into his hair. After running fingers through his hair, he washed the excess gel from his hands and completed the transformation with sunglasses.

"Voila," O'Neill said. "I wouldn't even recognize myself."

"Instead of looking like a hungover punk, you look like a hungover punk at a pool."

"Screw you. I look fine."

Ryder looked him over for a minute. "Take out the earring and take the sunglasses off. Otherwise, he'll think you're Jim McMahon."

"I'll take the sunglasses off after a few minutes," O'Neill said as he took off his earring. "The first impression is all that counts, and if you're doing all the talking, he won't pay attention to me."

Ryder reluctantly agreed, and they headed down the stairs and into Ryder's Chevy S-10. Larry's apartment was on Broom Street, a quarter mile from Johnson Street and a half mile from Andie's former apartment. The ride didn't give O'Neill enough time to fall asleep.

Unlike most of the area housing, Larry's apartment was a new structure and included underground parking. A security system was on a panel inside the building's foyer. Ryder rang the buzzer, and they waited. Ryder hit the bell three times before deciding to wait in the truck.

"He better show," Ryder said as he got into the truck.

"I talked to Myles' old roommate, Ralph Warzyn, last night," O'Neill said. "He was with Myles from basically twelve noon until they went to sleep after midnight. They then woke up before ten o'clock. It's a strong alibi. Myles couldn't have come back at night and buried Andie's body. There wouldn't have been time."

"Who told you to interview someone last night? I was going to do that today."

"I did. I wanted to be sure before we met with Larry."

Ryder didn't argue with him. "I'm thinking about the meeting with Harry. How is it we explain things to him? How do we explain that we think we solved this case? How do we do it without making the MPD look like shit?"

"The cops made reasonable assumptions. But I don't think the cops understood Andie. They didn't understand her motivation."

"But you do?"

"Maybe slackers think alike," O'Neill suggested.

"I agree. We can clear Myles Staley and bust Larry Marsh's alibi. But that still doesn't prove that Larry is the killer. What do you think happened?"

"Larry was heading home from class shortly after eleven thirty. If he drove up Johnson Street, he may have seen her, or he was home before she arrived at his apartment. My guess is he suspected something. She was probably wearing her running clothes, and maybe he spotted her turning off Myles' street. He grills her in his apartment and gets angry. He's learned he can't hit her because punches leave bruises. Instead, he chokes her, but he goes too far and suddenly she's dead."

"Inside his apartment?"

"That is how it makes sense to me."

"How does her body get to the arboretum?"

"I assume he carried her from his apartment to the parking garage late at night and put her in his trunk. He drove to the parking area on the southwestern end of the path, carried her to the spot, and used a shovel to bury her. The point is, he took her to the woods rather than burying her off a random country road. Who, besides Larry, benefits by bringing the body to that area of the arboretum? Whoever killed her knew she ditched her run in the arboretum woods. Only two or perhaps three people knew about that: Myles Staley, Carver Stringer, and Larry Marsh. Of those, only Larry had the opportunity and motive. It can't be a coincidence."

"Larry could claim he didn't know anything about her cutting the run."

"We have a witness to show she did the same thing earlier this summer. My guess is she told Larry about it, but you're correct that we can't prove it. Who, besides Larry, wanted her body found in the woods? If some other man killed Andie, he wouldn't want her body found anywhere. An attack on the arboretum path gives Larry an alibi."

O'Neill was staring at the college students as they crossed Broom Street, heading back from classes. The women were wearing either shorts or dresses, and he stared at their legs as they walked past. It seemed to be an unbreakable habit.

"Let's stick with our plan and hold part of the story back from Harry," Ryder said. "We tell him the part of your theory where someone kills Andie after she purposely left the path. We won't bring up Myles sleeping with Andie. Hopefully, it's enough progress for him to up the contract for two weeks, but it won't scare him off. If not enough, we will call him next week and drop the rest on him. If progress is what he wants, he will give us an extension." He tilted his body sideways, cracking his back. "If he demands proof and progress isn't enough, we'll work with the MPD. Ideally, we find someone who witnessed Larry putting something in his trunk, or heard fighting at Larry's apartment, or someone who saw him with a woman that afternoon, or who saw Larry pick Andie up in his car. Odds are slim, since we are talking about something that happened two years ago."

"What about physical evidence at Larry's apartment?"

Ryder considered the question before answering. "Strangulation doesn't leave blood, and the killer used his hands, so there's no murder weapon to find. We won't find signs of a struggle from two years ago. And if he drove her body over in the back seat of his car or in his trunk, it wouldn't be a big deal if we found her hair, since she'd probably been in the car dozens of times. Her hair could have fallen into the trunk in many ways. His car would leave tire tracks, but that was two years ago. And if he's smarter than a beach ball, he got rid of the shovel long ago."

"Yeah, but what apartment renter keeps a shovel? My guess is he bought the shovel after the murder."

"Could be, but I'm guessing he paid cash, so we won't have anything to tie him to the purchase."

"Have you looked into our librarian to be sure he's not a suspect?"

"Yeah, I did," Ryder said with a chuckle. "Carver Stringer is sixty-four years old, worked for the Madison Public Library for forty years, has a wife and two adult children, and no criminal record. He recently got two speeding tickets and his driver's license lists him as five-foot-nine, one hundred and forty-five pounds. You might even take him in a fight."

"I can't see our lead-footed librarian overpowering a gutsy, five-foot-ten world-class athlete," O'Neill said.

"Let's not bring Carver's details up to Harry. Unless something firms up against Larry, we want to show progress. The existence of a suspect whom the MPD did not identify implies progress," Ryder said, pausing as he glanced in the rearview mirror.

"What's up?" O'Neill said.

"Larry Marsh is here."

Chapter 27

O'Neill twisted his neck around. Behind John Ryder's Chevy S-10 was a silver GTO with "WINNER" license plates. Ryder waited until Larry walked past Ryder's truck, then he opened the door and stepped out. O'Neill followed.

"Mr. Marsh," Ryder said as he lifted his mass out of the truck.

Larry did an about-face. He looked relaxed, and, after sizing up Ryder and O'Neill, a slight grin slid onto his tanned face.

"You must be the detectives. I'm glad to meet you."

"I'm John Ryder, and this is my partner, Seamus O'Neill."

Ryder and O'Neill shook Larry's hand. Larry looked O'Neill over. For an instant, O'Neill thought he could see a slight twitch in his face as if he was wondering whether he recognized O'Neill.

"Let's go inside," Larry said as he slid his security key into the lock. "I'm sorry to have kept you waiting, but that is how teaching goes. I'm sure you fellows can imagine that there is always one student needing extra time and attention."

Ryder nodded.

"If I understand correctly, you want to talk about Andie Sheridan," Larry continued.

"It is routine," Ryder said, his voice cracking. "We're talking to everybody we can."

They stopped at the end of a hallway. Larry opened the door with a key card and waved Ryder and O'Neill inside. The inside of the apartment was large, well-lit, and smelled fresh. The apartment had a kitchen, a dining area, and a living room. A separate hallway led to what O'Neill assumed were bedrooms and the bathroom. The dining table and a part of the floor were littered with open notebooks, textbooks, and magazines. The kitchen and the living room were immaculate, and incoming sunlight glittered off a glass table.

"Please excuse the state of things. I've been working on a research paper, and I made a mess with my papers. Can I get you something to drink?"

"No, thanks," Ryder said.

"If you don't mind, I'm going to grab a soda."

Ryder and O'Neill waited as Larry strode in and out of the kitchen.

"Take a seat on the couch," Larry said, opening a can of Coke.

Ryder and O'Neill sat on the sofa with Ryder nearer to Larry. O'Neill pushed up his sunglasses, rested them atop his head, and pulled a notepad and pen from his pocket.

"Andie's death was a stressful thing, of course. I never lost a loved one before, not a grandmother, an uncle, or anything. It was a shock for me." He looked up, teary-eyed. "I apologize if I get emotional about this. It has been a long time, but it feels like it happened yesterday. Have you felt that way, Mr. Ryder?"

Ryder cleared his throat. "Yes, I understand how you feel."

"It seems like only yesterday she sat on the couch you're sitting on, and only yesterday we laughed and talked." His head was shaking again. "It seems only yesterday that I thought we had a future."

O'Neill wrote "Bullshit" on his notepad.

"I understand you were teaching a class at the time of Andie's disappearance," Ryder said.

"It was a special study group rather than a formal class. A special study group is for students who are having trouble or have specific questions relating to course material or assignments. The idea is the professor and I, as his assistant, catch problems and questions at one session. Running a special group is easier than having twenty or thirty hours when you're available for questions. We already had finals for the session, but there were outstanding assignments and opportunities for extra credit."

"I understand," Ryder said. "What time did this special study session finish?"

"Eleven thirty. The first one ran nine to ten, while the second ran ten thirty to eleven thirty."

"You left school then, soon after eleven thirty?"

O'Neill noted a slight change in Larry's expression.

"Yes, I went home," Larry answered. "Professor McLean and I left the building together. The police interviewed him, confirming the time."

"You drove home?" O'Neill asked.

"Yes."

"When did you realize Andie was missing?" Ryder said.

Larry looked to the side, reflecting. "I was busy, but we had plans for Thursday evening, the day after her murder. When I didn't hear from her, I called her, but I got Mary."

"Mary Gleason?"

"Yes, she was worried once she knew Andie wasn't with me, though I wasn't too worried. Andie loved life and did crazy things on a lark. I thought she had gone off with a friend."

"Had she done something like that before without telling you?"

"She and another friend once drove to a Wisconsin Dells water park. It got me angry at the time because we had planned on dinner. I couldn't locate her, and I got concerned. When Andie came back, I was sore."

"But you forgave her?" O'Neill asked.

Larry Marsh looked at O'Neill for the first time since they went inside. His gaze held steady on O'Neill for a full second before returning to Ryder. "Yes, I forgave her."

"When she wasn't at home," Ryder said, "it didn't worry you, since you thought she went on another trip?"

"Precisely, though I knew she didn't go anywhere with Mary. That was the only reason I was even somewhat worried. If there was no answer at their house, I would have assumed she and Mary went somewhere together. Yet Mary was worried, so I talked to the university police on Friday morning. I didn't file a report on Friday, but Mary and I talked, and we agreed to file a missing person report if we didn't hear from Andie by Saturday morning." He shook his abundant blonde hair. "I called Saturday morning, but Coach Lehman had contacted the police earlier that morning. The police had Mary and I come in, and we spent the next few days worrying about Andie. Our fears, unfortunately, turned out to be warranted."

"What were the police thinking when you first contacted them?"

"They thought she ran away or something. They thought she went to Hollywood like in *Pretty Woman* or something. It was ridiculous, but they say it happens all the time."

"What did you think?"

"I was worried by then," Larry said in a whisper. "I found out she hadn't finished her run on Wednesday, which was August twenty-first, so I knew something happened at that point."

There was a brief silence.

"What kind of person was Andie?" O'Neill said.

Larry leaned back in the chair. "I could talk about her for hours," he said in a quiet voice. O'Neill and Ryder waited patiently before Larry spoke again. "She was a lovely girl who loved music, friends, dancing, and talking. She was exquisitely beautiful." He paused and looked up at Ryder. "She was truly a beautiful woman, everything I wanted. She was both intensely competitive and sensitive. Everyone knew and expected the competitive fire, but most didn't expect the level of introspection and sensitivity she had. We were very much in love."

Ryder cast O'Neill a "what now" look. O'Neill shrugged his shoulders.

"We used to spend a lot of time at my apartment," Larry said. "It worked since some may have seen our relationship as inappropriate. In addition, she had a roommate, while I had none. It was as if she lived with me rather than with Mary. I think her mother suspected that Andie was spending most of her time at my place, which did not thrill her. At some point, I bought a bed for her. She grew up in a family where her mother and father slept in separate rooms, even before they separated. Andie wanted her own room, and I gave it to her. Andie needed her own space."

"Do you have thoughts about her murder?" O'Neill asked. "Any idea who killed Andie?"

"The bastard that raped her," he answered. "Plenty of guys wanted her, but I don't know if anyone was spooking her or coming on to her. She wasn't one to talk about those things."

There was another long pause, then Ryder pulled himself off the couch.

"I'm sorry to have bothered you, Mr. Marsh," Ryder said.

"No bother at all," Larry said. They shook hands.

"One thing before we go," O'Neill said. "Do you still have her things? I'm trying to get a sense of her personality, and it helps to see her world."

Larry's eyebrows pushed down, and he nodded. "I use her room for storage, though some of her things remain. I haven't had the heart to clean out the room. I doubt it will help, but you are welcome to look." Larry walked around the couch and into the hallway. There was a bathroom between two closed doors. "It's the smaller bedroom," he said as he opened the door. "I kept the room closed, and I left a few things as they were. This spring I gave most of her clothes to Goodwill."

A canopied, full-size bed dominated the room. The bedspread and black pillows had neither a masculine nor a feminine tone. A dresser drawer and vanity took most of the wall space. CliffsNotes to Hamlet were atop the dresser. Atop the vanity was a mirror, a hairbrush, a bottle of perfume, a container filled with hairbands and hair clips, and a framed picture. The trash container sitting alongside the vanity was empty. Larry opened the shades with a flurry, and sunlight filled the room. O'Neill took a few steps in, noting the lack of dust.

"You kept her brush. That's sweet. Who is with Andie in the picture?" O'Neill asked, though he had seen the picture before and knew the answer.

"Andie's parents. Anything else?"

O'Neill shook his head. "No, nothing at all."

* * *

"That was a waste of time," Ryder said, stepping outside the apartment complex.

They dragged themselves into Ryder's Chevy. O'Neill leaned back and closed his eyes. The upholstery was hot as always, but O'Neill didn't care.

"What did we expect to find, anyway?" Ryder said. "We should have just prepped for our noon meeting with Harry Bartholomew."

"I suspect we found out where in the apartment he killed her."

Ryder turned toward O'Neill and smiled. "How, my hungover friend, did you figure that out?"

"He laid those books and papers out recently. He didn't want us in the dining area. Everything else was super neat, and nothing's out of place in Andie's room, even though the room hasn't been used since the murder. You notice when he opened the shades in the spare bedroom, there didn't seem to be any dust? The guy is anal. Shit, he looks like he washes his hair more than Orel Hersheiser. And besides, he showed us her bedroom, so he didn't kill her there. He could have killed her in his bedroom, but I'll go with the dining room."

Ryder started the truck and pulled into traffic. "You come up with the strangest ideas. Even if he killed her in the dining area, she died of strangulation. There wouldn't be blood, or evidence, so why bother keeping us out?"

"Paranoia."

"That is something you know about."

"Screw you."

Ryder changed lanes and gave O'Neill a strange look. "Get that gel brushed out of your hair when we get back. You look like a pimp."

O'Neill's eyes opened, and he pulled his sunglasses off.

"Did you notice the brush?" O'Neill said.

"Brush? What brush?"

"The one in Andie's room," O'Neill said. "In Larry's apartment."

"What about it?"

O'Neill rubbed his chin. "That may just be our evidence. Maybe even our proof."

Chapter 28

It was a problem. Harry Bartholomew was due at any minute, and O'Neill could not keep awake. Ryder leaned back in his chair, his feet on the desk and the sleeves of his shirt rolled over his elbows.

"Shaaaaaymuuus, stay awake," Ryder said.

"Are you okay with us spilling everything to Harry or not?" O'Neill asked.

Ryder stood and walked to O'Neill's desk. "Yes, I agree. Though it's against my better judgment."

"Good," O'Neill said. "This way, you won't get pissed when I talk about it."

"Okay, well, here's the deal. We'll explain the path and the library. But we admit we're speculating on what happened at Myles' apartment and at Larry's apartment."

"Sure," O'Neil said, his eyes still shut.

"What's the deal with your new girl?"

"What?" O'Neill said. His attention had drifted, but he caught the change in the subject.

"That girl you said you haven't done it with yet."

"What about her?"

Ryder giggled like a child. "Still whipped?"

He was, but mentioning Jane brought memories from the night before at her apartment. Jane had cleaned him up and put him in her car. He tried not to vomit again as they traveled to his apartment. Jane didn't speak during the ride, and once at his apartment, she opened the passenger door and pulled him out of the car. He was standing on the sidewalk. She got into her car and left. She didn't help him up the stairs, and she didn't say goodbye.

"I think she's pissed and disappointed."

"With you?"

O'Neill nodded.

"Let me guess: she doesn't mind you drinking, but she doesn't want you drinking that much, right?"

"I suppose. It always seems to end that way since they decide they're going to dry you up or dump you."

"You should date another lush."

O'Neill chuckled. "I've done that plenty of times; it works about as well as you'd expect."

Ryder was rubbing a toothpick between his teeth. "Is it Sayonara then?"

"I hope not. I could cut down on my drinking."

"Would you really cut down on your drinking?

"Suppose it would be a good idea."

"If you do, try something definable. Tell her you won't drink on Sundays or something like that."

O'Neill gave a look of disgust. "Sunday's a great wine day. I wouldn't cut Sundays out."

"How about Mondays? Oh, wait, don't do that. If you did, you would end up binging on Tuesdays and missing work on Wednesdays." He paused, considering the problem. "The best approach would be to not drink on Fridays. Then you could get hammered on Saturday and recover on Sunday."

"Friday would be the last day I'd give up."

"What day then?"

"What day is today?"

"Friday."

"How about Thursday?"

"Something tells me this won't work," Ryder said, shaking his head.

O'Neill closed his eyes again. It could work, he thought to himself. He could abstain from drinking for one day each week. He thought he could do that, but he was unsure whether it would satisfy her.

"You should wash that shit out of your hair. Harry will think you're going respectable and trying to win your Sandy back."

A knock at the door interrupted them. Ryder hopped out of his chair and rushed to the entrance. He pulled the heavy wooden door open, revealing a smiling Harry Bartholomew. The lawyer was wearing a gray suit with a swirled mauve tie. Harry stumbled as he stepped in but recovered.

"Mr. Ryder, I presume?" Harry said.

"That's me," Ryder said as they shook hands. "And I assume you are Mr. Bartholomew."

"Call me Harry," he said. He turned toward O'Neill. "Seamus, I didn't recognize you with your new look."

"Good to see you, Harry. How is Sandra?"

"Fine. She's adjusting well and is excited to begin her new job. She has already met several interesting people. She wanted me to say 'Hello' to you for her."

Ryder offered Harry a seat. Then he offered him coffee, a cigarette, and a drink of water. Harry took the seat and declined the rest.

"I understand from Seamus that you two have busted this mystery open." The lawyer pulled a notepad from his jacket pocket. "You think the victim's boyfriend killed her?"

"Exactly," Ryder said.

"You realize he has an airtight alibi?"

Ryder described O'Neill's theory. O'Neill added a correction or two as Ryder explained why and how Andie had cut her run short, ending at the library. They explained how Carver Stringer saw her at the library earlier in the summer.

"Myles Staley was at the library we're referring to at nine thirty that morning."

"How do you know that?"

"It's in the police files. That was the alibi he provided. Emily Hawkins, a librarian who remembered Myles arriving just as the library opened, verified the alibi."

"Are you claiming that Myles was involved in this woman's murder?"

"No."

O'Neill then explained how they thought Myles had met up with Andie at the library on the day she disappeared. Finally, he explained that Larry Marsh was the lead suspect and had no alibi past eleven thirty on the morning of Andie's disappearance. O'Neill also explained that Myles had an ironclad alibi for the night of August twenty-first. He explained that was important since the killer almost certainly buried the body that night. When they finished the story, Ryder muttered a conclusion.

"I'm afraid I don't know enough about this case to judge your theory," Harry said, his gaze jumping between O'Neill and Ryder. "I wonder, what gave you this idea? Did this roommate of Myles Staley, this...?"

"Ralph Warzyn."

"Yes, Ralph Warzyn. Did Ralph tell you this story about Myles having sex with the Sheridan woman?" His big eyebrows shot forward in a frown.

"We never asked him about it," O'Neill said. "We only talked to him about the alibi he provided for Myles for the day and night of the twenty-first. I do, however, suspect he knows more. He traveled to the Cities with Myles on the night of the twenty-first. It would not surprise me if Myles told Ralph about the encounter he had with Andie. At that point, Myles would not have known that Andie was missing. We figured it would be better for Ralph to tell the police."

"The police?"

"We're assuming," O'Neil continued, "that Myles, or perhaps Myles' father, didn't want him to go to the police because he thought he would be a suspect, since the police found Myles' sperm on Andie's body. I understand his concern. He would have immediately been their number one suspect. Yet the police assumed the murderer came back on the night of the twenty-first to bury the body. We are sure that's the case. We simply go further since we believe the murder did not occur near the path."

"If it was Myles' sperm on the body," Ryder said. "We suspect he'll be able to explain it."

"How did you jump to the conclusion that the victim was murdered somewhere else?" Harry said.

"Did you read Myles' letter?" O'Neill asked. "That's where I got the idea."

"Yes, Myles' father showed the letter to me after he sent it out."

"Did you notice anything unusual about the letter?"

Harry turned pale. "Myles' letter was awkward. Don't tell me there was a reason for it?"

Ryder hunted through papers on his desk, then handed a copy of the letter to Harry.

"I'm going off memory, but the letter told me three things," O'Neill said. "The first was the hidden message."

"Hidden message?"

"Yes, the first letter in each sentence spells Larry Marsh."

"My God, it does," Harry said after a moment. "I should have read the letter rather than skimming it."

"Myles' letter also says Andie was killed 'late in the morning.' I wouldn't call nine fifteen in the morning 'late,' would you?"

"Probably not. And the third thing you got from Myles' letter?" Harry asked as he examined the sheet.

"It says we should ignore the 'basic premise' the police relied on. The police assumed Andie was attacked, raped, and killed while running on the path. Clearly, she was murdered, but the rape wasn't as clear. They assumed rape because they found her partially naked with a condom wrapper near her body and semen on her body and underwear. The police knew Andie changed her clothes in the morning, so they knew the semen was not from prior to the run. The assumption of rape was reasonable. As to the location of the murder, they inferred it based on where they found the body. The time of murder was based on when Andie was last seen."

"You're saying the police were wrong about everything?"

"Yes, but it was based on logical assumptions. And Myles' belief that they would blame him was based on logical assumptions as well. Myles knew there wasn't a rape, and he knew she wasn't attacked or murdered during the run."

"It seems to explain everything," Harry said as he examined a map of the arboretum path.

"It explains the main thing bothering everyone about this case, which was how improbable the attack was. It was improbable that someone would jump a runner in a group with no one hearing or seeing anything. Even more improbable was a killer *choosing* to attack someone running in a group. This led us to the theory that Andie left the wooded path on her own and was killed elsewhere."

They were quiet for a few minutes. Then Harry laid the paper on Ryder's desk.

"Can I use your phone?" he asked.

Ryder handed him the receiver and Harry dialed a ten-digit number. O'Neill's head was pounding.

"You calling Sandra?" O'Neill asked.

"Myles Staley," Harry said to O'Neill. He turned his attention to the phone. "Myles, it's Harry. Please come in and join me inside the office. Yes, now."

"Myles came with you?" O'Neill said, clearly surprised.

Chapter 29

Harry hung up his phone. The perennial smile was gone, as if he had taken off his mask. He looked at O'Neill and then at Ryder.

"Myles called me early this morning," Harry said. "He was upset and when he learned I was driving to Madison, he insisted he come along. Now I know why he insisted."

Harry walked to the entrance and pushed the door open.

O'Neill and Ryder waited. When they heard Myles' footsteps, O'Neill took a breath. Myles stepped in, stumbled, but recovered. He was tall with a full head of sandy blonde hair, bright eyes, and a lean figure. He was wearing casual pants, a yellow shirt, and white tennis shoes.

"Sit down, Myles," Harry said as Myles stepped into the office. "These are the detectives, John Ryder and Seamus O'Neill. Grab a chair."

Myles introduced himself to Ryder and O'Neill and sat beside Harry. Harry turned to his client.

"I want you to come clean, Myles, and tell me and these two gentlemen everything you know about Andie Sheridan."

Myles looked apprehensive.

"Go on," Harry urged. "Your father trusts my judgment, though you can call him first if you prefer."

"I don't want to call my father," Myles said. "I trust you. Where do I start?"

No one replied, so Myles took a long breath, giving the sense his story would take hours.

"Coming into my junior year, I was dating a girl named Mary Gleason. That summer, Andie became Mary's room-mate. Andie was fun to be with and rockingly beautiful. I ran into her at the bars or at parties, and I saw her when I was with Mary. I admit, I thought she had something for me by the way she looked at me and acted around me. Anyway, one night, I was out with my friend, and we ran into Andie and her friends at this place on State Street called Mondays. Mary stayed home that night because she had a test. Anyway, we ended up playing darts with them, and we moved to the Flamingo. Andie and I headed to the Flamingo's bathroom, and she was all over me. It was awful of me, since I was dating Mary, but when she kissed me, I kissed her back.

"The kiss didn't last long though since Ralph — he was my roommate — interrupted us. Andie and I pulled apart and acted as if nothing happened. When we went back to the table, she put her hand on my leg and I put my hand on hers.

"At eleven thirty, Ralph wanted to go home. I wanted to stay, of course, because I was feeling it and wanted her, but I didn't want Ralph to suspect anything since he was friends with Mary. When Ralph suggested we go home, I agreed. Andie and I kept talking, though, and I mentioned something to her about whether she'd have trouble running the next day." He paused and his gaze locked on O'Neill. "She was on the cross-country team, as you know. Anyway, she told me she planned to cut her run. I asked what she meant, and she told me she would drop to last place and stop on Monroe

Street. Then she would walk to a library on Midvale Boulevard and relax. She said the only concern would be if she got to the library too early, since it opened at nine thirty. She said she would rejoin after her teammates ran past. It turned an eight-mile run into less than a five-mile run. She said she could run five miles in her sleep.

"I didn't think twice about it, but that night, I couldn't stop thinking about her. And that next morning I thought about her too. At some point, I had to see her, and I had a silly idea. I knew she would be at the library just as it opened in the morning, and I couldn't stop myself from seeing her."

"You don't have to explain yourself," Harry said in a reassuring tone. "Continue your story."

"I figured out what library she was talking about and drove there. I got to the library just as it opened, though no one was there but a librarian. She was an older lady. I asked if she'd seen a young, tall blonde. She said I was the first person she'd seen, so I waited outside, and, within a few minutes, Andie arrived. She saw me and she had a look in her eye. I'll always remember that look since it was very sweet. But anyway, we talked for a minute, and she wanted to get in my car in case her teammates ran by. We talked for a moment longer, and she asked me to take her to my apartment. I asked about her run, and she said she'd tell her coach she pulled a back muscle. I drove her to my place on Johnson Street."

"And when you were at your apartment," Harry said, "you had sexual relations with her, correct?"

Myles nodded. "It might sound awful, being she was my girlfriend's roommate and all. But she was incredible, and here's me thinking about whether I can keep seeing her since she had a boyfriend and I had a girlfriend. It wouldn't be easy, though Mary and I had run our course. I could break up with Mary, but Andie wasn't sure she could break up with Larry. Anyway, Andie left around eleven thirty. She didn't think she could get into her apartment since her key was in her locker and she didn't know if Mary was home. But Larry had a key hidden on the back porch outside his apartment. She didn't think he would be home yet, so she planned to get changed at Larry's then go back to her locker. I assumed that was what happened. Meanwhile, Ralph and I drove up to the Twin Cities."

"Did you and Andie have vaginal sex?" O'Neill said.

Myles squirmed in his chair.

"I apologize if I'm being indelicate," O'Neill continued, "but it matters. The medical examiner didn't find semen inside her, but they found some on her crotch area, on her underwear, and in her hair."

"She wasn't sure she was protected," Myles said. "We fooled around and did mostly oral stuff. She wouldn't let me..."

"Okay, got it," O'Neill said. "How much semen got into her hair?"

"Why does that matter?" Harry asked.

"Andie has a brush in her room at Larry's apartment. We saw it last night and there's still hair on it. I think it's part of Larry's little shrine or something. Either way, if she brushed her hair once she got to Larry's apartment, she may very well have gotten your semen on the brush. There were also hairbands in a sort of ceramic thing. We know she was wearing a hairband when she was running, but one wasn't found on the body."

"It's been two years," Harry said. "Wouldn't Larry have cleaned the brush to hide any evidence?"

"I didn't study the brush, but there was blonde hair in it. I don't know whose hair, but I can't see someone as anal as Larry using someone else's brush, so I don't think it's been washed. Besides, he would have no reason to believe that anyone besides Andie's DNA would be on that brush. Keep in mind, he placed a condom wrapper near her body to explain the lack of semen. He didn't know there was semen on her or her clothes."

"What if my DNA is on that brush?" Myles asked. "So what?"

"Your DNA on either the brush or the hairband that matches with the DNA from the semen that was found in Andie's hair would prove she was at Larry's apartment *after* she had sexual relations with you. That would place her at Larry's apartment after eleven thirty on August twenty-first."

"It would," Harry said, straightening his back. He turned toward Myles. "You'll still have to explain why you never went to the police."

"I didn't know anything at first," Myles said.

"A few days later, I heard she had disappeared. I was upset, but Mary made a mistake and told me Andie had been missing since Thursday rather than Wednesday. I read a newspaper article which said she disappeared on Wednesday, but I thought they got it wrong. I thought she disappeared on Thursday until after they found her body. By the time I found out, word was she was raped as well. I realized the police would think I had raped and killed her. Anyway, I was upset and scared shitless. Upset about Andie and scared shitless about my predicament. It was an awful week."

"We understand," Harry said.

"I wanted to call the police. I was a key witness, and if I came forward, the police might realize they made incorrect assumptions, but they might think I was the killer. If accused, it would go to trial, and I might end up in jail. If they acquitted me, the murder would hang over the rest of my life. Anyway, I waited a day before calling my father. He came to town, and I told him everything — like I told you now — and he told me I should forget about it. He thought an accusation would ruin my career, and he said I knew nothing that would help the police solve the crime." His gaze dropped. "The police had already interviewed me, since I had seen her out the night before she disappeared. But they didn't ask me about the next day, and I didn't tell them anything other than that I was at the library at nine thirty. My dad made me promise to not approach them again, though I didn't like it. I felt worse when the police investigation floundered.

"I tried to talk my father into letting me come clean with the police, but he wouldn't budge. And since I promised I wouldn't go to them, I didn't. A promise is important to a Staley." He paused, emphasizing the statement. "Finally, I figured if I couldn't go to the police, I could hire a detective to identify the killer. Dad didn't like the idea, but agreed, provided he picked the detectives and I stayed out of everything. I assume that is how your agency got involved."

"Thank you, Myles," Harry said. "To go back to Mr. O'Neill's earlier question about semen in the victim's hair..."

"I wouldn't be surprised if there was a lot," Myles said sheepishly.

"That summarizes your involvement?" Harry said.

"Yes," Myles Staley answered. "Until last night when Ralph Warzyn called and told me a female private detective interviewed him about the murder. He wanted me to know, and I figured it related to my hiring a private detective."

Ryder's eyes lit up, and he mouthed, "Female?" to O'Neill.

"That is why you called me this morning?" Harry asked Myles.

Myles nodded.

"One other thing," O'Neill said. "Can you talk about the letter with the message that spelled Larry Marsh?"

"You figured out the puzzle? It was lame, but it got past Dad. I hoped you'd figure it out. He agreed to use my name, so he wanted a letter from me. He gave me two minutes to write something on his computer. He told me I couldn't say anything that wouldn't have been common knowledge. Yet, you needed to know Larry Marsh was the killer, and you needed to know the police investigation was off target. My dad would have none of it. He didn't want me in the investigation and wouldn't even tell me who he hired to investigate. The only thing I knew was that Harry managed the hire."

"So, you put a message into the letter. We also caught the comment about the murder happening in the morning and about ignoring the 'basic assumption' the cops made."

Myles smiled again. It was the smile of someone who had gotten a weight off his chest. "I'm glad you figured everything out and cleared me to boot. I wasn't sure how difficult my message would be to see or solve. I was glad my dad didn't figure out what I did in the letter. What did you mention about when the murder occurred?"

"Your note set the murder late in the morning, while the cops set it at nine fifteen to nine thirty."

"Oh, I guess I did that by accident."

O'Neill inwardly smiled, not sure if a Freudian slip or an error led him in the right direction.

"You say you thought Larry killed Andie," Ryder said. "We think so too, as you know. Do you have any evidence against Larry?"

"No evidence, but Andie was afraid of him. When she left, I told her I'd punch Larry out if she had a single bruise on her. She told me he knew how to make his point without leaving bruises. I thought she was referring to emotional abuse, but when I found out how she died, I wondered."

"Shocking," Harry said. He turned to O'Neill and Ryder. "I agree with you that there's a reasonable chance that there will be DNA evidence on the brush or on the hair thing. Do you have other evidence?"

"More time should give us evidence," Ryder said. "As you noted, we've made a lot of progress in less than a week."

"I don't think it will take much for us to convince the cops that Larry should be their primary suspect," O'Neill said to Harry. "Myles and Larry are likely the only suspects who knew Andie planned to skip from her run in the arboretum. They both knew the teammates would infer that someone attacked and killed Andie on that path. Yet, someone buried Andie near the path, leaving her partially undressed with a condom wrapper nearby. This implied sexual assault. Only one suspect benefited from her being found near the path and it was Larry, because a nine thirty attack gave him an alibi. But he likely doesn't have an alibi for the night of the twenty-first, while Myles does. Larry undoubtedly took her shorts and underwear off to make it look like a sexual assault. This provided a motive for the killing. He left the condom wrapper because he didn't know Andie had relations with Myles that morning. He was trying to explain a lack of semen."

"That's ironic," Harry said.

"Yes. Either way, the appearance of sexual assault helped Larry, but made things worse for you, Myles, since you didn't know that your alibi for that night was more important than the alibi you provided for the morning. Also, Ralph says he was with you that afternoon. That means that, even if you had killed her, you'd have to buy a shovel and get her body buried before noon. There was a nursery school on the path from ten o'clock until after eleven. There simply wasn't time."

"The police asked me about what I did the rest of the day, but they focused on the nine o'clock to ten o'clock timeframe."

"Once they thought you couldn't have assaulted her on the path, they basically crossed you off their list of suspects."

"What about other evidence?" Harry asked.

"There are several possibilities beyond the brush and the hairband," O'Neill said. "As I said, the police noted semen in her crotch area and on her underwear. Her underwear and shorts were buried with her, and the underwear was torn. None of that might seem odd, but I wonder where on the underwear they found semen. I'm guessing the location on the underwear will be consistent with semen getting on her crotch and her then putting her underwear on."

"Why does that matter?" Harry said.

"I'm assuming the location of any semen on the underwear will match with the location on her crotch. That implies she put her underwear on after getting semen on her crotch. Yet he tore the underwear off. Why would a rapist tear her underwear off, put it back on, and then take it back off again? We have seen nothing in the police files that details the exact location of the semen on the underwear, but that's how I see it."

"You're right," Harry said. "It would support Myles' story by illustrating consensual sexual activity on the twenty-first."

"Also, the police did not focus investigative effort around activity at Larry's apartment or the library on the afternoon and night of the twenty-first. Yesterday, he parked on the street in his GTO, but those apartments have underground parking. I thought it odd him parking outside when he apparently had underground parking. Perhaps he didn't like the idea of us thinking about underground parking. It's a new apartment complex, and with security cameras becoming more common, there could be cameras in the apartment hallways or in the parking garage that might show him leaving the apartment that night with a large package. The library could also have security cameras, though I have no idea how long they keep the footage. We'll look closely at the apartment, the parking garage, and ideally the trunk of his GTO."

"What could you get from his car trunk?" Harry asked. "There wouldn't be any blood."

"We might find hair in the trunk or the back seat. While not as good a chance as the brush, it's possible Myles' semen would be on one or more strand of hair. The brush, however, is the better chance since anal Larry probably vacuums his trunk at least weekly."

Harry nodded his agreement.

"Finally, whoever buried Andie's body used a shovel. Undoubtedly, he dumped the shovel that same night, but I'm doubtful Larry kept a shovel in his apartment. My guess is he bought one from someplace nearby on the twenty-first or the early morning of the twenty-second. He also likely purchased something to carry her body in, such as a tarp. I doubt he would be dumb enough to use his credit card for such a purpose, but who knows? Even if he didn't, there could be security cameras at the hardware store or wherever. I'm doubtful they would keep footage that long, but I don't know."

"And don't forget," Ryder added, "the Madison Police Department did not look for witnesses or activity at or near Larry's apartment. They never asked Larry's neighbors if they heard arguing around noon on the twenty-first because they thought Andie was already dead. In short, we have several opportunities for witnesses and evidence."

"I agree that, with more time, you likely could obtain enough evidence, but just as important to my client, we should be able to clear Myles with the information we already have. As you said, Myles and his father didn't understand the importance of his alibi for that night. It's doubtful he would have even had time, even if he wanted to risk burying her in the daytime. I'm thinking our best approach will be to go to the police at this point. We'll get Myles cleared, present our evidence, and let them work to get a search warrant for Larry's apartment and car. Was she killed at his apartment?"

"Myles just told us she left his place for Larry's apartment at eleven thirty, so Larry's apartment makes the most sense. Since he choked her to death, there likely is no opportunity for evidence in his apartment at this point beyond the brush and the hairband."

"Okay," Harry said, "Let me handle this. I'll confer with colleagues to verify a few things, but then I will contact Mr. Ryder and the three of us can go to the police."

"Three of us?" Ryder said.

"I think we're better off not involving Mr. O'Neill, at least in the first meeting with the police." Harry turned toward O'Neill. "I recognize the contribution you've made to this, but I suspect the police will take Mr. Ryder and me more seriously.

Besides, you're a bit of a loose cannon — if you don't mind me saying. We can't have a loose cannon going off until after Myles is clear."

"This means this nightmare will be over?" Myles asked.

"Yes, this will be over," Harry said. "I told your father this might require a decision, but he trusts my judgment." He stepped over to O'Neill's desk as Myles motioned toward the door. "I'm very impressed, Seamus. I'll tell Sandra."

"Another thing to keep in mind," O'Neill said, "is that Larry claims he loved Andie, yet he ripped underwear off her dead body and buried her partially naked in the arboretum. He is a Machiavellian asshole."

"Point well taken," Harry said.

"What a bastard," Myles said.

"Final thing," O'Neill said, as he pulled Harry to the side. "I am curious about you hiring me. Were you trying to pay me off?" His eyes met Harry's. "I know you didn't want me involved with Sandra. It's over and that's fine. You may have figured out that I'm a curious sort. I'd like to know."

"It was pure luck, honestly," Harry said after a pause. "Adam Staley came to me a while back, and I was dragging my feet in hiring a Chicago firm. I admit Adam wouldn't care who I hired because he didn't think anything would come of it, but when Sandra mentioned you, it seemed like an opportunity. Sandra would realize I was not dismissive of you or of her relationship with you. Two birds with one stone, as they say."

O'Neill nodded. It seemed a reasonable explanation. Besides, it no longer mattered.

Chapter 30

O'Neill laid his torn jeans on the mattress. He found his needle and thread inside his dresser. The needle was in a plastic container sitting under a silver-colored thimble and two spools of thread. He chose the white thread, tied it to the needle and put the thimble on his finger.

Jane had cut the pants at the knee from one seam to the other and down one seam to the hem. He would not sew the horizontal tear since that had already been torn, but it took fifteen minutes to sew the vertical tear. He put his repaired jeans on and returned the needle and thread to his dresser. The fix didn't look great, but they were his favorite jeans and it kept him with two pairs.

He stepped outside. Rain was coming down hard, and people crossing Frances Street held newspapers or umbrellas over their heads. O'Neill was used to being outside in bad weather, so he walked like the rain was not there. Once at the Red Shed, he took off his pullover sweatshirt, setting it on a bar stool.

"Bit wet, Seamus," the woman bartender said as she filled a pint of Berghoff.

"Observant," O'Neill said under his breath.

"The rain is killer and is keeping everyone away. Never seen such a dead Saturday."

She leaned closer as she handed him the beer. O'Neill caught her eye for an instant and when she pulled away, he looked her over. She was about five-foot-seven with an athletic build. Her eyes were brown, and her hair was long and dark black. He couldn't decide whether she was the same bartender he saw last time or whether she was a different one. Either way, she was too young for him.

O'Neill took a gulp from his beer and surveyed the clientele. At one end, a group of four men in their mid-twenties were talking loudly while another group played darts. O'Neill didn't realize that Amanda Preston was one of the dart players until she came over to talk to him.

"Hey Seamus, what's up?"

He twisted around. "Amanda. You're not mad at me anymore?"

"Nah, I can't be mad at anyone as wet as you." She put her bottle of Miller on the bar and sat next to him. "You said you were sorry, didn't you?"

"I didn't think that was enough. I thought you didn't like me seeing your sister."

"I didn't, but you're not seeing her anymore. That's what she told me earlier this morning, and she was emphatic." Amanda took a small drink from her bottle while O'Neill drank from his glass. "She had a crush on you, but she's over it. She said you did nothing bad to her, and Sandra sent me a text saying you two had broken up, so I can't be mad about that. Jane says you got problems she can't deal with. It's that simple. Thinking back on it, I was stupid to introduce her to you, but she brought you up constantly for the past few years and I was sick of it. I hope you don't have hard feelings. You hanging out?"

That had been O'Neill's plan, but not any longer. He finished his beer, put his money on the bar, and stood. He was not angry at Amanda but seeing her reminded him of Jane.

"Unfortunately, I got to roll," he said as he put his damp sweatshirt back on. He took a large gulp to finish his beer. "Catch you later."

Once outside, he pulled out his flask and took a sip of whisky. The rain was still coming down hard, rolling off awnings and forming puddles at intersections. He walked aimlessly to State Street, going into a bus stop shelter and sipping his whisky. Within a few minutes, a lanky guy wearing a brown shirt and green pants joined him.

"You gimme a sip?" the guy asked.

O'Neill handed him the flask. He took a few gulps, then handed it back. "Mighty fine Scotch."

O'Neill took a nip and realized the flask was nearly empty.

"You got a woman?" O'Neill asked.

"Do I got a woman?" he repeated, laughing. "The question should be: how many women do I got?"

The guy motioned toward the flask. O'Neill handed him the Scotch.

"How about you?"

"Not now, at least."

O'Neill took the flask back. It was empty, so he moved on.

He checked Topper's shop, but it was closed. He only had four dollars, so he would be best off stopping at the liquor store, picking up a six-pack of beer, and going home. But he couldn't stop thinking about Jane and felt drawn to her house. He wanted to look into her blue eyes and hear her voice. It was a bad idea, but one he could not suppress.

He replayed the time he first met her and the time she looked at his injured knee. He thought about Jane running on the path, and he remembered the night at her apartment. The melancholy feeling dispersed until he saw her Mazda parked in the driveway of her apartment building.

O'Neill stopped. The rain had slowed, but he was soaked, and it no longer registered with him. He wanted to pull out his flask, but he held off and instead he continued forward, touching the side of the Mazda as he passed and splashing raindrops into the air.

He rang the doorbell and the inside door opened. Jane was wearing her Green Bay Packer shirt again along with baggy sweatpants. It took a few moments before she looked him in the eye.

"Seamus, you are soaking wet."

"It's raining outside," O'Neill said meekly.

"I noticed," Jane said. She glanced backward and then at him, her blue eyes cutting through the darkness. "Just a minute while I put on shoes."

She closed the door, returning a few seconds later. The screen door pushed open, and she stepped onto the porch.

"Ryder and our client went to the police yesterday," O'Neill said. "Ryder said Garcia and the rest of the cops were receptive. They got a court order to search Larry Marsh's apartment."

"Great," Jane said. She stood on the porch, leaning against the building.

"Ryder is confident the police will charge him. He doesn't know how things will play out. It depends on whether they find anything at his apartment or whether they get lucky somewhere else."

"That's great. I'm happy for you, as well as for Mary Gleason and Andie's friends and family."

"Ryder said Garcia called Andie's mother, Jennifer. He said all she could do was cry," O'Neill said, suddenly feeling choked up. "She couldn't even say anything."

O'Neill couldn't remember the last time he had cried. He turned away from Jane and wiped his eyes with his wet shirt.

"That's great. You did a good thing."

"You helped," O'Neill said. "You helped a lot."

"Thanks. I hope I did."

There was a long silence.

"Did you want to talk about Thursday night?" Jane said.

"Yeah," he said, turning back to face her. "I'm sorry about that. I was so pumped. I guess I was too high. It's not something I do. I don't know what it was, but I..."

"Seamus, I can't do this," she said, motioning to the two of them. "I can't be with you and watch you drink like that. I can't see you like you were on Thursday night. It's not fair to you or to me. I want to see you, but only if you stop drinking."

"Jane, I've been drinking for twenty-one years."

"I thought you were thirty-one."

"Yeah. Ten was my dad's drinking age."

"You're kidding."

"No," O'Neill said as a rumble of thunder interrupted them. "We could only drink when we played, though. Sometimes he wanted a band. He'd be drinking and playing and suddenly he needed a whistler or an accordion. So, I joined in. He'd need a fiddle, so my sister would have to play. There was no saying no, regardless of the time of day or night. I drank a lot of cheap beer out of returnable bottles."

"That's crazy. But that just illustrates my point. I'm just saying you're important to me and I need you to stop drinking." Jane paused and wiped her eyes. "If drinking is more important than me, then that's your decision. But it's one of the other. I need to be clear."

"It's not choosing you or drinking," O'Neill countered. "I could drink less."

"I wish I could buy that, but I can't. You may say that you can cut down, but cut down to what? I'm a nurse. I've learned a lot about drug and alcohol abuse, and it's clear to me that drinking is managing you. It's past the point when you can manage your drinking. I recognize it's awful, and it's not your fault. You were drinking at ten years old. It's no wonder you have issues."

"Jane, I can't give up music."

"Who said you have to give up music?"

O'Neill took a breath before answering. "My sister stopped drinking about five years ago. But the only way she could do it was to give up music. She hasn't played a note since she quit drinking. She's afraid that if she picks up a fiddle or a guitar, she'll start drinking again. I can't do that. I can't give up my music. If I did, I might as well not even be. It's who I am."

"You don't have to give up music," Jane said. "That may be something with her. That may be what she thinks, but that's how she managed to stop drinking. That doesn't mean you have to do the same. Everyone is different."

"I guess I got to go," O'Neill said. "Goodbye."

O'Neill went down the steps, but as he walked past Jane's Mazda, he heard footsteps. He turned as Jane jumped into his arms. They hugged and kissed. Her skin felt warm, and he looked into her eyes as she said his name.

Finally, she pulled away and O'Neill wondered whether there might still be a possibility. He thought about saying they could see how things played out if he cut down on his drinking, but nothing came out.

"Goodbye, Seamus O'Neill," Jane said.

O'Neill mouthed, "Goodbye, Jane Preston."

She turned away and hurried into her apartment. His eyes continued to drip, and he walked away, not knowing where he was going or why.

Chapter 31

O'Neill ended up back at the Red Shed. Jane's sister was nowhere to be seen, but the woman bartender still poured him a tap of Berghoff. Someone was in the seat he had earlier, so he grabbed one at the end of the bar. The bartender smiled at him, and O'Neill wondered whether she smiled at everyone.

He finished the first beer in a few minutes then ordered another. As he finished the last beer he could pay for, the bartender handed him the phone.

"Phone call for you, a guy named John Ryder."

"Seamus?" Ryder asked. "Figures you're at a bar."

"Where are you calling from?"

"Why does it matter? I need to pick you up so we can meet with Garcia tonight. Results came back on the brush and the hairband. Believe it or not, both had semen on them. It will take time for them to check if the DNA matches, but it's obvious how it's going to play out. You were right."

"Holy shit. Have they arrested Larry?"

"Yes. He's lawyered up. They're negotiating and expecting a confession."

"What does Garcia want with me?"

"He knows you're the one that did the heavy lifting on this. He wants to talk through things so they can prepare for Larry and his lawyers. Also, I think he's pissed at himself. He's wondering where everything went wrong and why we solved a crime while they didn't."

"So, this is nothing bad."

"Definitely not anything bad. I'll pick you up on the way to the station. Also, I got good news. You will not believe this, but we got a five-thousand-dollar bonus for this thing from Myles Staley, or rather from his father, Adam. Five thousand bucks plus the two-week payment for one week's work!"

"You're shitting me."

"No, we did good."

"Do I get twenty-five percent?"

"It's not so clear, but I'm willing to go with it."

"One thousand two hundred and fifty bucks on top of the down payment," O'Neill said with a smile. "Make sure you bring a few bucks with you. If you don't, I'll have to wash dishes to get out of here."

"Okay, but cool it. I don't want you in the bag when we talk with Garcia."

"Course."

He hung the phone up, waved the bartender over, and ordered another pint.

When Ryder arrived, he paid for three of O'Neill's beers. He was wearing a tie and a sweat-stained white dress shirt. Ryder hurried O'Neill into his Chevy S-10.

"Don't you at least try to stay out of the rain?" Ryder said as he started the car.

"At least the seats aren't scorching hot," O'Neill said. "Will Harry be there?"

"No. He headed back to Chi-Town. His chief concern was to ensure that Myles was clear. That's accomplished."

When they got to the police station, Ryder pulled his Chevy to the curb. It was late, so they entered through a side door where a uniformed police officer waited for them. The Madison Police Department stuck Ryder and O'Neill in a small room with a table and four chairs. After five minutes, two men joined them.

"Ryder, thanks for coming in," the taller man said. He motioned toward the other man, then turned toward O'Neill. "I'm Detective Garcia and this is Detective Langley. He's been working with me on the Andie Sheridan case."

Garcia was a big man with dark brown hair and a thick mustache which covered his lips. Detective Langley was average in build, average in appearance, and average in manner. Ryder got out of his chair and shook hands with the detectives. O'Neill opened his eyes but didn't move.

"He's tired," Ryder said.

"Smells like a brewery," Detective Langley added.

The smile on Ryder's face disappeared. He glanced toward Garcia then back at Langley.

"Seamus was on the town, but he interrupted his night because you requested to meet with him. You know he was integral in identifying Larry Marsh as Andie Sheridan's killer."

"We appreciate that," Garcia said methodically. "Mr. O'Neill, has Mr. Ryder updated you on the test results from Mr. Marsh's apartment?"

"He told me you confirmed that there's semen on the hairbrush and the hairband. It will take time to confirm whether the DNA matches with the semen found on Andie's body."

"Yes. We'll be following up on various angles as well, but we're negotiating with the assumption that we have a DNA match. We believe that, along with the statements from Myles Staley and Ralph Warzyn, this is a slam dunk case. The DA is talking with Larry Marsh's lawyers as we speak. I expect a confession and don't see this going to trial. We're using the final DNA results as a bit of a bargaining chip. He knows the results will only improve our hand. My guess is he will confess by day's end to second degree intentional homicide. We could wait for the DNA results, but there's a slight chance they don't get DNA from the semen. That would be bad. DNA testing is in its infancy, so I take nothing for granted. That's why we're negotiating with them."

"What sort of penalty goes with second degree intentional homicide?" O'Neill asked.

"The maximum is twenty years. The DA and Marsh's lawyers will work through a proposal on what they recommend to the judge. That will be part of the deal to get him to confess."

"Doesn't seem like too much for murdering a nineteen-year-old woman. But I get it."

"That should be the minimum," Langley said.

"Ryder and you have been more than generous working with the Madison Police Department to close this case," Garcia said. "Ryder is allowing us to manage the messaging around the arrest. We'll certainly mention and thank the Ryder Detective Agency for the help in solving this case, but I realize you guys could have made this into a public relations nightmare for us. We appreciate that. I appreciate it."

"You shared your time and opened your files," Ryder said, "so it seemed appropriate."

"But we fucked up. I know that, and Langley knows that. I want to figure out where we went wrong and make sure we don't make the same mistake next time."

"Sure," O'Neill said. "Makes sense."

"You don't need to explain the entire crime again, but I'm wondering if you could give us your thoughts on what you think went wrong with us?"

"Andie disappeared while running in the woods," O'Neill said. "When you found her in the woods, it was only natural to assume the attack happened during the run, especially since she clearly disappeared while on the arboretum path. It was reasonable for the medical examiner to infer sexual assault since you could establish that the semen showed up after she started the run. Plus, she was found partially naked with her underwear torn off. Larry wanted it to look that way. Don't give yourself too much grief."

"Thanks," Garcia said.

"It was the medical examiner who gave us the time of death," Langley said. "Reynolds, yeah, Dr. Reynolds. That was off."

"Everything implied that the murder happened around nine thirty on August twenty-first. It was actually a few hours later, but the body wasn't found for six days. I'm not a doctor or anything, but they found the body six days after the murder. I can't imagine the medical examiner was able to specify beyond the day. If he said ten o'clock or whatever, he was just reflecting on what you thought."

"Yes," Garcia said. "I get your point."

"Ryder and I had a few advantages over you. First, we knew that your investigation didn't work. That encouraged us to go on hunches and try things differently. Second, Myles Staley gave us clues. You didn't have those advantages. Finally, I don't think any of you guys were runners. One runner even mentioned that to me. I mean, when one of them said they didn't see Andie on the path, it didn't seem like you took her seriously. Your detectives were just imagining a bunch of women running on a path and imagined how you thought it would appear. I think it would have been worthwhile to hire a cross-country consultant. She might have helped you to ask the right questions and might have helped you evaluate the women's statements."

"Interesting idea," Garcia said. "You are correct that none of our team are runners."

"Shit, no," Langley said.

"Finally, I don't think people really understood Andie. Everyone just saw this beautiful, talented woman. And that's all they really saw. Yet what she did was about her inner self. I don't know what your answer is on that for going forward."

"But it's another interesting point," Garcia said. "I appreciate it. And I appreciate your thoughts on this. One last question. Ryder said you were sure from the get-go that Larry was the killer. Why?"

"Like I said, Ryder and I could go on hunches. It was just a hunch. And I sensed someone who wanted control and attention. First time I saw him, he belittled me. You could say I was trying to pin it on him because I didn't like being belittled. That might be the case. But I also thought that a bully like that might be the type of person who was a control freak. And the more I learned about him, the more that made sense. He was an abuser and a control freak. And he was smart enough to have put together on the fly how this could all play out. He knew that if Andie disappeared, he would be the number one suspect, but he realized people might not know she had been at his apartment that afternoon. He suspected something, but he didn't know if anyone had seen her that morning. And if they did, was it one person or multiple people? Yet he was desperate, and it occurred to him that her teammates would assume she disappeared while running through the woods. He wanted it to look like the attack had happened in the woods. Burying the body near the path accomplished that, yet he didn't want the body found right away, so he buried her."

"What if someone else had seen her with Myles? Or what if Myles had come forward?"

"Your investigation would have taken a very different direction. Larry didn't know if his plan would work. But like I said, he was desperate."

"Staley should have come forward earlier," Langley said. "We interviewed him during the investigation, but he didn't admit to a relationship with the victim."

"If Myles stepped forward without evidence or a witness, you might have thought he was guilty," O'Neill said. "Odds are you would have figured out that he didn't have the opportunity to bury her body. It would have kept him out of the Waupun Correctional Institution, but the case would hang over him. Keep in mind, Myles didn't know who killed Andie, and he may not have known that the body was buried. He only knew she left his apartment at eleven thirty. Going to the police was a risk. He should have done it, but he lost his nerve."

They spent the next hour talking about the investigation, with Ryder doing most of the talking. O'Neill spoke when he needed to clarify. It was near midnight when the interview was over, and they were all exhausted. Ryder offered to take O'Neill back to the Red Shed, but even O'Neill was too tired to drink, so Ryder brought him home.

"What happened to your cane?" Ryder asked as O'Neill stepped out of Ryder's Chevy.

O'Neill had forgotten all about the cane. "I left it at a friend of mine's place. I'll pick it up Monday so I can return it to my neighbor."

"Did you leave the cane at that girl's place?"

"No, it wasn't at her place. If she's smart, she's done with me. And I think she's smart."

"I know how you feel. Are you going to go after her?"

"I want to, but I'll try not to. I think she's done with me and, even if I got her back, I'd eventually fuck it up. She deserves better."

O'Neill tried to close the car door, but Ryder stopped him.

"Sorry about the girl, but don't forget you did something good. We solved a murder that everyone assumed was unsolvable. It feels good knowing Andie's parents have closure. That is also true for her roommate and her teammates and her coach. By the way, Andie's parents invited us to a brief ceremony on Tuesday at Andie's gravesite. Jennifer Reilly's hoping you will come along."

"Sure, assuming you're driving."

"Maybe you're not as worthless as everyone thinks. It must feel good."

"I suppose, but I'd rather be sitting with Jane on my lap and a beer in my hand."

Ryder shook his head. "Get your drunken ass to bed."

O'Neill shut the car door. He heard Ryder drive off and he looked at the clouds as they pushed past the moon. He breathed in the damp air and leaned on his sore knee, wondering if it would feel normal in a day or two. If it did, perhaps he would walk to Monroe Street and finish the arboretum path run for Andie. Not the entire run, just the half-mile path.

He opened his apartment's outer door and started up the first flight of stairs.

Acknowledgments

Thank you to family and friends who supported me in writing this book. Special thanks to Dannielle Konz, Dianna Breen, Matt Breen, Sue Krumenauer, Dan Birrenkott, Kelsey Breen, and Dave Greenwell.

About the Author

Paul plays guitar poorly and spends far too much time on genealogy. A native of Columbus, Ohio, Paul Breen grew up in Madison, Wisconsin, and worked at the University of Wisconsin-Madison. Paul enjoys running, biking, music, sports, history, and visiting brewpubs. He lives with his wife and family in Madison.

9 798986 208305